BEAST OF ROSEMEAD

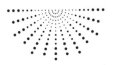

LUCY TEMPEST

FOLKSHORE

But he that dares not grasp the thorn
Should never crave the rose.

— — THE NARROW WAY, ANNE BRONTË

INTRODUCTION

Welcome to the magical world of Folkshore!

Fairytales of Folkshore is a series of interconnected fairytale retellings with unique twists on much-loved, enduring themes. It starts with the *Cahraman Trilogy*, a gender-swapped reimagining of *Aladdin*.

It is followed by the *Rosemead duology,* a retelling of *Beauty & the Beast*.

Join each heroine on emotional, thrilling adventures full of magic, mystery, friendship and romance where true love is found in the most unexpected places and the fates of kingdoms hang in the balance.

Coming retellings will be:

Cinderella, Sleeping Beauty, Hades & Persephone and The Little Mermaid!

MAP

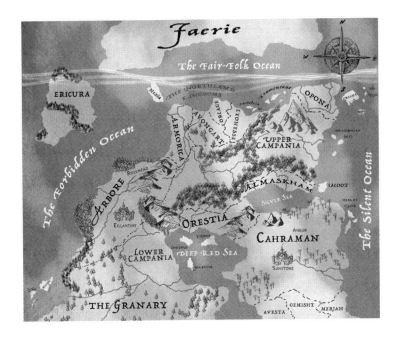

CHAPTER ONE

*D*istant voices echoed in the darkness, heated, angry, none distinct enough to discern. A tinny whistle followed the escalating shouts, drowning them in its blanketing sharpness.

It was like my head was submerged beneath murky waters, where I felt heavy and weightless at the same time. And I was slowly floating to the surface, towards the rays of light pouring from above, rising, rising until I...

I sat up with a gasp, kicking the woolen bed covers off me, the chill from the open window instantly gripping my body. My eyes filled with tears, if only from the scratch of dryness, for it wasn't that bright. A lantern hung from a hook across the room, and framed in the window, lilac-grey clouds blended with the pink-orange sunset as the top of the apple tree rustled in the breeze.

Disoriented, pounding head pressed into my palm, I disentangled my numb legs from the covers. I swung my feet to the dusty, wooden floor, and the yellow, silk nightgown fell to cover them as it hung off my small frame.

Why would I have gone to bed in Adelaide's clothes? We'd just done the laundry two days ago, and I couldn't have run out of clean sleepwear this soon.

Unsure if I was still dreaming, I gathered the nightgown up in a knot, shuffled towards the lantern and picked it off its hook. Needing to investigate the sounds of arguing, something I'd never heard in our house, I was almost at the door when a floorboard beneath me croaked like a giant frog. That one noise extinguished the haze of sleep from my aching head with a downpour of confusion.

Adelaide didn't own silk clothes. I didn't sleep in the attic. We didn't have an apple tree. And our house was made entirely out of stone.

Where was I?

I spun around, sluggish heart suddenly thundering. Taking in the unknown room, panic climbed up my every nerve, a feeling so foreign it shook me, rattling the lantern in my weakening grip.

There were no wooden places in Aubenaire. The only place I knew of was Miss Etheline's tavern, which was the last place I remembered being in. But this couldn't be one of the lodgings, as the tavern had neither an attic nor an orchard. Wherever I was, it seemed I wasn't just away from home, but I was out of town.

And I couldn't remember how I got here.

Suddenly, I felt much smaller, younger, the missing memories even more terrifying than the mystery location. I wanted to call out for my father, for Adelaide, but the cry died in my throat, exiting my spastic lips a rasp of fright.

There was only one answer for how I'd gotten here: I'd been kidnapped.

My heartbeat filled my entire body, each thud worsening my trembling. Why would anyone take me?

I could think of plenty of terrible reasons, some from my books, but mostly ones my father used to discourage me from straying away from home. But I didn't want to consider them now. I couldn't.

The question now wasn't what I was doing here, but what was I going to do about it. Do I hope whoever had taken me had made a mistake and would let me go, or was a merciful captor and would return me if I begged—or do I attempt to escape? If I did, could I find my way home?

I had always thought that my first brush with danger would be exciting, an encounter with the magical, or at least with the strange customs of the places we traveled through. "We" being myself and Adelaide, who'd handled life on her own for years, roaming the island, and dealing with all sorts of people and circumstances, and the danger both posed. She would have known what to do in this situation, would have escaped out the window and be halfway home by now.

Oh, Ada, what could she and my father be feeling now? They must have found out I was gone, must be going out of their minds with worry.

But—what if they were here as well? What if whoever had snatched me had taken them as well? If they had, I was certain they couldn't hold Adelaide for long. She would free herself and my father. So should I wait for them to come for me?

But if they hadn't so far, it probably meant one of two things: either they weren't here, or they were but unable to come for me. Maybe they were still knocked out? Had I come around faster for some reason? Or where they tied up? Or worse, injured…?

The thought felt like a stab in my chest, its pain burning behind my eyes, hitching my breath.

No! I couldn't think the worst. I'd be of no use to them paralyzed with dread. I had to find them, set them free. They'd take charge from there and lead us back home.

I took another step towards the door and almost jumped out of my skin when another floorboard complained below my slight weight like a discordant violin. I froze, expecting my captor to blast through the door and tie me up this time...or something. But long moments passed, and nothing happened, the sounds of argument continuing unabated from below. Gulping a shaky breath into my starving lungs, I finally tried the door's handle.

It moved. I thought it stranger still to find the door unlocked, but I didn't pause to think why as I cracked it open, peered out. There was no one outside.

Heart rattling my whole body, I rushed out to the landing and stumbled down the creaking stairs, sweaty hands sliding over the polished-wood banister.

The floor below was spacious, sparsely decorated with leather-upholstered furniture. It was perfectly silent, making the argument from below fill the entire house. Breathing in labored puffs, I carefully peeked inside each room, and thought over escape plans.

I'd never needed to run or hide, not beyond schoolyard games. I'd never faced any kind of emergency, let alone danger. But if I were to be confronted by someone right now, what could I do? Eighteen I might be, but plenty of younger teens or even children towered over me. I couldn't fight anyone even if I wanted to. But what if I had to?

It didn't look like I'd have to so far. While it drenched me in disappointment that I didn't find my father and Adelaide, there were also no other threats in sight. The entire floor was empty. And there was an open balcony across the hall.

It immediately reminded me of Adelaide's many stories of climbing in and out of houses through balconies, windows or even chimneys. This was lower than the attic's window, could be my only way out.

I was crossing towards it when a yell speared through the cacophonous debate, stopping me dead in my path.

"Whatever game you're playing, it's not working!"

Dad!

Caution thrown to the wind, I spun around and barreled down the steps, sobs of relief tearing through me.

I was almost atop the last flight of stairs when I came face to face with a bear.

I screamed.

The scrape of wooden chairs followed by the scramble of hurried feet encroached on me as I fell back on the steps, their edges digging into my back.

Someone rushed up the flight, yelling something, but I didn't hear anything over the roar of panic as I swung the lantern at his legs.

With a surprised yelp, he crashed sideways, landing on the steps below me, clutching his knee.

"Crazy as your old man, I see," he growled.

"Who are you?" I said shakily, whatever hope of acting tough gone.

His groan was pained as he pushed himself up. And in the light from my lantern and the floor below, I saw his face.

Breathtaking beauty was a common sight in nature, from blackthorn blossoms in late winter, to butterflies in the summer. But in people, I always thought it only existed in books.

Except for him.

I could draw a line down his face, straight through his linear eyebrows, elegant nose, defined philtrum and lower-lip crack, all the way to the cleft in his strong chin. Each feature was better than the last, from his intense, thick-lashed eyes to the jut of his firm, triangular jaw. I'd never seen a face so chiseled and symmetrical.

"I am Castor Woodbine," he huffed, back on his feet. "And you are in my family's hunting lodge."

"What am I doing here, Castor?" I wheezed as I tried to sit up.

"Recovering." He held his hand out to me. "Or I hope you are. From the way you're shaking, I'd say you're still way out of sorts."

"Why am I here?" I asked warily, searching his face in the dim stairwell, trying to pick out more details, colors, imperfections, intentions—anything. "Recovering from what?"

My father's voice traveled up from below, cracked, urgent. "Bonnie? Bonnie, is that you?"

"Dad!" I jumped to my feet, but they buckled beneath me. Before I could fall on the steps, Castor stuck his arm around me, lifting me up and against him.

I was used to feeling small, but right now, pressed against his tall, broad frame, I felt minuscule, the thrush to his hawk.

There was no way I could fight him, and I honestly didn't want to anymore. He was so big and strong, felt so secure, my mind stilled in his steadying hold. I wanted to lean against him, trust him not to let me fall again as I searched his face with all the wonder I did the night sky.

He chuckled, a sound that quieted all my trembling into one last shudder. "How about you take it easy from now on?"

Struck dumb, I could only nod as he scooped me off my

feet and carried me down the remaining steps. He smelled like smoke, pinewood and rainwater, an outdoorsy blend that reminded me of the last days of summer before I retreated indoors for months to read by the fire.

We crossed to a large, blanched door and entered a sitting room that was decked from wall to wall with curious decorations. At least, at first glance. On my second look, I recoiled with a squeak, curling up in his arms.

Rows of mounted heads stared down at me, each from a different animal, from antlered deer and elks with glassy eyes, to silently roaring bears, mountain cats, and wolves. Hides hung off the backs of the leather furniture facing the wide, roaring stone-brick fireplace, and lay on the floor as carpets.

One bear looked up at me as if in reproach, with its dead eyes and open mouth, the rest of it flat beneath the wide-backed armchair that held my father. He had his back to me, facing four men on the seats and couch, still arguing, gesturing wildly. As Castor took me closer, relief flooded me, until I saw my father's leg bound by a chain ending in a large, metal ball.

"Dad!" I cried out. "What did they do to you?"

My father swung around, and the instant he spotted me, he leaped out of the chair, arms outstretched. "Bonnibel, I was so worried—" The ball yanked him back, but he struggled nonetheless, trying to drag it after him.

I struggled in Castor's arms until he set me before my father and we met in a desperate hug. Father picked me up, but an alarming pop in his back had me kicking to be set back down.

Once on my feet, I found myself lecturing him like we were in our sitting room, rather than a stranger's house. "You have to stop hauling heavy stuff. Your back is bound to give out."

"I can still lug my work around, and it's much heavier than you," he grumbled, broad, kind face looking worn, his thick, greying-brown hair mussed, but his grey eyes brimming with joy.

A sharp clap cut our reunion short.

I swiveled away to its source; a muscled, bearded man with reddish-blonde hair, wearing a fur-lined blue cloak, with a sword at his hip.

"Now that we're all here, we can finally discuss what's going on," he said.

But my focus remained on the sword. I'd never seen one outside of books. The engravings on its golden hilt said: *To my lord, to the realm, I pledge my service.*

I'd read those words before. In a book about an old kingdom in a faraway land that I'd been told all my life didn't exist.

"You're a—knight?" I hugged my father closer, my words slow, my mind racing.

The man proudly held out his arms and bowed his head. "Sir Dale of Roxborough, at your service."

But Ericura didn't have knights. Not in the way folktales and my novels did. Which meant this sword must be an heirloom from a forgotten past and this man had inherited some honorary title. Yet somehow, I didn't think this was the answer.

"Where are we?" I tried to sound assertive, but my voice shook and spoiled the attempt.

"I already said you are in my family's hunting lodge," Castor said, entering my view.

This lighting added more depth and dimension to his face, revealing his eyes to be a dark blue and his hair to be an intriguing cross between ash-blond and warm brown, the sides cropped closest to his head shimmering in the overhead light.

I couldn't put a name to this new feeling that came over me whenever I looked at him. I'd spoken to plenty of boys and men in my town, some even from beyond it, but not one had grasped my attention this wholly. It was like someone had sculpted him, a commission for a temple. A vision of the utmost perfection to represent a god.

Getting a precarious grip on my wits as I stared at him, I managed to ask, "Yes, but where?"

"As we were just telling your father," Sir Dale began with a sigh, sharing a longsuffering look with Castor. "You are in Rosemead. We found you unconscious in the woods while on a hunt for a sacrifice. We couldn't tell whose family you belonged to, so we brought you back here."

"A sacrifice?" My voice came out a squeak, fear crashing back into me. "A sacrifice for what?"

Castor's smile dimmed, rage gripping his body, shifting his features from welcoming to intimidating. "For the Beast."

I looked up at my father, whispering for his ears only. "Are they these mad cultists you once warned me about?"

He shook his head. "But they keep trying to sell me this silly story."

"What story? What part of Ericura is Rosemead in? I've never heard of it."

Castor poked his head between us. "That's because Rosemead is in the Kingdom of Arbore, not the fabled island of Hericeurra, where your father claims to come from. *That's* the silliest story we've ever heard. But whatever the reason he's telling it, and whatever you're here for, you've come to the worst place, at the worst time."

CHAPTER TWO

*C*astor's words spun in my mind, refusing to make sense.

But in the maelstrom, fragmented recollections started to rain down, lodging together like a shattered window reforming. Still, none led back to the point that had brought us here.

I now clearly remembered the past week, as the town had gotten ready for our midsummer bonfire. I remembered everything up to yesterday, when Adelaide had gifted me books she'd stolen from the Dufreyne mansion.

One of the books, a magnificent leather-bound tome, was called *The Known World*. It had held a map of the Folkshore, a world our entire land knew nothing about, or had forgotten. According to everyone in Ericura, our island *was* the whole world, and we were the only ones left in it. Aside from the fairies we believed lived across the border of Man's Reach, what manifested in our town as the Hornswoods that no one could cross.

I'd always hoped everyone was wrong. And as I'd stared at that map, I'd become certain they were. *The Known World* told of a vast world beyond our island, reigniting my desire to leave home, not to travel the island, but to go beyond it.

The words on Sir Dale's sword had come from a tale I'd read years ago, about a land called Arboria. On the map of the Folkshore, it lay across a Forbidden Ocean that separated it from fairies in their Fair Folk's Shore, with our island caught between them. That Arboria, what I'd thought our ancestors had hailed from, had been my desired destination.

And Castor had just said I was there. *If* this Arbore he'd mentioned was the same place.

I swayed, feeling faint. "Do you mean Arboria? And what do you mean 'fabled island?'"

Castor came closer, offering me a soothing smile. "Your father here is trying to convince us he's from the lost island of Hericeurra. Don't worry, it's nothing a visit from the town's nurse and a good week's rest won't fix."

He called Ericura *Hericeurra*, just like the book had. So the world had forgotten about us as we'd forgotten about it.

"There's nothing wrong with him," I said. "We *are* from Hericeurra—Ericura. And the people there think *your* land is the fabled one, or that it got swallowed by the ocean."

Castor shared another look with Sir Dale, who shrugged and sighed. "One person is concussed. Two people are delusional."

"What about three?" I looked around the room, briefly checking the three other men. One was tall, slim and dark-haired and was twirling throwing knives. Another was as tall and big as Castor, but strangely wearing a green, hooded cloak indoors that totally obscured his upper face. The third appeared the youngest and to be Dale's brother, with the same face, but beardless and with redder hair.

"Who's the third loon?" Dale asked only to be elbowed by Castor.

A sudden chill settled over me, like being drenched in cold sweat on a midwinter morning. "You don't have Adelaide?"

All five men now looked at one another, each offering up a gesture of confusion or ignorance that made me cling to Dad for support.

"We only found the two of you," said Castor. "Perhaps another hunting party got your...sister?"

"Cousin," I said, a half-truth, as our late mothers had been friends prior to our births. Apart from becoming my best friend, I felt that also made us the only family we both had. "She's very tall, as tall as you." I pointed to the one with the knives. "Black-haired, brown-eyed, was in men's clothes, possibly wearing a wooden mask."

"Men's clothes and a mask. What kind of place is this isle of yours? One where the men wear gowns and the women farm the land?" Dale's brother laughed, earning a quick knife-toss that buried the blade in his cloak, pinning him to the wooden wall. He gaped at the slim man. "Will, what gives?"

"My sister was a better hunter than you ever were, Glenn," Will said sarcastically, pointing the other knife at him.

"Yes," Glenn snapped. "And her insistence on doing what no girl should and you letting her join our hunts was what got her carried off by the fairies."

Will stiffened, anger straining his voice. "I wouldn't talk about missing sisters if I were you, considering yours got gobbled up by the Beast."

Face twisted with fury, Glenn launched himself at him but got yanked back by the knife in his cloak.

"Enough!" Castor's shout filled the room, his furious intensity raising all my hairs. "Scarlet, Quill—we'll avenge your sisters soon. We'll avenge all our loved ones. But first, we must find out if theirs is still alive."

"Why wouldn't she be alive?" My father asked in alarm, his step forwards hindered by the ball-and-chain.

Dale rubbed his forehead with a sigh, looked at me with solemn eyes. "Since you're not from here, you clearly don't know that Rosemead is home to a monster that no one has survived an encounter with. Every month, the people offer it a sacrifice to stave off its fury, keep it away from us all."

"We started off giving it the best cuts of meat, then entire animals, going from birds to elks," Castor said bitterly. "The best we catch has to go to it every month to ensure that it doesn't do to us what it did to the inhabitants of the duke's castle. But nothing seems enough for it."

"So you now give it *people?*" I gasped, horrified.

Sir Dale shook his head. "But it does seem to want more every month, and since we couldn't find your cousin, we're afraid the Beast might have taken her."

Imagining Adelaide in some monster's clutches had weakness invading my limbs with a vengeance. My heartbeat hammered too fast, and sweat cascaded from my scalp down my back, like I'd been running for hours and was about to collapse.

But no! Ada couldn't have been taken by the Beast. Even if she had been, she'd escaped so many terrible situations, from the dangers of harsh nature to those of predators of all sorts. Surely she'd given it the slip. After all, no one was more slippery than an accomplished thief. And she was the very best!

She was fine. She *had* to be.

"How exactly did you get here?" Castor asked my father before either of us could ask anything more. "If you're really from this place that has been so isolated it has forgotten the Folkshore, how did you venture here?"

Instead of answering, my father raised his bound leg. "Do you mind?"

Castor gave him a sarcastic smile. "Will you attack me again? The gods have given me this face, and it's survived several swiping claws and snapping jaws unscathed. I'd hate to accidentally lose a tooth to a flailing old man."

"You'd be surprised how much damage this old man can do," my father said gruffly.

If I weren't too caught up in my worry, I would have been puzzled by this statement. Though years of hammering metal and working in a forge had toughened my father up, he wasn't the type to argue, let alone fight. And he didn't only seem ready to, but they'd bound him because he'd already attacked them.

Castor took a key out from his pocket, kneeled to unlock the anklet. Leaving my father struggling to get it off, he rose but stopped on my level. Nose almost against mine, I could see nothing but his face and feel nothing but the restrained intensity radiating off him. It was like standing too close to a furnace, the warmth pleasant at first but quickly becoming too much, prompting me to step back.

Then he spoke, and all those reservations melted away. "You have the most beautiful eyes I have ever seen."

I flushed, not knowing what to do with myself. It was one thing for older people to tell me I was pretty to flatter my father or in an attempt to secure an acceptable wife for their sons, or the sons themselves paying me clumsy compliments to the same end. It was a completely different feeling to have someone as beautiful as him look at me that way.

"How about we settle down, have some tea and discuss all this from the start?" he said. "Get to know each other?"

I nodded enthusiastically and only managed to intensify my dizziness.

He set a hand on my shoulder in a steadying grip as he led me to the couch where Will had sat back down. Castor kicked his legs. "Up."

Will rolled his head towards us lethargically. "Get her her own chair."

"I'll stick your stupid knives up your nose if you don't get up," Castor bit out, his sudden temper startling me. "Make us some tea while you're at it."

Will opened his mouth to object, but the hooded man grabbed him by the arm as he passed, dragging him along. They left the room, squabbling. Glenn left us, too, saying he'd go downtown to get some supplies.

Castor and I settled on the couch, while my father and Sir Dale did on the armchairs across from us, framed by the animal remnants that decorated the room. If anyone could call this macabre array a decoration. Between the smell of wolf hide draped along the back of the couch and the unblinking eyes of every mounted head, distress crept within me, different from the one elicited by our displacement or Ada's disappearance.

I supposed this was deep, primal disgust, a feeling I'd never felt even towards things like rotting food. I found flaunting the animals they'd killed this was at once outrageous and sickening.

"So, Fairborn, was it?" Sir Dale asked my father, seemingly willing to go along with what he clearly thought a delusion. "Sounds Arborean. Perhaps your ancestors were from here."

I forced my thoughts away from our surroundings and situation, the new topic capturing my attention. "That's what I thought." All the men turned to me, and I continued, my voice sounding small and breathless. "I had a book that detailed the Folkshore, or as it was centuries ago. It said that our island had two waves of migration, people who settled in the north and ones who populated the south. I figured the north population had to be from Arbore. It's why I wanted to come here."

My father raised his dark brows at me, wrinkling his forehead. Guilt pricked at my sides, making me slide further down the smooth couch. I hadn't mentioned any of this to him, partly because I hadn't known how.

"So, though you planned on coming, you don't know how you got here?" Castor summed up.

"Yes," I admitted.

My father gaped at me. "You and Adelaide were going to just up and leave?"

"No! Well, yes, but not anywhere too far," I said hurriedly. The last thing I wanted was to upset him, but with our situation, that intention was as pointless as it was late. "We discussed traveling to another city, like a trip to Galba so I could go fishing and walk on the seashore. Leaving Ericura was just a fanciful idea."

"Now a grim reality," he huffed, settling back in his seat, hand going to his chin, stroking it thoughtfully. He suddenly ripped his hand away, looking startled.

It was only then that I noticed it, too. A beard! How had he grown one?

He beat me to the question. "How long have we been here?"

"In Rosemead or at my house?" Castor threw an arm along the back of the couch as he turned my way, watching me intently. "We've had you for a week. You were asleep the entire time, then within an hour of each other, you were both up."

"Going by the condition we found you both in, covered in moss and cobwebs, you must have been there at least as long," Dale added. "I'd say you were put under some enchantment and left there, by a witch or a fairy, I can't tell."

"Going by my state, I'd say you're right." My father stroked his beard, gloominess seeming to weigh him down. "Two weeks, if not more."

I couldn't sit up anymore, sagged back in a boneless slouch, breathing heavily.

My dream of coming here had gone from the frivolousness of a grasp at trailing smoke, to the reality of being pitched into a flaming wicker figure. Like the ones we were meant to burn at the bonfire the night before. No, the *fortnight* before.

"And we somehow ended up in the one place where you wanted to be," my father said, his disappointed tone making me want to curl up into a ball, hide my face in shame. Even though this wasn't my fault, couldn't be my fault, I had intended to leave. Most likely without telling him, because he would have said no.

But he was looking at me as if he needed an explanation why I'd wanted to leave, and I finally felt compelled to tell him. "I'm sorry, Dad, but there was nothing more I wanted than to leave home. You let me do nothing, in the house or outside it, and the idleness became too much, especially after I finished school. I wanted to see new people, other places, do things myself, get some answers, and that feeling intensified when Adelaide came to town. She'd traveled the island bottom to top and was full of stories of places, people and adventures."

"Ada lived a difficult, *terrible* life," he said, his voice roughened with emotion. "She came to us so her struggle would end. She wanted the life we had."

It was true. Once she'd settled with us, she'd refused to budge any further. Aubenaire—with its cyclical schedule and humdrum society, packed with people who didn't care to know anything new or to have their patterns disrupted—was where she'd made her home. She hadn't wanted any more surprises, had only wanted the mindless routine and a quiet future with a local boy. A desire I couldn't grasp, a life I couldn't continue in.

"I can't believe you were going to drag her along on this ridiculous journey of yours," he continued. "You know she didn't cross the land for the fun of it, but because she was forced to, and that she hated it. She came looking for family, because her mother abandoned her."

"Her mother died!" I objected, even when I knew my father would never excuse Ada's mother for inexplicably leaving her before she had. "Just like mine did. When Ada came looking for her, it was the first time I knew we knew anyone beyond our corner at the end of the world. How else did you expect me to react? I had to know more about what she's seen, maybe find out where Mum came from—because you won't tell me anything about her!"

His face hardened with what looked like a dozen objections, but when he answered, he only said, "She must have tried to dissuade you."

"She did," I said sadly, remembering our argument in the tavern, the distress she'd expressed at the idea of leaving the prison that she considered a haven. "It's why we compromised on traveling to a seaside town, not sailing beyond it."

"I would have been fine with that trip. I would have locked

up shop and chaperoned you." He stopped, grimaced, looking pained. "Was our life so bad?"

There was no easy way for me to explain my feelings, not without coming off as silly or shortsighted. But I'd wanted the chance to be both, to experience something, anything, see with my two eyes that life did exist beyond our dirt roads and open fields. I'd hated the idea of living my life where people found me bothersome and bizarre, and thought my interest in our past, in the fairies and anything beyond our town disruptive and dangerous. I'd hated knowing that all my reading would win me nothing but a teaching position at our local school, and if I were lucky, the title of schoolmistress in a decade. Though I was grateful for the tomes Schoolmistress Bertha had lent me, and the history books she'd borrowed for me from the nearest monastery, I'd still hadn't wanted to be her successor.

But I'd resigned myself to that fate, until the instant I'd found that map in *The Known World*. It had been then the hope of finding a world beyond our island had fired up my urge to leave town. When Ada had resisted the idea, I'd instead suggested that we tried to go through the Hornswoods to Faerie and...

"We saw something in the woods," I gasped, a memory bursting in my mind, vivid and overpowering. "Some kind of creature with big, glowing yellow eyes."

While it had scared Ada, it had only encouraged me, solidified my belief in life beyond our borders. And I'd wanted to see it at any cost. If not through the woods then across the sea to Arboria, if it still existed.

And it did. The Kingdom of Arbore, a land of blossoms, knights and adventure, with folk heroes in every city and mystical creatures breathing magic into its history and…and I was in it!

My father frowned, looking like he was remembering, too. "Was it that woman—the one who said came from beyond them, whose carriage you brought me to fix?"

I shook my head. "She came to the tavern asking for help the next day, before we left for the bonfire. I left to fetch you, and Ada went with her to the woods to search for the piece that fell from her carriage…" Suddenly my last and haziest memory flared in my mind. "…we arrived to find her and Ada in front of a hole in the air, made of revolving wind and light, and…"

Nothingness. Until I awoke upstairs.

"Things are starting to make sense," Dale commented.

Castor looked at him as if he too needed treatment. "They are?"

Ignoring him, Dale looked at me with sympathetic eyes. "It seems your Adelaide was taken by a fairy. And you must have tried to follow it. The same thing happened when they took Will's sister, Marianne. Fairies plucked her from their group through a portal and flung the rest across the river. But when you plunged into that fairy's portal, your urge to visit our land must have influenced its magic, sending you here."

I gaped at him. Could it be? We were here because of me, after all?

"But at least that means the Beast didn't get her," said Castor, his arm now off the couch and around me.

The foreign intimacy made me sit up rigidly. "Is a fairy kidnapping her any better?"

Castor shrugged. "At least she won't eat her." He bent over me, staring into my eyes intently. "But it's a good thing we found you, or else the Beast would have gotten *you*."

Shaking myself out of my stunned numbness, I waved a hand at the room's morbid décor. "What kind of beast could you not have stuffed and mounted by now?"

"The biggest and deadliest of them all," Castor spat venomously, his arm tightening around me in an uncomfortable grip. "But don't worry, I will catch it soon. I will kill it, slowly, then I will have its head placed outside my home, as a warning to anyone or anything that I am to be respected and feared."

Confidence radiated from him as he puffed out his chest, making him look so fearless, so capable that I believed he could do anything.

Will returned, carrying a tea tray. "We've already told you, we're not hunting the Beast."

"Yes, we will!" Castor growled.

"It's not a moose or a bear, Woodbine." Will dropped the tray on the table before us, rattling the cups and spilling tea from the pot's spout. "This is the King of the Beasts we're talking about, something we've never seen the likes of. And then, it dodged every attempt you made to capture it. It even once led you into your own trap. You remember how *that* ended."

Vicious determination shone in Castor's eyes. "It only means I have to try harder, with better weapons."

"No, it means it can outwit you," Will scoffed. "Which isn't saying much."

Castor ignored him, continued, "The army now has hand-held firearms that some nobles use to hunt. If I could get one—"

The hooded man stomped into the room, eyes still obscured and fists clenched as he yelled, "You're not hunting the Beast, and that's final!"

Castor got to his feet, confronting him. "Just because you're all cowards doesn't mean I have to cower with you. If you're content to live under its threat, fine. But I'm not going to continue offering it sacrifices and praying it won't slaughter me like it did everyone in that castle. Maybe you choose to forget, but among those it devoured was Dale and Glenn's sister, who was to be my wife!"

Dale came between them, glaring up at Castor. "Stop bringing her up!"

Castor only persisted. "I will not stop!"

Dale unsheathed his sword, holding it up like he was about to smack him with it. "Don't make me use this."

"How dare I want to avenge your sister, right?" Castor drawled bitterly. "Someone has to, seeing as you both refuse to."

Dale's eyes hardened to the frozen-blue of icicles. "It's not your place to avenge her."

"It is! She was mine as well as yours!" His anger melted into hurt, as if the thought of the knight's sister reopened a wound.

I was debating my urge to reach out and comfort him when Dale stormed out of the room and up the stairs. I turned to my father in time to notice Will pouring something into the teapot.

"What's that?" I asked.

Will poured two cups, dark fringe shadowing his eyes. "Tree sap. We're out of sugar, so this will have to do as our sweetener for now." He offered me a cup with a crooked smile. "Drink up, it will make you feel better."

Suddenly realizing how parched I was, I eagerly accepted it. We might have been in some kind of magical coma for two weeks, and that was why we'd survived without food or drink, but my body was now waking up and screaming for sustenance. My father must be feeling the same way, as he, too, reached for his cup and drank thirstily.

I'd downed the first cup and poured another when Glenn burst back into the lodge. I choked on my tea at the sight of his face, so pale it appeared almost grey in the amber firelight.

"The Beast was seen out of the castle!" he stuttered. "They're saying it's on the prowl!"

Castor rose to his feet. "But both we and the Bentleys left it a whole elk each."

My eyes went to the largest set of antlers on the wall as Glenn shook his head. "It must have rejected them. We have to try something else before it starts picking off our people!"

Will cut off Castor's demand to attack short. "*Not* a suicide mission, you meathead."

"No." Glenn agreed. "No one will consider an attack, so give it a rest, Castor."

Will's eyes turned to me before flitting away. "We might soon be down to doing what our ancestors did in times like this—sacrificing prisoners of war to their gods and demons."

Glenn's lips thinned into a line. "But we no longer sacrifice those. And the war itself might soon be over." He jerked his head towards the hooded man. "It's why Rob and Dale were sent home, with King Florent said to be negotiating a treaty with the regent of Avongart."

"King Florent is only rotating the forces on the frontline so far," huffed Rob. "But I hope he can end the war, if only so we can be done with Prince Jonquil's idiocy."

"You mean Prince Jon's regency," Castor corrected.

Rob made a rude noise. "You heard me right." He nudged my father's arm. "Drink up before the steam's all gone."

My father obliged him, gulping the tea down, then setting

the cup upon its saucer with a soft *chink*. "Very sweet—interesting flavor. What sort of tea did you say this was?"

Before Rob could respond, my father slumped forwards, head hitting his knees.

"Dad!" I tried to get up, but I couldn't feel my legs, and the numbness was creeping up my arms, making it impossible to push myself up.

Panic flared in my mind, but nowhere else. My heart was steady, pumping a soft, lazy beat that left me warm and sluggish. My vision was blurring at the edges as my eyelids grew heavy, then it went sideways when my head hit the armrest.

What was happening to us? Was this a side effect of what that fairy woman had done to us, or was this something else…

The tea! They'd put something in it!

Castor shook me. "What's going on? What's happening to them?"

Rob pushed Castor away from me, before punching him, knocking him to the floor. "We're doing what we must to appease the Beast."

Castor struggled up, glaring daggers at Rob. "I won't appease it, I'll kill it."

"Suit yourself then." Will kicked Castor in the head, knocking him out this time.

Rob bent to pick my father up, giving Glenn a warning look. "As we've already said, this Beast is intelligent, and if it doesn't want prey, then there's only one thing it could want. The only animal that can hunt all others: a man."

Will came to help Rob haul my father over his shoulder. "Not just any man, but a live one it can chase itself."

Even against the downwards spiral of numbness, my pulse spiked in horror. I wanted to jump up, to attack them, stop them—to even scream. But I was paralyzed by the unstoppable invasion of drowsiness that had begun to claim my mind.

Glenn stepped before Rob, and hope soared within me. He'd stall them, call Sir Dale and they'd stop this madness in its tracks.

But Will pushed Glenn aside, knives out, face serious with intent. "Don't play the hero, Glenn, and don't call out to Dale, or we'll just knock you both out like Castor. It's either the old man or the girl. We have no better options."

"They're our guests," Glenn hissed.

Will shoved him out of the way, making him stumble aside. "They're random strangers we found in the woods. We owe them nothing."

"In fact, I'd say the Fates led us to them at the most opportune time," said Rob. "Just think of the Arboreans we lost in the war, especially conscripts from Rosemead. This one foreigner will spare countless of our countrymen from the Beast's wrath. Spare many families from losing loved ones like you did. Anyway, there's nothing you or Dale can do to stop us, and you know it."

My eyes were starting to droop, but I still saw conflict gripping Glenn's face. Then with a long, weary exhalation, he stepped aside, head hanging in defeat.

NO!

I struggled for every last drop of willpower so I could beg for my father's life. But I had none left. I screamed inwardly at my helplessness, at the horror of their intentions. Outwardly, only a strangled whimper escaped me as they exited the lodge. My father's inert body dangling over Rob's back was the last thing I saw before I was reclaimed by the dark depths of nothingness.

CHAPTER THREE

*L*ight tickled my eyelids, chasing the darkness away.

They felt fused together, almost tore apart when I cracked them open. And found a snarling wolf staring down at me.

I bolted upright with a strangled yelp. Swaying, my head swam, realizations sloshing within it like muddy water in a metal basin.

It hadn't been a bad dream. The wolf was a mounted head and I really was in Castor's family hunting lodge, in Rosemead. From the faint, rosy light pouring through the high windows between antlers, it was dawn. But there was no telling how long I'd been unconscious this time. It could have been two more weeks.

The possibility horrified me. There were no gaps in my memory that staved off the onslaught of sickening recollections. This time they hit me like a lightning bolt, instantaneous and debilitating, tearing a shriek out of me.

"Dad!"

Castor's friends had given us some sort of sleeping-draught. They'd taken my father up to some castle, as a sacrifice—to the Beast!

I heaved up to my feet, but on my first step, my legs gave and brought me down to my knees with a crash that must have echoed throughout the lodge's wooden floors.

I dragged myself up with a groan, pain screaming in my knees, sweat pouring down my back. My pace was sluggish, my body heavy, like my bones had been coated with lead. Whatever they'd given me, I had to shake it off. I had to get to that castle, had to...

Had to what? What would I do? What *could* I do?

What if I was too late and the Beast had—had—

"Ah, you're up." Castor came into the sitting room, a wooden chest under one arm and a covered wicker basket hanging from the other, sweet smells wafting from it. "I was about to come wake you."

"Where is my father?" I rasped, stumbling to grab his arm.

Eyeing my clawing hands in surprise, he offered me the chest. When I didn't make a move to take it, he sighed. "We can discuss this over breakfast. How about you get dressed first? I had the maid change you out of your ruined clothes when we first got you, but I thought you'd appreciate some fresh clothes, so I brought you some of my mother's."

I stared at him, stunned by his nonchalance.

"I don't want breakfast," I snapped, my harsh voice alien in my ears. "I want my father."

His smile stayed put, but his gaze flickered. "So do I."

"What do you mean?"

He pressed the chest at me. "We'll talk over breakfast. Now, please get dressed."

"But—"

"Please," he stressed, his loudness making me wince.

I reluctantly took the chest, if only for the promise of something other than the drenched in sweat nightgown to wear. Inside, I found a wrinkled, emerald green tea-gown, woolen slip and socks and a pair of black flats. Predictably, everything but the shoes appeared to be too big.

"You don't have to worry," Castor said as I retreated to search for a place to change. "You're not alone now."

I didn't have a name for the feeling that stalled my response. It could be the warping effects of the sleeping-draught, or that I couldn't process his meaning. All I knew was that his words had the oppressive emotions storming through me at my father's and Ada's absence crushing me even harder.

I found some storage room and struggled out of the billowy nightgown and into the equally roomy but dry clothes before padding back out. I found him sitting at the dining table on a chair turned sideways, sharpening a cutlass with slow, precise slides, each a painful scrape along my every nerve.

At my approach, he perked up, giving me a big, smoldering smile that melted some of my jitters away.

Kicking out the chair next to him, he patted the seat. "Sit. Eat."

I glanced around the table. There was oatmeal, raspberries, a rusting creamer, a small jar of honey, a block of cheese, a basket of bread rolls, and a pot of tea. Almost the same as the typical home breakfasts in my land. But not what I'd been eating for the past few months. I'd been starting the day with Adelaide, mostly eating what she served at the tavern.

The thought of her, on top of my dread for my father, had bile creeping up my throat, sparking a wave of overwhelming nausea I'd never suffered before. "I'm not really hungry."

Though his smile stayed put, his eyes hardened as he repeated, "Eat."

"But—"

"Not going to listen to you unless you talk with your mouth full."

Finding no energy to resist, I settled beside him and poured cream and honey in my oatmeal. He watched me as I stuffed the first lukewarm spoonful into my mouth then relaxed.

"That dress looks lovely on you," he began. "There's a lot more upstairs, all yours, along with shoes, coats, hats and riding boots, too."

The uncertain reaction was back. I couldn't peg what I was feeling, towards anything he said, and now about this offer. "Thank you?"

Beaming, he gestured for me to continue eating. When I began to shake my head, he dumped a handful of berries in, nudged the bowl closer. I knew he was right. I had to eat, to keep my strength for whatever came next. So I struggled to tamp down the nausea, picked the bowl up. It was only when I began shoveling more in that he sat back with a satisfied smile.

When I set the bowl down empty, feeling like food was up to my neck, and nausea up to my eyes, he nodded approvingly. "Now, what did you want to talk about?"

I goggled at him. "You know what. My father being kidnapped by your friends."

He shook his head. "They're not my friends. Hunting partners, yes, and we occasionally patrol the borders of the city together for any kind of fairy activity. Other than that, I tolerate their cowardice and ineptitude because they're still the best I could find to partner with and, well, I am a generous person. I was even going to do Dale the honor of marrying his sister, giving her everything her family couldn't. He certainly couldn't achieve much with his simple knighthood. But that future got destroyed when she was lost."

He poured me some tea, and I found myself more interested in the bubbles that roamed its surface than in what he was saying. I'd heard that some witches read one's future in tealeaves. In one of the books I'd read about the lost lands, what I now knew to be the east of the Folkshore, they read coffee grounds. But this brew was a clear light yellow rather than red, with no tea residue, and smelled strongly of mint. Even if I knew how, I couldn't look in it for answers about my fate, or those of my loved ones.

He ordered me to drink, and I only said, "You said Glenn and Dale's sister was killed by the Beast?"

Anger seemed to brim within him, twitching various muscles around his perfect face. "She would still be here if she'd listened to me. So would my father."

His father. So that was what he'd meant earlier, when I'd said I wanted my father. He'd lost his, too. "What happened to him?"

Castor's mouth twisted as he answered my earlier question. "She was going to marry me and I would have elevated her family's station by making her the lady of my house. My family has properties that bring in a great sum yearly. But she insisted on taking a job up in the castle. Why would a woman want to be someone else's servant rather than have her own?"

"Maybe she wanted to have her own money?"

"For what reason? I would have given her an allowance." He nudged my arm. "Drink your tea."

I glared at him. "I don't want to."

"Why not?"

"The last time I drank tea, I lost my father," I ground out.

"I am deeply sorry about that. I, too, lost my father to the Beast." His eyes darkened with a heartache that quieted my annoyance, and made me want to reach out, share mine. "We were attempting to hunt it a few months ago, and against my demands, my father broke off from the group to chase it deeper into the woods where we'd set traps. By the time we found him, my father was caught in one of them, mauled to death."

The thought of my father suffering the same fate finally solidified what was happening in my mind.

I was lost in a new land, with my best friend taken by fairies and my father sacrificed to a monster. And it was all my fault.

None of this would have happened if I hadn't clung to that map, hadn't hounded Ada about going to the Hornswoods where those eyes had seen us, what must have been the fairy's. I'd wanted to leave home, leave my father alone, all to see either Faerie or Arboria. Now I'd lost them both in those places.

Something horrible welled in my chest, spread up to scream in my head, burn behind my eyes. I gasped with its agony, cried out as it scorched my blurring vision and ran down my sizzling cheeks. I'd always read about people crying with desperation or desolation, had seen some doing so, but had understood it only on a mental level. I hadn't had anything to cry about, not since my mother died when I wasn't yet six.

And because I'd never appreciated that, I now had everything to weep for.

Castor set his hand on mine, shocking me out of my surrender to guilt and misery. I lurched, rearing my chair on its back legs before it slammed back down, jostling a tearing hiccup from my throat.

"It's all right," he whispered, gripping my hand.

"No—it's not," I wailed, tears running thicker, sobs hacking in my chest harder. "My family are gone. And there's nothing I can do about it."

"I know how you feel, so believe me when I say I can help you through this." Before I could respond, he rose, bent to pick me out of my chair as if I was a child. Stunned, I went limp against him, the last rise of tears squeezing from my swollen eyes as he took me back to the sitting room. "Stay with me and we'll move to my family's estate where you will have everything you could want—clothes, flowers, sweets and servants to tend to your every need. You'll never need to leave the manor."

I stiffened against him then struggled, to piece together everything he'd said so far, and so he would let me back on my feet. "What do you mean, stay with you?"

"I'll take care of you, and we can rebuild the family we lost." He set me down, pulled back to eye me appreciatively. "With your beauty and delicate poise and my, well, everything, we could have the perfect family and household."

I gaped at him until the chokehold of shock allowed me a breath. Then everything crashed in place as I squeaked, "You want me to *marry* you?"

He nodded, hands keeping my unsteady form in place, earnest eyes roaming me, searching for things he seemingly approved of. "Small as you may be, you look quite healthy. Together, we will have children so beautiful the fairy queens will scratch their eyes out in envy."

Of all the ways I'd imagined a handsome hero would propose to me, this certainly wasn't one of them. What did one say to something this blunt, this abrupt and unromantic?

"But we just met!" I finally stuttered. "You don't know anything about me, or I you."

He waved off that concern. "I am a minor lord, a hunter, from a good family with reasonable wealth, and am prepared to care for you forever, for very little in return. What more do you need to know?"

When he put it that way, it seemed so reasonable, so—pragmatic. I wiped the tears that clung to my lashes as I mumbled, "I suppose you're right."

"So you'll marry me?"

I shook my head, feeling as if I was sinking in quicksand. "I—I can't. I'm not ready for that. I've known you for barely a couple of hours. I just lost m-my father…"

"Well, I don't mean right this second." He chuckled, tapping my cheek lightly as he straightened up. "Before you become my lady, you'll first need to be shown the ropes of running the woman's side of things around my estate. I'll send you to my aunts and cousins a town away, where they'll polish you up, and get everything ready for our marriage." He faced the window beside us, glaring into the distance, drawing out and re-sheathing his cutlass by his hip. "In the meantime, I'll avenge both our fathers."

It was only then that I noticed it. High in the deep distance, beyond the town spreading below us, above the tree-tops surrounding its craggy hill was a massive, bleak castle. That was where they'd taken my father. Where the Beast had received him as a sacrifice.

I swallowed the jagged lump in my throat. "Do you…do you think there's a chance he's still alive?"

Castor worked his jaw, still focused on the view. "He might

be. The air here is quiet. I would have heard him scream if it already ate him. Unless it bit out his throat first."

A sob strangled me, a terrible mixture of horror or hope.

My father could still be alive. I had to know if he was.

"If there's any chance we could save him, we must— please," I begged, spastically gripping Castor's arm.

He covered my hand with his. "I told you, you don't have to worry anymore. I'll take care of you."

"What does that have to do with saving my father?"

Castor blinked at me as if he couldn't fathom what I meant. "You won't need him, or your cousin, if you have me."

All weepy drowsiness evaporated in a flare of affront. I pulled my hand from underneath his, stumbling out of his reach. "I don't want him back because he provides for me, Castor." He just frowned at me, as if my reaction bothered him, or as if he feared I was crazy. I tried again, "I want him back because he is my father, my family, and I love him. He's a wonderful man that everyone loves and the last person who deserves an ending like this."

His frown deepened. "I get that, but you have to understand that he's lost and move on. And I just said we'd have a new family—"

"Do you think this means I should forget about my old one? That's not how family works. And then relationships don't magically form because you say they will."

Still looking confused, he stepped around me, heading towards the sitting room door. "You're being very odd, but perhaps it's grief. You will be more amenable after you have a chance to come to terms with it, I'm sure. So eat up and sleep some more."

Though it did nothing to slow him down, I latched onto his arm, staggering in his wake. "You can't tell me you didn't love your father when you want to avenge his death this badly."

"Of course, I did! But to me it isn't about love but honor." He scowled down at me as he dragged me behind him. "The Woodbine men have been great hunters for generations, and for my father to be struck down so easily is an affront to our family name. To be killed by your own prey is the greatest dishonor, and by killing that creature and hanging its head with my ancestors' trophies, I will restore my pride, as well as my father's."

He stopped at the threshold of the unsightly trophy room, with the massive antlers of the largest moose in my direct view. They reminded me of the unsightly statue of the Horned God at the end of my town, where it sat guarding the Hornswoods. It supposedly made sure no one went in and nothing came out. Ada had always had an irrational fear of it, calling it "nightmarish." She'd once said it looked as if it might spring to life and chase her down. I'd laughed her fear away that day. I'd always believed such things only happened in my fiction books and the town's folktales. I'd heard of fairies, gods, witches and monsters all my life, but I'd never seen any proof of their existence.

But not only did these things exist, now Ada and my father were each the victim of such a supernatural being.

To cling to what I could of my wits, I had to convince myself that Ada was in a far less dire situation than my father. She was so resourceful that I had to believe she could handle herself until we found her. But first "we" needed to survive then get out of here to go after her. And to do that, I needed Castor, and he was proving too dismissive and single-minded.

No, not single-minded. Stubborn. Stupid.

He had a premade plan, and nothing would dissuade him

from it, no new developments would make him consider adjusting it. Though he'd already decided he'd attack the Beast, he wouldn't do it now to save my father, having already given up on him.

It seemed behind that beautiful face was the simplistic drive of a woodpecker. And I had a feeling it would one day lead him to blindly peck a beehive, unleashing a swarm of disasters.

Apart from the terrible circumstances of our arrival here, this was yet another distressing disillusion. A sad departure from my stories, where along with good looks and a fortune, the hero was also in possession of a great mind and character, either on par with the heroine, or above her in life experience and hard-won wisdom. In all my readings and daydreaming, the hero was always able to eloquently debate with the heroine, to empathize with or at least understand her situation or dilemma and help elevate her from them.

Castor had all the attributes of every classical hero, and he seemed to have the required instant interest in me, to the point that he wanted to make me his Lady Woodbine. But he couldn't, or worse, wouldn't listen to my concerns, or understand that what he offered wasn't what I needed right now, or even what I wanted in life.

But I'd never done anything on my own. Without my father and Ada, I was totally helpless. I needed his help, had to convince him to offer it. But to do that, I had to try a different approach with him. I hated to be manipulative, but I had no other option. I had to play on his pride, inflame it even more so he would do what I needed him to.

I caught him back again. "Why wait? You can restore you and your father's pride now! We can go up there, so I can save my father while you kill the Beast! You'll be the hero who slayed the monster who's been terrorizing your land and returned triumphant. You'll be the toast of the town, and there will be renderings of your victory all over your kingdom." He stared at me over his shoulder, unmoving and unmoved, and I rushed to add, tongue so rough with the lie I was about to utter, I felt it could sharpen his blades. "Everyone will admire you even more for saving your—your future father-in-law!"

He continued to watch me, but he finally seemed to be mulling my suggestion over. Then he finally exhaled. "You're right, that would be especially heroic. And I suppose I do need your father's blessing. He would be a fool to refuse me, though."

"Yes, he would be!" I was so frantically relieved he'd relented I would have agreed to anything he said. I turned on my heel, pulling at his arm. "Now, let's go!"

He peeled my fingers off his sleeve and clasped my hand between his, chuckling amusedly. "Don't be silly. I can't go now. I won't."

I gaped up at him. I hadn't swayed him at all?

I would have stomped my foot in frustration if I didn't fear I'd crumple to the floor. I still nearly yelled, "Why not?"

"I'll go at night, when it can't see me coming."

"By then it could be too late. We have to go now!"

"It's adorable that you think you could join me, but you're not going anywhere." He smiled down indulgently as he steered me back towards the dining room. "You stay here, explore the house, try on the clothes, wash the dishes or pick apples from the backyard. You know, things you can handle."

"What makes you think I can't handle going with you?" I didn't know if I could, but why would he assume it so readily?

His sigh was longsuffering as if he had better things to do

than explain anything to me. "It is going to be dangerous, and I guarantee it will get ugly and gory and you'd faint at the least opportune moment and put my hunt at risk. Someone as sweet and delicate as you has no business being near such a situation. And as we said yesterday, when girls behave like men, it ends in the worst kind of outcomes."

"How is attempting to free my father behaving like men? Will it make me shoot up twelve inches and grow a beard? And then my cousin is a girl and she did everything you and your friends can do. She lived and traveled alone, worked in many establishments, climbed walls, helped around my father's forge, and was tougher than most men in our town."

"And she, like Will's sister, got snatched up by fairies. Don't be stupid enough to do the same, or end up lost like both." His rising anger ended in a shout that filled the entry-way, its echo buzzing in my bones. "Girls who stay put, stay where their husbands and brothers can defend them, live longer, safer lives. Now, do as I say and finish your breakfast."

I twisted in his grip, irritated enough to be confrontational. "It's not like I'll be doing the hunting. I'll leave that to you."

My exasperation became reflected in his eyes. With one swift move, he picked me up again, unaffected by my kicking and squirming, and planted me back down on my chair.

"We'll discuss this when I get back," he said, gem-like eyes hard as stone. "Now I have to go search for a weapon worthy of that Beast's neck."

And with that, he stomped to the back of the lodge.

I stared after him, frustration almost boiling my blood.

If my father, who could still be alive, died, it might be because I couldn't change Castor's mind. Because I couldn't do anything. As Castor advised me to continue doing.

He'd said that girls who ventured nothing would be safe

from trouble. I'd been told that my whole life. But I'd also always known that there were never any guarantees. My mother had died in her own bed.

All my father's precautions and sheltering, if he'd treated her the same way he had me, hadn't protected her, had probably only stopped her from living life to the full. She'd still died young, her life cut short in a backwater town. She'd never gotten to see my father grow grey hair, or see herself in me as I grew towards womanhood.

But no one was letting me grow up. If I didn't do it on my own, I never would.

Before all this had happened, there'd been nothing I'd wanted more than new experiences and adventure. I'd dreamed I'd find both with Adelaide, then go back home to my father, laden with splendid tales and gifts. But they'd both been taken from me. And though I'd never done a thing on my own, I'd do anything to get them back.

I knew Castor wouldn't let me go. He might actually imprison me to make me "stay put." Which meant one thing.

I had to escape.

The decision solidified between one breath and the next and I called out, "Castor?"

I bated my breath as only the ruckus of his rummaging for a weapon carried back to me.

I waited until I became certain he was too far away to come running back, spoiling my plan, the one I didn't have yet. Then I bolted out of the main door.

CHAPTER FOUR

A plan started to form in my frantic mind as soon as I cleared the lodge. At least, the getaway part of one.

I came across a wooden enclosure where a satiny, light brown mare was tied in front of a water basin. Heart racing, and dreading hearing Castor's shout at any moment, I ran to one of the apple trees filling the yard. I plucked a couple of ripe ones and approached her, extending my offering. I was greeted by her snuffling snout, her warm breath blowing loose hairs off my face.

After she was done checking me, she went straight for the apple. I gave it to her, and while she was busy munching, I untied her reins from the fence, which I used to boost myself onto her. Etched along the middle of her saddle was MAPLE.

The one time I'd ridden a horse had been when my school had decided that riding lessons would be a useful addition to the curriculum. But after a few got bucked off and one lost a few teeth to a stallion's kick, the idea had been scrapped. I'd thankfully been among those who'd remained on horseback without incident. Now I had to rely on faint memories of a six-years-ago, ten-minute trot to sit astride the mare, and remain there.

"I hope you can take me up to that castle, Maple." I steered her head towards the winding cobblestone path I saw in the distance, leading down through the town and seemingly back up to the castle.

She began to trot away from the lodge, still munching. But the pace was too leisurely, and I was too agitated to wait for her to gain momentum.

"Sorry, girl!" I kicked my heels against her sides, eliciting a startled whinny.

I just had enough time to wrap the reins around my hands before Maple burst into a gallop that had me shooting up and slamming back down, over and over, expanding and compressing my insides like an accordion. Heart clattering in my chest, I pressed my knees against her sides with everything I had, threw myself forwards, almost lying flat over her back, and hung on for dear life.

After feeling reasonably secure I wouldn't go flying over her head, I turned my head and watched where we galloped. Maple seemed to know her way to the castle, must have taken it many times with her master, who was obsessed with the Beast.

Soon we were speeding through Rosemead, blasting past whitewashed, two-floored houses with speckled, black-tiled roofs. Their terraces and gardens teemed with laden fruit trees and vegetable patches, twining vines that covered walls and archways, and sprawling bushes filled with bursts of glittering flowers of every hue.

Though Aubenaire was rainy and green, and we planted many things, it had nothing to compare with Arbore's exquisite flora. Apart from that, and the massive castle looming over the town, it seemed Rosemead wasn't too different from my own. Cobblestone covered its roads, stone fountains seemed to hold more birds than the trees and children ran amok in alleys and in backyards.

The streets were thankfully not busy yet, and those occupying them on horseback, in carriages or on foot were startled by my haste. Others emerged from houses and shops to investigate the racket of Maple's clomping hooves. Though small towns were generally unused to urgent riders, everyone didn't seem curious but alarmed at my passage. It seemed living under the Beast's threat had made them wary of anything that would draw its attention or wrath.

When no one tried to intercept me, I began noticing their details. The women were mostly in high-waist gowns with locks of hair artfully spilling from their updos, and the men wore loose shirts and tight pants, their hair ranging from close-cropped to flowing past their shoulders. Everyone's complexion was almost the same as in Aubenaire, either fair or freckled, their hair in shades of browns, blonde and the rare redhead. One man I passed almost within an arm's reach had eyes as grey as my father's.

It was more evidence that my ancestors had come from here. But my dream to discover my roots and maybe connect with distant relatives would have to remain on hold. This dream had turned into a nightmare anyway, and if I couldn't save my father...

Unable to complete that thought, my throat convulsed with those new, awful emotions that had been assaulting me since I'd woken up here. I now understood why so many books I'd read ended with the moral "be careful what you wish for."

We'd just breezed past the common part of town and were

climbing up towards what looked like the elite one, formed in arcs at the foot of the hill with smoother paths and stranger trees with green trunks and unfamiliar fruit. The castle loomed larger above me by the minute, its closest tower a massive structure silhouetted ominously against the rising sun.

Arms burning and legs shaking with the unbelievably strenuous effort of riding, I had to slow Maple down as we reached a town square, surrounded by large, luxurious buildings with cast-iron balconies—what could be official courthouses or homes of mayors, merchants or lords. But one thing caught my attention in the middle of the square. A ten-foot marble sculpture of a woman with long, wavy hair, wearing a wreath of peach blossoms and clutching a solid gold cornucopia flowing with silver grapes, corn and strange fruits I had no name for.

I knew her. The goddess of fertility and harvest we called the Field Queen in Ericura. She was among a pantheon whose names and tales had been lost to time, likely during the migration from Arboria to our island. Our depictions either had her holding a bundle of wheat or a horn-shaped wicker basket.

Her podium declared her to be ROSMERTA. She had to be the patron goddess of Rosemead. Perhaps it was named after her, like Aubenaire was for Saint Alban, who'd led my ancestors out of Arboria and onto Ericura.

Finding out the Field Queen's true name ought to have been exciting. This was precisely the kind of discovery I'd longed for all my life. But now it only had me sinking past anxiety and spiraling into melancholy. This goddess wasn't just a reminder of my people's forgotten past, but of what I'd personally lost.

My mother's effigy above her grave had been based on her.

All this landmark did was remind me that I'd already lost one parent.

It hurt to look at her, and also away from her, but I had to turn from what I had lost and focus on what I still had. At least, I hoped I still did.

A couple of miles past the square, Maple slowed from a trot to a walk as we were engulfed by the castle's shadow.

Perched on its worn, stony hill, it was a menacing sight. The main structure was a gigantic, sheer rectangle, its facade made entirely of dark, rain-stained slate. It had conical, capped towers and a smattering of turrets that bordered arched, curtained windows and towering stone fences topped with sharp, metal spikes that glistened with simmering threat.

When Maple finally came to a stop before the towering black iron gates, fog emerged from beyond them in thick, curling clouds, turning this midsummer day to a chilling autumn dusk.

Shaking down to my toes, heart stumbling in my chest and cutting off my breathing, I stared up at the castle. Half a dozen gargoyles stared down at me from the distance. And there was no discernable way in, aside from the locked gate.

With a loud huff, Maple turned her head, gearing up to leave. I pulled on her reins, the sudden chill intensifying the tremors of exhaustion and dread.

"Wait! We need to find a way in."

She stomped her hooves and made complaining noises. I could feel her growing fear, feel her itching to leave. I didn't blame her. If not for my father being held captive in there, in danger of being the Beast's next meal, I would have run and never looked back.

I dismounted, and almost crumpled to the ground. I clung to her mane to steady myself, giving her the other apple as I stroked her neck in encouragement and gratitude. Then I squinted up at the nightmarish edifice.

It was as if it absorbed light and radiated danger, exactly what I'd imagined an evil creature would reside in. All it was missing were a murder of circling crows and cracks of perpetual lightning.

Setting my hands on the cold, damp gates, I let out a shuddering breath. I'd come all the way up thinking I might find a way in once I got here. In my books, the hero or heroine always had a plan, or found a convenient one when they most needed it. It was clear none of those stories had anything to do with reality. Reality was the harsh, ugly and merciless place both my father and Ada had been trying to protect me from...

A metallic creak startled me, had me stumbling back a few feet. A carpet of thick, freezing fog taller than me rolled out, encasing me in an instant layer of frost that turned my hands slippery, my hair damp and set my shoulders shaking. A gust of wind followed, dispersing the cold spirals into blanketing vapor and carrying a low, hair-raising hum coming from behind the gates. A chorus of rustling leaves or of sinister whispers, I didn't want to know which.

But the gates were open. Somehow. All I had to do was run in, find my father and lead him out to Maple.

So why wasn't I running?

I was stuck to the spot, lips and fingers going numb, eyes drying out as I stared up at the Beast's abode.

As much as I hated to admit it, I was too terrified of going in there. I...

"Bonnie!"

The shout hit me between my shoulder blades, almost had me keeling over. It was only then I heard the approaching stomp of hooves.

Teetering around, I saw Castor on a white stallion, galloping up the hill towards me. I didn't need to see his face to know he was livid.

"Get back here *now!*"

The imperiousness of that order gave me enough spiteful courage to stagger past the threshold. Before I lost my nerve, I broke out into a sprint through the gloomy grounds, splitting the eerie fog in my path, cracking the glaze of ice that had settled over me, and regaining body heat in a burning surge.

As I ran, I caught glimpses of my surroundings in the ghostly illumination of the fog-blanked sun. But it was only halfway between the gates and the main castle door that something caught my eye, what I'd thought a short oak tree from a distance. As I passed it, I couldn't credit what I saw. It had no fruit, only flowers. Not blossoms, but the biggest *roses* I'd ever seen. About a dozen of them, in different colors. One was even blue!

Shaking off the entrancing sight of the impossible tree, I ran up the cracked stone steps towards the massive oaken doors, my mind racing with my two options. Either put Adelaide's lock picking accounts into practice or bang on the door and take my chances begging the Beast for my father's life. I decided to try the former first, as it had a slightly lesser chance of ending in certain death.

I'd failed to find the door's lock and was frantically concluding that it was bolted from the inside when I heard a shuffle of movement. Before I could draw another breath, let alone retreat or hide, the left door creaked open.

Without giving myself a chance to wonder about what was letting me in or why, I rushed in and the door slammed shut behind me.

I stood in total darkness for heart-uprooting moments

thinking I'd only succeeded in providing the Beast with an extra live meal.

After moments, when nothing attacked me, my eyes adjusted enough to realize that subdued light was struggling from the iron-boarded windows on both sides of the door. Then with a faint buzz burst above me. It was a bulbous glass lantern, like the bottles from an apothecary. Its soft light was still not enough for me to scope out the place.

Clenching and unclenching my damp, freezing hands, trying to control my tremors, I walked further in and more lights burst to life with my every step. What I could see of the inside of the castle was nowhere as scary as the outside, with the walls spread in panels and paintings and the floors paved in multicolored mosaic patterns and images.

Swallowing down my rioting heart, I forced myself to think. Every book I'd ever read that was set in a castle had prisoners locked in a dungeon or a tower. My father was probably...

Something collided into the front door with a shuddering crash. I leaped with a muffled shriek and torches burst into white flames, lighting the way up a spiral staircase.

"*Bonnie!*" Castor shouted from outside, muffled but incensed. "Get out this instant and leave all this to me."

I wanted to yell back that I wouldn't be here if he had come in the first place. But that would be a waste of time I didn't have. I also didn't know if I'd be able to walk out, or if I was trapped. All I could do was go further in, do what I'd come to do.

As I headed towards the stairs, I passed through pitch-dark halls on either side. Suddenly all my hairs stood on end. Something big and heavy was shuffling in tandem with my footfalls. The strangest and worst ideas burst in my mind's eye at once, that of a giant worm slithering across the floor or a bloodied body being dragged in a bed sheet.

A faint memory flickered through my morbid imaginings, of people wrapping my mother's limp form in her sheets, then lifting her out of the bedroom. At the time, I'd thought she was sick. It had taken weeks of waiting for her to be brought back after she recovered for me to understand that she was gone forever.

The dragging noise distressed me more than it frightened me. I didn't want to consider what creatures inhabited this place, but it was better that than imagining the ravaged remains of my father being taken out for burial.

Castor slammed against the door again, this time many times in a row, like he was trying to shoulder it down, all the while shouting orders at me. But I was too far now to hear him clearly. And the trail of whispers I'd heard earlier was now louder, some coming from above, some from around me.

I still saw nothing. But I felt a sudden draft that blew my hair over my face before the flutter of massive wings reverberated in my ears.

Another burst of panic propelled me to the stairs where the torches seemed to be guiding me. I was halfway up the first flight when a rasp grated from above. I almost ran back down until I realized what the voice had said.

"Follow me!"

Unthinkingly, I did. The white flames flickered as I passed among them, darting behind the voice. At the first bend, another prodding hiss came from above me.

"Hurry!"

Shock at how close it sounded made me slip on the red carpet covering the stairs. I arrived at the second floor on all fours before scrambling up. A loud flap, followed by hard stomps, like someone walking on stilts, led me further up, where the whispers diverged, becoming distinct if overlapping, as if in argument.

At the fourth and apparently final floor, I was panting my lungs out when a single hiss from far above urged, "He's through here."

Dad. It had to be him they were leading me to. Whatever they were. He was alive. He had to be.

A rush of exhilaration washed over me, unbalancing me into seesawing towards the direction the voice came from. A doorway that I wasted no time stumbling blindly into.

One instant I was on a spacious landing, the next I was in a tubular space with nothing but stone stairs that wound up steeply all the way to a dim-lit end.

Heart racing, I dropped to my hands and knees and crawled up the stairs. I could barely see with sweat spilling into my eyes, blurring my vision. I didn't come all this way to sabotage everything with a bone-crushing stumble to the bottom.

The light led me up into an endless chamber with cells along both sides. I got up, snapping my head around. "DAD?"

"Bonnie?"

I burst out running towards his voice. The moment I saw him, I threw myself at his cell, shakily clinging to the bars. "Dad! Are you all right?"

He struggled up from a pile of hay, rushed to wrap his hands over mine. They were even colder than mine, but in the light from the tiny, high window, I could see there wasn't a scratch on him. He just looked pale and disheveled.

His relieved expression vanished like smoke in a gale, soaring fright replacing it. "You can't be here." He unwrapped my fingers from the bars frantically. "You shouldn't have come, Bonnie. Go away—*run*."

I stretched my hands out to him through the bars. "No, I'm not leaving without you!"

"I can't leave." He shook his head as he staggered out of reach, then back down on the hay. "But you have to get out before it finds you!"

I opened my mouth to argue, only to close it. Of course, he thought he couldn't leave. He was still locked in there.

My spastic fingers trembled as I took pins out of my hair as I looked around, hoping that if I didn't find anything better, I'd be able to pick the lock like Adelaide had told me how.

The flap of wings came from above again then something clanged at my feet. I looked up then down, found a long, black key on the ground.

Not pausing to think who was helping me, or why, I snatched the key up. My hands were shaking so hard it took three tries to slot it in.

As soon as I unlocked the door, my father's breath caught in his throat as his eyes rounded in fear. Before I could utter another word, a shadow grew behind me, its darkness smothering us both.

I could barely inch my head back to look over my shoulder, suffocating with dread.

And that was before I saw it.

Silhouetted against the light at its back, a huge, hunched creature with clawed hands and eyes that glowed a terrifying yellow towered above us.

The Beast!

A shriek of horror escaped from my gut as I tore the door open and streaked inside the cell, slamming it behind me. It only tore it back open and advanced on us.

Sobs wracking my body, I spread my arms protectively in front of my father, who was struggling to get up. Eyes clinging in terror to its glowing ones, knees about to give way, I braced for the worst.

When it came, the blow I expected wasn't a swipe of flesh-shredding claws, but a rib-rattling, marrow-congealing rumble.

"How did you get up here?"

CHAPTER FIVE

*I*t spoke.

I'd expected a hundred things from the Beast. That wasn't among them.

But—if it could speak then maybe—maybe I could reason with it?

I kept my arms spread in front of my father, who was now on his feet and trying to push me behind him. For all the good either of our actions would do. That Beast was twice our sizes. And it had already eaten the inhabitants of a whole castle.

I still had to try. There was nothing else I could do. "Please —please let him go!"

At my ragged plea, it cocked its head sideways, the golden light dimming in one eye. They didn't glow as I'd first thought, but reflected light, like other predators' did.

"Who are you, and how did you get in here? I won't ask again."

Its voice was literally hair-raising, sending goosebumps flaring up my limbs to my scalp, riding a body-shaking shudder. "I-I came for my father."

Not answering its question was risky, stupid even, testing its temper. But, true to its word, it didn't ask again, it just slowly straightened to its full size to look down at me in a way that made my teeth clatter.

"You can't have him."

"Are you going to eat him?" I blurted out, shudders spiking. "Please, please don't do this. We'll get you another sacrifice—a deer, an elk, a bear—all of them! My friend is a hunter—he'll get you whatever type of game you want. Just please—let him go."

"I did."

My chattering and shaking stopped dead, leaving me stiff and gawking at its statement. "Do you consider imprisonment rather than slaughter 'letting him go?'"

It growled in answer to my scoff, reminding me just what I was dealing with. As if I could forget.

"When your father was dropped on my property, I left him to wander the grounds and find his way out." Menace blasted off it as it glared down at my father. "But then he stole from me, and for that he must be punished."

Offense boiled within me, fueling my reckless shout. "My father is not a thief!"

Not that I considered stealing bad on principle, with my best friend a thief who'd always had good or even necessary reasons for her thefts. But my father had a very black and white moral code, and would never steal a thing.

The Beast came closer, sending me stumbling back with a gasp. I could see the outline of its sharp fangs and long hair now, but the rest was still shrouded in shadow. "And yet, he still ripped a rose from my garden."

Its deep, chilling voice sent shockwaves through me. But even through that level of shiver-inducing fear, I couldn't hold my tongue. I'd already disrespected it, anyway, and if it was going to punish me for it, there was nothing I could do about it. So why stop now?

"What bizarre logic is that?" My father gripped my shoulders, whispered for me to please stop, but I couldn't. "On what grounds does plucking a rose warrant a life sentence?"

"On my grounds," it growled.

"How much is a single rose worth to something like you?" I choked, on the verge of breaking down. "You spared him before, why not spare him for something so insignificant?"

It didn't answer me.

"Please—please, let him go," I begged. "If you don't consider him a sacrifice, there's nothing you can possibly achieve from keeping him here. I'll do anything you want. I'll plant you a whole new rosebush if you need."

"The rose wasn't from a bush."

My thoughts flitted back to the peculiar tree I'd spotted on my way in. I was about to ask what its significance was, if my father and I had stumbled into a fairy situation, but a slam from below had us all jerking in its direction.

"Bonnie!"

At Castor's distant scream, it rounded on me. "How many others did you bring here?"

"None! He followed me, but I can explain—"

It had no interest in listening to me as it pushed my father back deeper into the cell and pulled me outside. Then it slammed the door, locking it again before tearing away, heading down towards Castor's approaching bellows.

The Beast was sure to tear him to the pieces. He'd die a gruesome death, all because he'd come for me. I couldn't let that happen.

I spun around to my father, gasped, "I'll be right back!"

My father's cries for me to escape trailed after me as I sped away like wildfire was at my heels. Climbing down the steep steps was harder than the journey up, and I fell a couple of times, and miraculously didn't tumble the rest of the way down.

I finally made it to floor below to find Castor with his back to me, holding a crossbow, looking around rabidly.

"Come out and face me, Beast! I know you have her, and I won't leave without her or your head!"

"Castor, you have to get out of here!"

He jumped with a shout, shooting an arrow that chipped the wall beside my head, and had me falling back through the doorway.

The Beast emerged from the shadows, a towering, terrifying figure in the wavering torchlight, and ripped out an ear-splitting roar that had Castor leaping back, fumbling another arrow in place.

It was on him in a heartbeat, slapping the crossbow from his hands. Castor only whipped out a serrated hunting knife and yelled for me to run.

That moment of distraction was his downfall. My warning shout left my mouth too late, accompanying his pained screech as the Beast struck him down.

The Beast bent over him, no doubt to swipe a killing blow, and I was across the space before I knew it. I latched onto its arm, stuttering, "Don't—p-please—don't kill him."

"You're making a lot of demands for someone who has no leverage here," it grumbled as it raised me high in the air. But instead of tossing me away, it only kept Castor pinned under its foot, pressing his throat.

I clung to its massive arm, kicking the air, panting, like I'd once done as I'd hung from a tree branch in our backyard.

After my father had saved me, he'd immediately cut down the tree and forbidden me to climb any again. And here I was, hanging from a murderous monster's limb, bothering it enough it might smash me on the ground at any moment.

I could barely breathe, but I still had to beg for Castor's life. "H-he wouldn't have come if it weren't for me—and I wouldn't have trespassed if my father hadn't been kept here."

When Castor went limp, it removed its foot, but still dangled me, raising me higher. "Your father earned his sentence."

I squirmed, trying to no avail to make it put me down as I gasped, "He wouldn't have been brought here in the first place if you didn't require sacrifices from the people!"

"I will not be held accountable for your people's stupid assumptions." Its snarl struck me still and stiff as plaster, fearing it would finally end my annoyance by snapping me in half.

"I'm not from Arbore!" I pleaded. "I have no role in or knowledge of whatever has been happening in this place. I just want my father back!"

It ceased its threatening noises, head tilted up quizzically. "Where are you from?"

"You wouldn't believe me if I told you."

After a thoughtful pause, it lowered its arm and me along with it to the ground. "Do you know anything about Arbore at all?"

"Just that it exists. Why?"

The whispers from earlier suddenly returned, gripping its attention.

"Do you really think so?" it said to seemingly no one, looking behind me.

I followed its line of sight and found an obscure outline

with what looked like horns sticking out from behind a suit of armor. The shape seemed to respond, if only from the Beast's reaction. I could hear nothing but that whispering, as if it spoke in a pitch and volume not meant for human ears.

The Beast finally nodded at it. "I will spare him, but he will join your father in the cells."

"No!" I cried out.

"Then what is it that you want? For me to set him free, so he returns with more hunters to attack me?" It kicked Castor with an exasperated growl, making me flinch. "If I release your father as well, then that gives the people more incentive to attack."

I shook my head, confusion swirling in my deepening shock. "How?"

I could have sworn it rolled its eyes at me, a strangely human reaction from such a creature. "A man who was sacrificed to me resurfaces unharmed with his daughter, and so does a hunter who broke into my castle. Everyone would assume your boy fought me and not only lived but rescued you both, and he goes out urging people to help him finish what he started. Knowing that I didn't kill either of them makes me less fearful, a possible target after I was an impossible one. Do you understand?"

I did, and I had so many other questions for it. But they were all my insatiable curiosity being roused at the worst of times. Our immediate situation didn't call for them, neither would they be of any use to me right now.

"What if we all immediately left Rosemead?" I said. "Our disappearance would keep the people's fear, wouldn't it?"

"I'd sooner believe in benevolent fey than I would in this hunter abandoning his plan to slay me."

"Then w-what do you want?"

"To be left alone!" Its bellow blasted around the hall, shaking the stone ground beneath my feet.

The whispers returned, faster, urgent, and I caught another glimpse of the horned entity before it disappeared.

"There has to be a way around this," I wheezed, panic pounding my heart against my ribs until I felt it would bruise, or burst. "There has to be something I can do—something to exchange for his life, for my father's freedom."

"There is nothing you can give me."

It was right. I didn't have anything, had nothing to offer, to trade, nothing but...

Myself.

"What about me?" I blurted out.

It went totally still. "What about you?"

"Take me in their place."

Its voice dipped deeper, becoming a wolf's growl. "Why would I do that?" The whispers rose like wildfire, until its frustrated snarl doused them. "Let me think!"

It turned its attention back to me, prompting me to continue, and my teeth chattered until I had to clamp them shut and speak through them, already regretting my words, yet seeing no other solution. "When you let them go, Castor won't tell anyone that you spared him or that he failed to save me. He's too proud for that. While people will assume that you found my father insulting as a sacrifice, and took me as a replacement. Everyone will accept that since girls are always considered better sacrifices."

Everything went unnervingly quiet, only my frenzied heartbeat drumming in my ears.

Then it bent over, bringing its face down to mine. "What is your name?"

In this lighting, I could see the outlines of its face, where its eyes, nose and mouth were. A configuration that seemed almost human.

"Bonnie..." My voice cracked. I cleared my bone-dry throat, tried again. "Bonnibel Fairborn."

After a long, nerve-wracking moment, it finally said, "Miss Fairborn, I believe we have a deal."

I only stood staring up at it, unable to utter another word.

It stepped over Castor and bellowed, "Ivy!"

The heavy slithering noise from earlier approached, dragging up the stairs until something slammed onto the ground beside us and sprouted upwards to the Beast's eye-level.

At first, I thought it was an abnormally tall woman. But when the rest of her silhouette became clear, I realized that she had no legs.

From the waist down, she was a giant serpent!

I didn't scream at the horrific sight. I couldn't. I must be beyond exhausted, my capacity for shock depleted.

"Take the two men away. Make sure no one sees you."

The snake-woman bowed her head at the Beast's terse instructions. "Yes, Master."

Mind-bogglingly fast for something that size, she slithered past me and shot up the tower. In a minute, she came back down with my father wrapped in her tail and scooped up Castor in her arms.

My father ceased his struggle to reach out to me, gasping, "Bonnie—what did you do?"

I winced as I met his stricken gaze, croaked, "What I had to do to set you free."

Ashen-faced, he resumed his struggle against Ivy's inescapable hold. "No! I told you to leave, to save yourself! Why didn't you listen to me?"

"I couldn't leave you up there! But I can explain—wait..." I chased after them, barreling down the stairs. "Wait! Slow down!"

Ivy ignored me, continuing to wind down the staircases like a worm through an apple.

As she reached the entrance hall, I leaped down the last stairs, no longer caring if I broke something, landing with a slam that shot up every bone and snapped my teeth over my tongue.

Pain screaming in every nerve ending, I ran, arm outstretched to meet my father's reaching hand as I tried to tell him it was going to be fine, that I had chosen this. But my lungs felt filled with broken glass and I could only wheeze incoherently. Then the door slammed shut in my face.

For a stunned moment, I stared at the soaring barrier. Then a wave of panic overcame me as I desperately pulled on the handle. But it wouldn't budge.

I staggered to the nearest window in time to see Ivy slithering out of the gates. I could hear my father's anguished shouts for me echoing up to the castle as they swung shut, a final barrier between us. I doubted they'd ever open again.

The deal with the Beast had been settled far faster than I could have processed. Now the reality of it sank in. And its dreadful implications.

My father had no one else but me. Neither did Adelaide. By striking that deal to separate us forever, I hadn't fixed anything.

I'd only ruined all our lives in a different way.

CHAPTER SIX

$\mathcal{H}$opelessness felt like an anchor that dragged me down to the bottom of crushing despair.

I'd stayed there with my face pressed to the window, my hands clutching its iron bars, numbly watching the shadow of the gates shift with the eerily muted sunlight until the day died.

Now it was pitch dark outside with nothing but a chilling glow from the gates illuminating the castle grounds, and I still waited. I didn't know what I was waiting for. The monster that had carried my father and Castor to freedom wasn't going to come back for me. She only obeyed her master. And he was never letting me go.

I was stuck in here, with no way back to my father. He was just as stuck as I was away from home. And Adelaide? Now I'd never know what had happened to her.

I sank deeper in self-recrimination with every passing second. There had to have been a better way to resolve this, one that wasn't a rash decision with terrible and permanent consequences. But I'd never had to talk my way out of a bad situation, let alone survive a risky ordeal. I'd never been exposed to danger of any sort. My father had made sure of it. Then had come Adelaide, and they'd both joined forces in coddling me, creating an impenetrable shield of love and protection around me.

If only they hadn't. It might have saved us all if I were more like her, experienced, resourceful, able to bargain, to lie, to struggle. But I wouldn't have needed to be, if we'd remained as we'd been, blissfully unaware of this old, forgotten world.

None of this would have happened if I hadn't insisted on going into the Hornswoods.

Now we were torn apart, each lost and alone forever. And it *was* all my fault.

"Miss Fairborn."

The Beast's voice rumbled in the ground beneath me, buzzed in my bones. I paid it no mind, continued watching the faintly glowing gates, as if my focus alone would force them open.

A huge shadow engulfed me. I listlessly sank to the ground and tipped my head back, saw the Beast standing over me, holding an oil lamp.

From this perspective, I could have seen its face more clearly. But I didn't care to. My curiosity, once a furnace fire, was now a dying candle's flame.

It offered me a hand. It was only then I registered that it wasn't some grizzly, clawed paw, but a large, hairy man's hand with long, sharp nails. "Come with me."

I sniffled loudly, wiped at my sore, swollen eyes, tears sticking my lashes together. "Why?"

"Do you plan on staying here forever?"

"This is as close to the outside as I'll ever get again, isn't it?"

"That was your decision. Now get up." Its order was harsher this time.

Ignoring its hand, I stood up, every muscle trembling, every bone aching. He moved the lamp as I looked up—and I saw it.

Saw *him*.

At first, I'd thought him one of the talking beasts in children's stories. But he wasn't an animal with human attributes. He was a man with beastly traits.

In a loose white shirt that failed to obscure a massive torso and shoulders and fitting navy pants that hitched up thick, muscular legs, he stood upright, if with a slight hunch. And that was the extent of his civilized getup, as he wore no belt or other accessories, and no socks or shoes on his huge, fuzzy feet. He also couldn't properly grip the gas lamp, thanks to his overgrown nails, and abnormally large, hairy fingers.

Reluctant yet fascinated, my weary gaze traveled up his thick, veiny neck to a broad, bearded face, housing an unsettling merge of features, all framed by his rioting, chest-length, wavy brown hair. He had a protruding lower jaw, a wide mouth full of sharp incisors and long canines that pushed his full lips forward. Above that was a large, slashed nose with loose skin along the bridge that crinkled with his every heavy breath. Two big, angular ears stuck out of his hair. In his entirety, he was the closest thing to the wolfman I'd read about in many a folktale.

There was only one thing that was fully human about him. A pair of thick-lashed, blue-green eyes that shone under his thick, sinisterly arching brows like polished turquoises.

And those eyes were drilling into mine in a searing glare.

Hunching further, yet still towering two feet above me, he snapped, "Are you done staring?"

Lurching back, I nodded, a painful flush of embarrassment surging to my face. He immediately turned and shuffled stiffly away, leading me back upstairs.

Several torches had been lit around the castle where there'd been darkness before, showing me more of the interior, solidifying my earlier observation that it wasn't as macabre around here as I'd expected coming in. After all, this had been some nobleman's castle before the Beast had seized it. What was chilling were the sounds of slithering bodies, fluttering wings, and stomping hooves that accompanied us as we ascended. The unseen horrors must be the Beast's underlings that had supplanted the castle's original staff.

Sir Dale's sister tragic story flared in my memory. It seemed I was to suffer her fate now.

Too numb to panic at the thought, my sore eyes roved around, taking everything in. I could now see the carpet covering the stairs was red velvet bordered with floral patterns of gold thread, and that up to a certain level, the walls were marble, like the stairs. Above that, beveled plaster of interlocking loops of thorns took over, contained in panels between the flat spaces. A look below as we got higher revealed the entrance floor pattern that I'd failed to see at ground level. A spiraling mosaic of a massive pink rose with a couple of fallen petals.

The second floor looked like the museums I'd read about, if like an abandoned one. In every corner, rusting suits of armor stood holding lances, axes or swords. On every silver-and-gold-wallpapered wall hung dusty paintings of natural panoramas or historical scenes. And by every column stood mahogany tables or marble pedestals displaying an array of exquisite ornaments covered in cobwebs.

Whoever the original residents of this castle had been, they could have probably answered my questions about my ancestors. But all that was left of them were these neglected treasures, their legacy desecrated by whatever creatures now roamed their spaces.

The Beast stopped before a whitewood door with a curling, golden handle.

"I had this prepared for you," he said as he opened the door.

I peeked inside, expecting to find a torture chamber or a blood-splattered area reminiscent of a butcher shop, but it was a bedroom. Neat and clearly recently cleaned, the spacious room had a queen-sized bed, with gossamer drapes bound to its four posters like sails, and a massive, ornately-carved wardrobe with alternating mirrored doors.

Apprehension kept me in my place. "I don't understand."

He gestured impatiently. "This is your room."

"Why won't you put me in the tower?"

His frown created ridges along his forehead and united his brows, hitching his top lip up and baring his fangs. "Because you did nothing wrong."

I turned away. I couldn't look at him without imagining those teeth disemboweling me.

He made a gruff noise and shoved me inside. "Enter."

Though I didn't think he meant to be forceful, he was so strong, and I was so tiny compared to him, I stumbled all the way to the bed, landing on my side on the decorative champagne duvet. I struggled up on it, and my feet dangled above the floor.

I nervously ran my hands over the cotton-filled satin

bedding, drying my sweating palms. "A-are you going to eat me now?"

He looked taken aback before he snorted what I felt was a laugh. "There's not much of you to eat."

"Don't you eat your sacrifices?"

"Do you believe everything you hear?"

"They weren't wrong about you being a beast."

His nose wrinkled like a wolf as he snarled like one, chilling me to the bone. "Don't call me that!"

All previous numbness evaporating, I hiccupped. "W—what do I call you then?"

He turned his head away as if to an invisible presence, angrily mumbling, "Why should I give her my name? What if she's heard?" He stopped, listened, then snapped, "She can't truly know nothing about the kingdom..." He stopped again before growling, "*Fine!*"

Turning back to me, he reluctantly grumbled, "Leander. My name is Leander."

Leander? While I didn't know if it meant anything, it didn't sound like a name I would have associated with him. But then I hadn't expected something like him to have a name at all.

I nodded slowly, eyeing him warily. "What are you going to do with me?"

"I'm not sure yet." He turned away, starting to close the door. "For now, you will freshen up and join me for dinner."

The blurted out "No!" was out my mouth before I could think.

He turned back, an angry eye staring at me through the door's crack. "What was that?"

I gulped my heart down, but had to answer. "N-no, I won't join you for dinner."

The door rattled in his grip as if it would rip out of its frame. I slid further into the bed, quaking, and heard another voice. Not a whisper this time, but a hushed shout.

What sounded like a heated if subdued exchange followed, then he finally mumbled, "I'll give you some time to relax. Then you *will* attend dinner."

He didn't give me an opportunity to object before slamming the door shut.

I drew my shaking knees against my chest, stared at the door. Unable to admire its carved design of a blooming bouquet, I dreaded his heavy, retreating footsteps would reverse, and he'd come force me to "freshen up" then drag me to dinner himself.

But he continued receding, along with that clomping noise. Once the floor grew quiet, the feeling returned to my limbs enough to roll myself off the bed.

I gave the room one more sweeping glance. It was the size of our home's entire top floor, was spread in opulent furniture I'd never seen the likes of even in storybooks. The upholstered, pale pink sofa, matching chairs and white marble table all stood on gilded legs and the carved hairdresser and a giant wardrobe looked like works of art by the open double-door that led into an adjoining bathroom.

It was a strangely exquisite cage for a monster's prisoner. I couldn't begin to think why he'd put me here.

And I didn't want to. I could only think of getting out. And now was my only chance.

I rushed to the window on unsteady feet. Despite the room's size, there was only one. But it was proportionately large, with a painted wooden frame and curtains that matched the bedspread, if covered in a pattern of pink roses. To my relief, it wasn't fitted glass and mortar, but opened inwards, letting cool air rush in, biting at my heated face.

Beyond the unnatural darkness cloaking the castle, the city below was languishing under what looked like the last traces of dusk. I could also see that the distance to the ground was far higher than I'd hoped. This second floor was three times the height of our two-story house in Aubenaire.

But this was my only way out.

It was ironic that when I'd last seen my best friend, I'd chastised her about breaking into our local lord's mansion through its second-floor window. She'd done it to rob his unbearable wife, to avenge me for when the harpy had ruined my book. She'd stolen me *The Known World* to replace it, and my obsession with it had resulted in our current tragedy. Now I needed Adelaide's experience in climbing out of windows and her hooked rope.

I just needed *her*.

But if I were to ever see her again, I had to get out of here.

Eyes filling again with a burning oppression, I rushed to the wardrobe. A quick rummage revealed shelf upon rack of neatly folded and hung clothes and organized shoes, all sorted by color, but nothing to be used as a rope.

Trembling with frustration, I searched my mind for any tips Ada might have mentioned. But nothing struck me, not until I found a shelf of bedding.

It was the earliest memory of our friendship, when Adelaide had finally agreed to come over for tea. She'd regaled me with what I'd considered thrilling stories from a life lived alone and on the streets since her mother had died. One was about how she'd snuck out of an inn she'd worked at after robbing some abusive patron by climbing down a line of sheets.

Dragging a chair over, I got down everything I could reach, almost tipping myself back a few times. Once I had all the sheets on the floor, I got to work.

Excitement and urgency burned through me, shaking my hands as I tied the sheets' ends together. I secured one end of the knotted snake to the bedpost before throwing the other out of the window. It went all the way down to the ground.

This was it. All I had to do was climb down and run to the gates. I counted on being able to open them, now I was on the inside. Without Maple, it would take me hours to walk back to Castor's lodge, but that was the least of my worries. Once I arrived, my father and I would be free.

Holding on tight to the ledge of the window, I looked up and down the side of the castle, making sure no one was around to see me climbing down. The towers, the roof's battlements and the gargoyles perched on every ledge seemed to be looking down at me warningly.

Shaking off the spooky sensation, I put one leg over the edge, gripped the sheet—

—and rolled out the window with a startled squawk.

Suffocating in fright, I clawed at the sheet, only for my hands to slide down their soft length, finding no traction. I closed my eyes, not wanting to see the plummet to my death...and slammed against the wall.

The collision emptied my lungs, snapped open my eyes. My hands had snagged on a knot, stopping my slide. Heart bursting out of my chest, I grappled with the sheet, kicking to bring it between my knees. I bumped into the rough façade again, flaring a rush of chafing pain at every point of contact. But that was nothing compared to what could have happened. I could have been lying on the ground in bloody, broken pieces right now.

That fate could be still in the cards. I was too far down to climb back into the room, and too far up a fall would surely kill me. And this was far, far more difficult and frightening than Adelaide had ever made it out to be.

Heart convulsing in guilt that I'd ever thought her life on the run exciting, I poured all my waning strength into clinging to my lifeline between hands and knees. This was the position I should have assumed from the beginning. There was still the risk I'd slip again and be unable to catch myself. But remaining in place was quickly wearing me out. I'd soon fall anyway.

Teeth clattering with gut-twisting dread and exertion, I moved my hands down a few inches below the knot, then lowered my legs by the same measure.

It worked. Now I had to do it again, and again, without any further disastrous slips.

After moments of trying to calm my breathing and gather my strength, I repeated the motion five times in a row, every muscle screaming.

I did get lower, but not by much. I still had what must be a fifty-foot drop beneath me, and I was fast losing strength, wriggling like a worm on a hook between the watchful gargoyles.

Then one of them moved its head towards me. "I knew you'd try to escape!"

Sheer terror slammed into me, snapping my grip. I left my scream high up in the air as I plummeted to the ground.

CHAPTER SEVEN

I grew ten times heavier as I plunged.

I couldn't grab at my makeshift rope.

I couldn't flail or scream or even close my eyes.

I was going to die, and I could only watch as the ground hurtled closer—and as the gargoyle abandoned its perch and dove after me, hands outstretched.

"I got you!"

It caught me in a swoop a few feet above the ground. I was as limp in its hold as wet blanket, paralyzed, everything inside me shutting down.

It soared back up to the room and deposited me just inside the window. Finding ground beneath my numb feet, I staggered to the bed, wrapped myself around the bedpost and sank down to the floor. I remained there for what felt like hours, stomach and heart squeezing each other in my throat, the whole world spinning in a violent vortex.

When everything finally stopped churning, I raised my eyes, found my savior hovering outside the window, flapping its wings. It looked decidedly less a stone demon and more a giant vulture.

"May I come in?"

It also sounded decidedly human. A polite one who was asking my permission to enter, after it had saved my life. I could argue it had endangered it in the first place, but I wouldn't. I would have fallen even if it hadn't startled me.

I could only nod dumbly, and it whooshed in through the huge window, my makeshift rope trailing behind it.

Once it landed before me, I finally saw what it was. "It" was a "she," a redheaded girl with gnarled, talon-tipped feet and huge, scarlet wings sprouting from her back. She appeared a bit older than my eighteen years, with a lanky frame, a perfectly put together, oval-shaped face and creamy skin dusted with tiny freckles. Apart from the vulture's feet and wings, she had big, bright yellow eyes, like an owl's.

Though I vividly remembered the Beast's annoyance, it was impossible not to stare. I'd never seen anything like her, not even in my storybooks, couldn't even name what she was.

Licking chapped lips, I tried to speak once, twice, only to finally manage a wavering, "W-what are you?"

Hurt flashed across her face, but she dipped into a quick curtsey, smiling and sweet-voiced. "Pleased to meet you, Miss Fairborn. I am Jessamine. I am to be your lady's maid."

I'd heard of handmaidens and ladies-in-waiting, who frequently featured in my novels, working for nobility and royalty, but never a lady's maid.

She shifted uncomfortably, avoiding my eyes and fidgeting with my makeshift rope. It was as if she was anticipating an attack, verbal or otherwise. One she was resigned to tolerate in silence.

She was afraid of *me* of all things? But why?

Though I couldn't grasp how or why she was wary of me, I knew one thing. Whatever she was, she was clearly a person, and I had to put a stop to that immediately.

Peeling myself off the floor, I stood up, swayed before steadying myself. Then wiping sweaty hands against my dress, I tentatively offered her one, along with what I hoped was a friendly smile.

"Jessamine is such a pretty name, almost as pretty as you."

Her face snapped up, rosy lips parted and eyes wide with surprise. "I—why thank you, Miss Fairborn."

"Please, call me Bonnie."

She bit her lip, twisting the sheets. "It's not appropriate."

"You saved my life." I reached for one of her hands, gripped it. "You can call me whatever you want."

She blinked at our hands confusedly, a hint of panic rising in her eyes. "But I am meant to serve you."

I blinked up at her. "Why would a prisoner need a servant? Also, what exactly is a lady's maid? Is it like a chambermaid?"

She let out a nervous snort before flushing and covering her mouth. "No, but I used to be a chambermaid. The Master just elevated my position from cleaning and tidying—caring for the chambers, to caring for you. I am supposed to be helping you get ready for dinner right now." She raised the wrinkled, knotted sheets. "It would be wise to not mention this—little incident to anyone."

At the mention of the Beast—of Leander, the mood soured.

"I don't want to have dinner with him."

Her hand dropped from mine. "Why?"

"Because he planned to imprison my father for life for plucking a rose, and now holds me hostage!" I wrapped my arms around my middle, trying to contain the still reverberating shock of my first brush with death. "It sounds like a fairy's sense of justice, a rose being worth someone's life. Are you all fairies here?"

"No, Miss." She shook her head vigorously, flapping out the sheet she'd undone. I instantly felt guilty at the wrinkled, distorted material she'd probably spend ages ironing, or if she couldn't, maybe get punished for ruining them—if she didn't let on it had been my doing. She sighed. "But it wasn't just any rose. If it were, well, none of us would be here."

My extinguished curiosity suddenly reignited. "What do you mean?"

Jessamine made a pained face. "I'm sorry. I wasn't supposed to mention that."

I gripped her by the arms, trying to convey my confusion and desperation. "You have to tell me what's going on here, please. What happened to this place? Where did you all come from? Is there any way I can get out?"

She shook her head again. Answering which question? The last one? Or was it a refusal to answer all of them?

A knock on the door had us jumping apart.

It was loud enough I thought the knocker would punch through the door. And I had a feeling I knew who it was.

Jessamine hurried to stuff the sheets under the bed before rushing to open the door. But there was no one there. Only a tray sat on the floor. She scooped it up and came back to me.

She extended the exquisitely worked silver tray and I shook my head. It had a glass bowl full of crystalized fruit, an expensive treat I'd only been able to afford once every midwinter. Putting the tray aside, Jessamine still insisted on handing me the accompanying note.

In a script too neat to be Leander's, it said: *Join me for dinner.*

Enraged, I dropped the note back on the tray, hoisted it out of the room, clattered it where it had been left and slammed the door shut.

I woke up on the edge of the bed, as someone banged on the door.

It took me disoriented moments to put together my situation. I hadn't gone down to dinner last night, to Jessamine's utter horror. I'd gone to bed without eating or changing.

Judging by the gloomy light outside, it was the crack of dawn. Or maybe that was what midday looked like in this miserable castle.

The banging came once again, and groaning, I flung off the covers and stomped to the door.

This time I found a small powder-blue box with a note on top of it.

Come to breakfast.

Clearly Leander's demand, but still in someone else's script.

I considered leaving the box unopened, but curiosity got the best of me. I bent and opened it, found a brass and jade ring on a velvet cushion. Not even up to wondering why he was sending me these things, I slammed both box and door shut.

Shuffling back to stuff myself under the heavy covers, I poured frustrated tears into the satin pillowcase. I escaped my new terrible reality by sleeping all day.

On the third day, Jessamine insisted on getting me out of bed, telling me she'd be punished if I didn't. Hating the beastly Leander even more for that, I forced myself up. I *was* in urgent need of bathing.

The bathroom was as spectacular as my room, way beyond anything I'd ever seen or read about. After a luxurious bath I could only distantly appreciate, I sat at the vanity dresser, resigned to letting Jessamine primp me up. She'd sifted through the drawers, producing too-pale face powder containers with their own mirrors, decorative tubes of lip pigments, flower-shaped hairclips and colorful powder palettes she called "eyeshadow."

Though she'd told me she only knew how to style hair, here I sat, with her attempting to paint my face. Once she was done, I would try my hand at braiding her hair. I wanted to see if I'd been complex-braiding my hair or just knotting it unevenly.

Trying to ignore the ridiculous colors being applied to my face, I watched it intently in the clear, unblemished mirror. I'd never seen my reflection with such clarity.

I'd always been told that I'd gotten my impish features from my mother. But I could barely remember her, so I searched my face for hers, for what wasn't from my Fairborn side. It meant she'd had a heart-shaped face, with big, upturned, vivid-blue eyes, high cheekbones, a small nose and a full mouth that encroached on her rounded chin, making it appear smaller than it was. The one feature I'd evidently inherited from my father was my chestnut-brown hair, which fell into big waves down my back when I let it down. I always preferred to hold it up in a ponytail.

"Do you have any sisters?" I asked Jessamine, trying not to flutter my lashes as she ran her brush over my eyelid.

"I wish. I have two brothers, one older, one younger."

"Are they like you?"

"Like me how?"

"You know…" I flapped my hands at my sides.

She let out a dry cough. "No. No, they're not. I was not. Always like this, I mean."

A soft knock at the door made Jessamine's hand slip, smudging the lip pigment on my mouth. She'd given up on answering it after the first two days, so we remained in place, watching the door crack open.

A man's voice said, "Mind if I come in?"

Jessamine shot up straight, anxiously adjusting her hair as she called out, "Come in!"

And in came something that overfilled my lungs with a trapped scream.

It was one thing for the snake-woman who'd carried my father off to exist, for me to be held captive by the wolfman and for my newest friend to be part bird. I'd either never heard of such things or heard very little about them. This one though, I'd heard and read plenty about.

The source of the eerie clomping I'd been hearing everywhere was a red-bearded, auburn-haired man in a slate waistcoat and a blue dress shirt—with fuzzy brown legs, iron-grey hooves—and big goat horns!

A satyr! A being of dark magic, worshipped by occultists in my island, and a staple engraving in tomes about monsters.

"Good afternoon." The goat-man stopped a few feet into the room, his smile and tone shockingly good-natured. "I thought it was about time we met."

As I rose on shaking legs, snippets of books and town elders' stories, with demonic depictions and anecdotes popping to the surface of my mind like bubbles in boiling stew. My instinct was to hurl anything heavy at him and hurtle to lock myself in the bathroom. I instead tried to swallow my fears—and the memory of a particularly nasty rendering of a goat-man maniacally chasing a young girl. In that story, the girl had prayed to be turned into a flower or a fountain to escape capture by the satyr.

But Jessamine was certainly not fleeing, or praying the gods would save her from this satyr at any cost. If anything, her reaction to his presence was—peculiar, as she played with her fingers and fluttered her big mesmerizing eyes at him.

It was clear she didn't fear him, not like she did her master. And it was as clear he could see my agitation as he broadened his smile as he tried to cover his horns with his curls. "I am more likely to eat flowers than I am to chase you, I promise."

I blinked, taken aback. Had he read my mind? Or did he know the tales told of his kind?

Not knowing which was worse, and if he was toying with me, I stiffly said, "To what do we owe the visit?"

He made a staying gesture before rushing back out, returning in a moment with a tray spread in covered dishes. "You refused to come to every meal, so I thought I'd bring one to you."

The clip of his hooves was hair-raising until he reached the carpet. But as he approached, he appeared less like the embodiment of pastoral evil and more like Jessamine, a mostly human, somewhat animal creature. Different enough to cause initial fright, but not to the point they were hard to look at, once the first alarm had passed.

There was also the fact that he had a human head, rather than a goat's. Or the ghastly hybrid of Leander's. His eyes were almost as big and as blue as mine, matching his wide, youthful face that shouldn't have been capable of sprouting such a thick beard. His warm, welcoming grin filled them, an easy and artless expression that only grew when he acknowledged Jessamine. For the stuff of nightmares, he was pretty dreamy.

"Good to see you keeping our guest company, Miss Quill," he greeted her, stepping around us to set the tray in the sitting area.

She avoided his eyes, her lips wobbling, as if unable to smile back at him.

He and Jessamine each took a chair and I settled on the couch. Jessamine started serving us, unveiling the first dish, and my nauseous stomach rolled out a startling growl, sparking a chuckle from my companions.

Jessamine handed me a plate of fried eggs, sausages, bacon, black pudding and toasted bread. After days of being unable to contemplate the idea of eating, the aromas were so maddeningly delicious it brought back hunger tearing into me. I stuffed a whole sausage in my mouth, earning me a stare from the satyr.

"Sorry," I mumbled around the food. "I haven't eaten in days. Actually, weeks."

His eyes widened, but he thankfully didn't ask me to explain my weird claim, only said softly, "Then my visit is even more timely than I thought."

Jessamine offered him a plate, nearly dropping it when their fingers brushed, before breathlessly asking, "Won't the Master be upset about this?"

His lips twisted. "Oh, I'm counting on it."

She sat back, wringing her hands. "He said she's not to eat if she isn't eating with him."

"To the staff he did," the satyr scoffed. "But I can share my meal with our guest if I want to. I'm not one of his servants."

I swallowed my mouthful this time before asking, "So who are you?"

I made sure to say *"who"* since *"what"* in my question to Jessamine had upset her.

"Oh! Where are my manners?" He bowed his head to me, giving me a better view of the curve of his lethal-looking, bronze-ridged horns. "I am Lord Clarence Gestum."

I gaped at him. "Lord? Lord of what? All cloven men and mad witches who dance with them in the woods?"

He choked on his food, doubling over to cough in between painful guffaws. "Life would be a lot more interesting if I was."

Jessamine beat me to thumping him on the back, until his harsh coughs faded into whistling wheezes as he sat up, his eyes still twinkling with merriment. "Well, if we're being specific then I am—or I was—the Duke of Briarfell. But do call me Clancy."

Judging by how Jessamine stiffened up, neither of them was supposed to tell me any of that.

"You weren't born like this?"

Timidly, she unfurled one huge wing, displaying the varying shades of crimson, vermillion and even ochre in her plumage. "None of us were."

"Did you think we all holed up in Rosemead for a monster getaway?" he said cheekily.

"I haven't given it much thought beyond what they told me about this place," I admitted, ravenous appetite suddenly gone. "They said the King of the Beasts moved in here and slaughtered everyone in the castle."

Jessamine nodded, fluttering the small feathers in her wings. "I at first thought they might think we're held hostage, but when no one came for us, I knew this must be how they explained our disappearances."

Clancy looked at her, his gaze kind and soft. "It's better that they think we're dead."

The realization hit me like a punch in the head. People. These two, along with whatever else populated this place, used to be normal people. And that meant...

"You're Sir Dale's sister!"

She winced, leaning forward so she wouldn't sit on her wings. "I'm sorry that his friends brought your father here. He should have stopped them."

"He wasn't around when they took my father, but I doubt he could have. Those Rob and Will seem to be very dangerous goons."

She pursed her lips. "I would have given them a piece of my mind, but I couldn't risk them seeing me."

"Why not?" I looked back and forth between them, baffled. "Why can't you tell them you're alive? What happened to you all to begin with?"

Clancy brought one hoof down in a sharp *thunk*. "We can't tell anyone, or show ourselves. They would kill us on the spot."

To say I was horrified was an understatement. "But they're her brothers!"

A bitter smile twisted his lips. "They're also hunters and one has even been to war. They're used to killing what they believe are threats. I bet their first reaction to a harpy wearing their sister's face is to panic and shoot it down."

So, that was what a harpy looked like? I'd only ever heard that term as an insult, usually from my father and other business-owners who complained about Lady Dufreyne. But Jessamine didn't fit any of the traits usually ascribed to one, was wholly sweet and even-tempered. The idea that her own family would kill her on sight made me feel ill.

"What about you? If you're a duke, how did you end up here?" I asked him. "Where is Briarfell, and while we're at it, where is Rosemead exactly?"

Clancy attempted to adjust his pose, but the stiffness of his goat-legs kept him from crossing them. Frustrated, he grumbled something under his breath about fairies and rolled to the side, fully facing me. "Rosemead is in the northeast of the kingdom, Briarfell is between Rosemead and Arbore's capital, Eglantine, which is a bit more south. I was here on a visit when I, along with the staff, got—transformed. I haven't been able to leave since."

"You were visiting the Beast?"

He coughed into his fist, sounding more like he was smothering a laugh. "Yes."

"Why?"

He opened his mouth to answer, met Jessamine's eyes, then shut it.

"What? Why won't you tell me what happened to you?"

Jessamine shivered, more feathers shaking along her wings. "It will upset the Master."

"What she means is, it's best that he tells you everything himself," Clancy then added. "Over dinner."

Dropping my fork with a clatter, I scowled at him. "You've been writing those notes, haven't you?"

"Guilty." He scratched his head awkwardly, one nail scraping against a horn. "How did you know?"

"You have human hands, he doesn't. The script was too neat to be his." I crossed my arms and legs, raising my chin defiantly. "Tell him that if he wants someone's company so bad, he needs to ask for it himself."

"He did the first day."

I narrowed my eyes at him. "Ask *nicely*."

"He'd sooner chase mammoths into the desert." As soon as the joke was out of her mouth, Jessamine clapped her hands over it.

Clancy laughed, hard. He rocked in his seat, his fair face turning red. "Forgive me, it's just the visual. The thought of Leander, on all fours, charging across the continent to herd mammoths down to Cahraman is just—" He broke into harsh guffaws.

Jessamine watched him in rapt attention, the corners of her mouth curling up behind her fingers, a rosy blush spreading beneath her shining eyes. It was as if she couldn't believe she'd made him laugh. "Was it that funny?"

"Funniest thing I've heard in a while," he huffed, wiping at his eyes. "In all honestly, Leander would go to such lengths to avoid something as simple as an apology."

"Then he's going to be dining on rejected invitations for a long time." I dropped my chin into my palm, looking over the room. The beautiful cell I'd remain in, probably forever.

There had to be another way out of here, a way back to my father. I didn't want to consider what the past few days had been like for him. Hopefully, Castor was taking care of him and planning to come back for me. With a better plan this time.

Suddenly, I got an idea. "Jessamine, how far can you fly?"

Her pleased smile faltered. "Um—why?"

I jerked my head towards the window. "There's no point in me remaining here, and you can't stay here forever, either. You can fly us out of here and to the Woodbines' hunting lodge. I'll tell your brothers everything so they're prepared, then you come in and—"

Clancy let out a disturbing sound, a merge between a goat's bleat and a man's bellow. "No!"

I started, suddenly wary all over again. "Why not?"

He got up, running his fingers over his horns as he stomped towards the door. "You can't leave, not yet." Before he shut it behind him, he ordered Jessamine, "Don't let her out of your sight, do you understand?"

The fading clomps of his hooves remained the only sound on the whole floor for stifling moments. But I couldn't handle the vagueness, the amount of missing pieces in this puzzling place, couldn't remain silent anymore.

I finally exhaled, looking entreatingly at her. "Jessie?"

"I'm sorry, Bonnie." She rose to her feet, twisting her fingers together. "But I can't do what you want, even if I wanted to."

My disappointment was too overwhelming to hide, even for her sake. The last thing I wanted was to make her feel worse about her situation, get her in trouble with her brute of a master. But I couldn't pretend her rejection was fine by me. She'd been my last way out of here.

She excused herself and left, and I sagged back, limp with the reinforced realization of my helplessness.

After what felt like an eternity of lying there, a heavy rap shook the door.

I rushed to open it, hoping Clancy had changed his mind. All I found was a big, floral-printed box topped with a pearlescent bow.

Inside it was a luxurious yellow gown, a diamond tiara with a matching set of diamond-and-citrine-studded jewelry—teardrop earrings, two hard bracelets and a choker necklace, whose worth alone might buy half the town below. The accompanying note was covered in a shaky scrawl that said:

Dear Miss Fairborn,

I cordially invite you to dine with me tonight.
Please wear these precious items I gift to you. I will await you in the
dining room.

Respectfully,
Leander.

I kicked the box, spilling its contents. Before I slammed the door shut, I tore up the note and let it rain over the mess.

CHAPTER EIGHT

"What's a mammoth?" I yawned, bleary gaze unfocused on the canopy above me.

It was my fourth day here, and what I now recognized as mid-morning light around here centered on the bed, with me on my back and Jessamine on her belly, stretching her wings.

"It's a big, wooly elephant," she mumbled into the duvet, face squished against it. "It lives in the northeast of the Folkshore, usually in Opona and the Mjallands. Some islands have pygmy sorts as well."

"What's an elephant?"

Her eyes widened, seemingly stunned again at how much I didn't know about this Folkshore. "It's this huge animal with large floppy ears, curved tusks and a long trunk for a nose. I've never actually seen one, but the Master has some foreign sculptures shaped like them. He can show them to you."

As if summoned, a series of heavy thumps assailed my door. The very sound of entitlement and impatience. It was a wonder he hadn't splintered the wood by now.

I rolled off the bed with a frustrated growl and marched to

the door. I wrenched it open to find not another box, but the Beast himself.

"Yes?" I demanded venomously.

Leander's fist was still up, poised to knock again, and his thick brows were raised in chagrin or confusion, or both. "Why do you keep rejecting my gifts?"

I stuck my fists at my side. "Why do you keep giving them to me? What do you expect me to do with them?"

He shrugged his massive shoulders. "I don't know what women usually do with the things they expect or demand. But I've never met a lady who snubs the most expensive clothes and jewelry. If that does not please you, then what will?"

"My freedom!"

His eyebrows descended ominously, almost obscuring his eyes. "I can't give you that. I'll give you anything but that."

"Then I want nothing from you." I slammed the door in his face.

I stood facing it, shaking, unable to believe I'd done that. It seemed he didn't either as a moment of total silence passed. Then he ripped out a harrowing howl.

"If you don't come out I'll break the door down and drag you out!"

"Do it!" I dared recklessly, too desperate to care if I was provoking on my own doom. "Do it and see where that gets you."

No one like me, tiny and useless, ought to be antagonizing anyone, let alone a giant barbarian like him. But I couldn't bear giving in to others' demands anymore. Or always feeling trapped. Now I literally was, and helpless to find or help my family. And *that* was all his fault!

He slammed himself against the door with a rattling crash

that blasted through me, sending me spiraling down a conflicting mixture of dread and defiance.

"Break down the door, do any harm to me, and you'll live up to the name '*Beast!*'" I shouted, frantic and incensed.

"I told you not to call me that!" He rammed to door again, making the hinges squeal and the wood moan. I knew it would soon give.

"But that's what you are!" I shook from head to toe as I shrieked back. "You not only look like a beast *but you behave like one!*"

Abruptly, he stopped.

I waited, breath shuddering out of me, to see if he would resume his tantrum or if he'd stepped back to charge the door and knock it down. But he did neither.

"Did he leave?" I whispered to Jessamine.

A stilted grumble from behind the door answered. "What. Do. You. *Want?*"

Irritation replaced all other feelings. "I told you what I want."

"AND I TOLD YOU—" He stopped, heaving in a loud breath before letting it out a long, noisy exhalation. "And I told you I can't give you that. Anything but that."

I approached the door, cautiously peeking through the keyhole. "If you're not going to let me go, you can at least tell me why."

He was pacing before my room, like a beast in a cage. "I don't know if I can."

"What? You think I'm too stupid to understand?"

"It's not about whether you can, it's about what it can change."

"If you think anything will make me hate you more than I already do, then you underestimate my feelings for you."

He shook his head with a dismissive snort, the tips of his angular ears wiggling. "I was hoping to change your mind about being here before telling you."

"Good luck convincing me to enjoy my stay with your attitude."

"You're very disagreeable," he grunted. "Very loud, too."

"You're one to talk," I scoffed.

He stopped his pacing, shot an exasperated look in my direction. "Do you have to answer back to everything I say?"

"Would you rather I go back to ignoring you?" I taunted, something I'd never done.

"I would rather that you'd do as you're told, like all young women of polite society ought to. I would like for you to accept my gifts graciously, to dine with me, to possibly get to know me, as I am your host."

"You're not my host, you're my jailer. I'm your hostage."

"Would you *stop*?" His shouted last word echoed down the hall like a crack of thunder through a night sky. "I'll have you know that if you spoke like that to anyone else you'd be punished severely."

"Oh, dearie me, what punishment could possibly surpass captivity by a monster? Being speared by a unicorn?"

"How did you know they did that?"

My heated annoyance went up in a puff of steam. "What do you mean?"

"That unicorns use their horns to impale threats or adversaries."

I was instantly gripped with a sense of childlike wonder. "Unicorns exist?"

"Of course, they do." He gave a mirthless huff. "Most may think them peaceful creatures, beings of pure light and beauty, but I learned about their tempers the hard way with my sister's mare."

In that instant, despite seeing no change in him through the keyhole, his image somehow shifted, became more human, reminding me that this Leander creature used to be a man at some point, like Lord Clancy, though it was much harder to believe with him.

But the way he spoke, his mention of a sister...

Perhaps if I did speak with him on less hostile terms, I could finally get some answers about this madness, maybe negotiate my release.

But when I opened my mouth, I found myself saying, "Your sister has a unicorn?"

He seemed surprised by my questions, coming closer until I saw nothing but his ill-fitting pants. I felt him touching the door, and I straightened, leaned against it, too, listening to the vibrations of his deep voice through the wood.

"Yes, she got it as a gift when she was seven. I, on the other hand, got an ordinary horse. You'd think people would like to keep things fair among siblings. If she got a unicorn, I ought to have been gifted a pegasus."

Joking. He was joking, the humor so subtle but so strange, even shocking coming from him.

I swallowed a sudden lump in my throat. "What's a pegasus? Is that the horse that is half-fish?"

"You're thinking of a hippocampus." He sounded significantly calmer as he huffed again. "Though I can't believe you know about those but not pegasi. Where did you say you were from again?"

"I didn't. Say where, I mean."

Neither of us said anything for a while, lingering on either side of the door. I had to assume he was waiting for me to speak again first.

"I can show you a painting of a pegasus," he finally said when I didn't, uncharacteristically quiet. "It's on the ground floor, in the main sitting area."

Jessamine piped up, startling me. "You could have afternoon tea there!"

His corroborating rumble was instantaneous. "Yes, we could."

Uncertainty filled me, along with lingering anger, a stubborn insistence for me not to leave my room, to give in to his demands.

But afternoon tea hadn't been a part of his plan. It was a random stop on this odd path the conversation had taken.

Giving myself no chance to overthink this, I unlocked the door.

He gaped at me when I peeked out, as if taken aback. It seemed he hadn't expected I'd relent. I hadn't either.

I looked way up at him, trying not to fidget. "Tea would be nice, I guess."

He gave an awkward nod, letting out a loud exhalation, the sound of deflating frustration.

Either I'd forgotten how beastly his appearance was or he'd further morphed since I'd last seen him. His lower fangs were bigger than I remembered, jutting his jaw further forward, and his beard had migrated further up his cheeks. His body had grown more bowed, arms bigger and longer. He was closer to the snake-woman than to half-human Clancy and Jessamine—a confused merge of man and animal, though I wasn't sure which one. Lion? Wolf? Both?

"Wouldn't you like to get changed first?" Jessamine pulled me back before I stepped out, sounding excited. "I can set out a nice tea gown for you. There's this periwinkle one that would go with your eyes."

"He doesn't deserve the trouble of putting on a nice dress," I said between my teeth.

She looked crestfallen for a second, before nodding and heading to the open window. Jumping on the edge, she looked back at me. "Can't say I haven't tried doing my job." And with that, she spread her wings and dove down in an effortless glide.

The urge to rush after her, watch her fly and yell questions about the mechanics of her wings rose tenfold.

Leander cleared his throat. "This way."

Reluctantly stepping out of my luxurious cell, I followed him downstairs.

It was no different than following him up had been, the interior of the castle captivating me all over again. From the soaring ceilings to the shift in decor from one floor to the other, with more lights, there were new things to notice everywhere. Like the gloss of some parts of the wallpaper, or the curled oak leaves holding the banister, and the detail in the rose mosaic in the entrance—though it seemed there were more fallen petals than I remembered.

A part of me wanted to break for the main door again, see if it would open this time. But I knew it wouldn't. Even if it did, I wouldn't escape him.

Exhaling in resignation, I said, "Whose castle is this?"

"It's now mine."

"Whose was it before you?"

"My father's, before he married my mother at least."

"So, you're like Lord Clancy?"

He shot me a half perplexed, half exasperated look. "Lord *Gestum* has paid you a visit, I see."

Not wanting to get into another argument, I ignored his comment. "What's the difference? In the books I read, people would always refer to noblemen by either their first or last name, and the same went for knights. Was that a writing error?"

He contemplated my question before his response echoed in the hallway we entered to the right of the entrance. "A reigning lord, the head of the family, is referred to by his surname, while other family members are by their forenames. The same goes for the lord's wife and his daughters. When Clancy was young, he was as you referred to him, a lordling among many. When his uncle died, he became Duke of Briarfell, head of his family, and Lord Gestum."

"And knights?" I asked, remembering Sir Dale and his friends.

"With knighthoods, it depends if the man is of noble birth or not. If he is a knighted peasant, then he is known by his first name. Though if he is a lord, his title takes precedence. I made the mistake of calling the Earl of Sherwood 'Sir Loxley' while I was being fostered at Loxley Hall. The old man wouldn't let me hear the end of it, and neither would his son."

There was an undercurrent of sadness at the mention of the son. I had a feeling they'd been friends. Had he lost all his friends because of his transformation?

Refusing to ponder this or to consider feeling bad for him, I said, "What do I call you then, if you're the Duke of Rosemead?"

His upper lip curled in what looked like a grimace. "Just Leander is fine."

He looked ahead, seeming to consider this enough questions, so I went back to admiring the hall. The whole place looked more taken care of than the first time I'd seen it. The paintings on the walls and the woodwork displays weren't draped in cobwebs and the endless carpet wasn't dusty. Its emerald green background was woven in an intricate design of tiny fragments of varying colors, and bordered by an interlocking pattern and a frame of alternating symbols.

My interest must have been apparent, since he asked, "Admiring the craftsmanship?"

I nodded. "I've never seen anything like it."

"You wouldn't have. It came from Cahraman, a land far from here."

And even further from my island.

Exiting the hall, we reached a circular room that opened onto many others. As Leander held open one door for me, I looked up at him. "Where did you send my father?"

He gestured for me to enter. "Not back to the Woodbine lodge, if this is what you're thinking. I sent him to a friend. He's safe, and well-cared for, I promise you."

And this put an end to any hope of finding my father, even if I managed to escape.

Heart sinking deeper in my chest, I passing beneath his arm into the room, grumbling, "Why should I believe you?"

Offense wrinkled his nose and brow. "We made a deal, remember?"

"It's a bit hard to believe you'd honor any deal when you locked him up over a rose."

Anger radiating from him again, he slammed the door shut. "We've already gone over this!"

"*You* think you did, but you explained nothing. I thought such a disproportionate punishment is very fairy-like, but now it makes less sense from someone who used to be a man."

"*DON'T!*" he shouted, the ferocity taking even him by surprise, tempering his follow-up to a harsh hiss. "Don't ever compare me to a fairy. Call me an animal all you want, but animals can feel. Fairies cannot."

His impassioned words only added more questions to my ever-growing mountain of curiosity. But whatever his dealings with fairies were or had been, this wasn't the time to ask.

I turned from him to the seating arrangement, four chairs around a low, walnut table before a stone fireplace. On the mantelpiece was four figurines, and above them, the room's centerpiece.

In a ridged, copper frame, hung an exquisite painting of a majestic white stallion, front legs curled mid-gallop, head turned up towards the hidden sun. Massive wings sprouted out of its back, spreading among the clouds, its feathers in shades of platinum, pearl and silver.

It took my breath away. "It's so beautiful."

"Not as beautiful as you."

The sheer randomness of his comment wrenched me from my wonder. I didn't even know what to say to that.

Avoiding my gaze, as if he regretted saying it, he crouched by the fireplace to stoke the flames. Deciding to pretend he hadn't said anything, I returned to admiring the painting's subtle variation of color. I reveled in the idea that something like this creature existed, that something as large and earthbound as a horse could be capable of flight. It comforted me to think it was free to venture beyond its realm, when I was bound by so many limitations.

The name signed at the bottom-left corner was his. LEANDER SILVERTHORN.

Had he really painted this?

Unable and unwilling to consider how such an unexpected talent changed my view of him, I turned to examining the porcelain figurines on the mantelpiece. They were of two boys and two girls, with the boy with the dark hair also bearing his name. The blond one was FLORIAN, and the two dark-headed girls ESMERALDA and FAIRUZA. The last name was as foreign as that carpet.

Were those his siblings? Were they here as well, transformed into maybe a lizard, a rodent and a quail?

Hard as he was to look at, he was becoming less fantastical and more real to me. This was a nobleman of all things, trapped in his own castle, one who had friends, a sister with a pet unicorn, and even a rare gift. Not that I could imagine him painting with those large, clawed hands. This must have been painted before his transformation. Which begged a few more crucial questions, ones I should weave into a conversation.

But I never had much tact to speak of.

Since I didn't, I sat down near the fire and just shot my questions. "How long have you been like this? And how old are you?"

"Almost three years, but it wasn't always like this." He abandoned the poker to sit across from me, waved around his face, wide mouth twisted in distaste. "It's getting worse the more time passes."

So, I hadn't imagined the change in his appearance?

"I am twenty-one-years-old," he added. "How old are you?"

This was a common question, even from people who'd known me for years. Some still believed I was twelve. That never helped with my father's overprotectiveness or people's refusal to hire me.

"How old do I look?"

Scrutinizing me, he raised a hand to cup his chin, but removed it with a grimace when an overgrown nail scratched his nose. "Not that much younger than me."

I goggled at him. "I'm eighteen. But most people think I'm still a child."

"I thought the same at first." His eyes bore into mine, their amazing blue-green intense in the firelight. "But now I've gotten a good look at you, you're definitely older than my sister."

"The one with the unicorn?"

His gaze flitted to the figurine labeled *Fairuza* and his brilliant irises darkened. "Yes. She's seventeen, for now."

Jessamine chose that moment to burst in, pushing a small cart laden with a delicate tea set and a plate of cookies.

She served us before lingering to arrange one utensil at a time as we spoke. Eavesdropping?

I popped a cookie in my mouth, spoke as I crunched it, "What do you mean 'for now?'"

His broad shoulders sagged as he picked up his cup, a subdued kind of anger I didn't think him capable of. Anger at something old or constant, something he'd gotten resigned to. "It is unlikely she'll live to see eighteen."

My heart gave a flutter of dismay. "Is she sick?"

"Worse. She's cursed. And so am I."

CHAPTER NINE

I couldn't believe a curse hadn't been the first thing I'd thought about.

But then, I'd just discovered the castle beastly inmates were originally human only yesterday. And I hadn't exactly been thinking straight since I'd woken up from whatever spell the fairy who'd kidnapped us had put us under.

But now I knew his sister's curse was premature death rather than metamorphosing into a beast, a different yet equally terrible fate, it led me to one question.

"What did you two do?"

He paused his sip, glowering at me over the rim of his teacup. "What makes you think either of us did anything?"

I pushed away my plate along the table. "How else would you have been cursed?"

"By a malicious being that enjoys ruining lives?"

"Judging by your attitude, you must have provoked it."

His calmness was gone, and back was the marrow-chilling rage. "I did nothing, and neither did my sister!"

In spite of quaking in my flat shoes at the brunt of his

temper, I pressed on. "Witches can't be going around casting curses all willy-nilly. You had to have done some serious offense or injury."

"Stop it."

"Why? It's not like I said anything unfounded," I shot back. "Going by how you've behaved so far, how defensive you're being now, I bet I'm right."

He had nothing more to say to me. Nothing in words. His response was to crush the cup in his grip with a deafening roar that had me bursting to my feet and running away with my heart in my throat.

Jessamine flew after me all the way up to the bedroom, blocking the doorway with her wings. "Please, go back. Just give him a chance!"

"I already did, and look what happened." I tried collapsing a wing to pass, but she wouldn't budge.

"But it was going so well!" she argued.

Residual fear still coursed through me, and I was on the brink of tears. I had to get out of this place, even if it meant breaking my neck climbing out the window again.

I dropped to the floor and crawled inside between her legs. Once back on the bed, hugging a post to ground myself, his roar still ringing in my ears, I looked at her.

She remained on the threshold, shoulders slumped, wings limp, and yellow eyes unblinking. She wasn't just upset, she looked defeated, like this disastrous meeting had dashed her hopes for something vital.

Before I could ask, she closed the door, headed to the window. "I'll come back in a while. I need to go clear my head."

And with that, she dove out the window and soared up with the winds.

Not long after she'd left, another of his knocks came at the door.

I didn't know why I bothered checking, but I did.

It was a box of chocolates with a solid gold rose on top, with a note that said: *I'm sorry.*

Back in Aubenaire, chocolates were a luxury that got imported only during winter holidays and a tiny box cost as much as a new season's outfit. I used to wait a whole year for them and devour them in an hour. But now I felt sick to my stomach, being at the mercy of someone this aggressive and volatile.

The gold rose felt like a taunt as well. Something worth more than my house was given freely, but a regular rose was what had doomed my father and I to this place. I didn't bother kicking the gift this time, just shut the door and curled up on my bed, watching Jessamine fly outside in circles, refusing to fly me to freedom.

In this moment, I was the fairytale princess locked in a tower, guarded by a monster that wouldn't yield. There was nothing I wanted more than for a knight to come rescue me.

After hours of motionless melancholy, an idea struck me.

Jessamine hadn't returned, making it possible to sneak outside. I went downstairs as quietly as possible, in search of the kitchen. It most likely was on the ground floor and had to have windows that opened, to air out any smoke or trapped heat. That could be my way out.

I reached the darkened entrance, found patches of subdued moonlight shining on the floor mosaic. The rose seemed to have wilted since the afternoon, surrounded by more petals. I was sure I wasn't imagining it this time.

Pushing the weird observation to the back of my mind, I took the opposite direction to the one we'd traveled earlier, which I was certain didn't lead to a kitchen. I hoped there wasn't anything lurking in my path.

I couldn't tell which corridor led to what, scrambled aimlessly, getting more desperate by the second. Then suddenly, I stopped dead, my ears straining.

Was that the sound of wind?

It was! At the end of the corridor. An open window!

I hastily followed the sound into an office whose balcony was wide open. Through it came not only the whistle of wind, but also the gallop of horses.

Could it be someone had come for me?

Hope filled me, blinding me to the risk of vaulting over the balustrade and into the garden below. I landed on my feet with a stab of pain up each leg, tipping me into the dirt.

With an ear almost on the ground, I could pick out the gallops of maybe half a dozen horses and the voices of as many men. I had to meet them at the gate!

Ignoring the ache in my knees, I heaved up and ran through the grounds, blind to my surroundings—until a glimmer snagged my vision. That impossible rose tree.

For some reason, it was more visible this time, as if with an internal light. There were giant thorns covering its green trunk, disappearing up into the rough leaves that surrounded the roses. And this time there was a pink one that wasn't attached to a stalk, just placed among the leaves, drying up and missing many petals.

Something crunched beneath my foot. Jumping back, I

found the dead pink petals, now as hard as crystals, a couple I'd crushed into glittering dust.

Was this the rose my father had plucked? But why would he have done so? What had compelled him to interrupt his escape for this? Had it been meant as a gift for me?

As strange a compulsion came over me, making me relinquish my own escape and remove it from the leaves. I hissed as a thorn pricked my finger, but gripped it even harder.

Something heavy landed behind me, shaking the ground and rattling my bones.

I didn't have to turn to know what it was. My massive captor was bearing down on me. Unprecedented anger was radiating from him like a furnace blast.

He snapped his jaws at me, deadly fangs gleaming like polished silver in the diffuse moonlight. "Put it back."

My feet felt they'd been cast in iron, heavy as anvils. But my mouth had no trouble moving. "You put it back. And let me go."

"You're the one who has to put it back," he growled, menacingly advancing. "Then you'll go to your room."

"I'll put it back if you let me go."

He snarled like the beast he was, clawed hands reaching for me. I stumbled back until I pressed against the thorny trunk, throat bobbing on a jagged lump of tears. I'd failed to escape, and this time he seemed maddened enough to throw me in a dungeon forever, or even to kill me.

But if I were to die, I would at least defy him to my last breath.

I crushed the rose in my grip.

He reared back with a pained howl as if I'd stabbed him. Then as the pulverized petals poured between my fingers, he threw himself upon them. He gasped and wheezed as he dug through the dirt, trying to gather up the glittering dust like it was the last drops of water in a wasteland.

Watching him desperately trying to reassemble that rose, heaving like he was suffocating, a bizarre sense of pity for him assailed me, had me in a chokehold.

A deafening boom at the gates extinguished that thought and snapped him out of his frenzy.

He rose back up, swiping at me. "You want to leave? Then go! Get out!"

I screamed as his claws scratched the bark off the tree. If they'd been a few inches closer, he could have taken my head off!

"GET OUT!"

His bellow shot feeling back into my legs, and I ran like I'd never done before.

I was almost at the gates when a battering ram burst them open, and six men rushed in, lead by Castor.

Never had I been this happy to see anyone.

But he didn't appear to see me, gaze focused behind and above my head, no doubt at the Beast.

I caught his attention by running to intercept him, slamming into his chest. "Castor, you came back for me!"

Blinking in shock, he nearly dropped his crossbow as he reflexively wrapped an arm around me. "Bonnie—you're alive!"

"Yes, but not for long." I tried to push him back. "We have to go now!"

He only pushed me behind him, arming his crossbow. "Not before I kill the Beast!"

"Don't! Let's go, before he comes after me." He might change his mind about letting me go when my transgression sank in. If innocently plucking the rose earned my father a lifetime of imprisonment, willfully destroying it might warrant me a slow, painful death.

"I'm hoping it does," Castor said fiercely. "When it comes close enough, I'll shoot it."

I pulled on his coat, urgency and frustration almost bursting my heart. "Shoot it and miss like you did last time?"

He glared at me from over his shoulder as he strode forwards. "Last time I was taken off-guard, was too focused on saving you first. Now that you're here, it will have all my attention." He patted his crossbow proudly. "And this time they're not just any arrows, but sharp metal that'll pierce right through its skull."

As I ran after him, needing to convince him to give up his moronic need to kill the Beast, movement came from both sides as reflective eyes advanced in the dark. The castle dwellers, coming to defend their haven and prison.

Castor and the men aimed their weapons at them and my blood froze. Before, I wouldn't have hesitated to sprint away to safety and letting them take care of the problem. But now I knew these weren't monsters that had eaten the staff. They *were* the staff.

I jumped on Castor's back, screeched, "Don't shoot them! They're harmless!"

He tried to shake me off, shouting, "Harmless? Are you mad?"

I clung harder. "Castor, listen to me! Just let them be and let's go!"

"To what end?" He shot at a set of eyes, but I yanked his arm at the last moment and thankfully I heard no cry of pain. He'd missed. He tried to tear me off his back again, infuriated. "Till the next month when we have to give it another sacrifice? Keep doing its hunting for it, so it doesn't hunt us? Or sacrifice more girls to keep it at bay?"

"I was in there for days, so believe me when I tell you it's not like you think. Nothing in that castle wants to harm us!"

"You sound hysterical." He bucked me off this time, pushing me towards one of the other hunters. "Get her out of here. We'll catch up once we're done."

He shot another arrow, right into the eyes' midst. One set blinked out with a hair-raising yowl and the rest scattered.

The man threw me over his shoulder with an effortless toss. I kicked, squirmed and screamed, but he was unfazed as he ran back towards his horse, and threw me like a sack of laundry atop it. It was Maple!

"What is that?" another man shouted from the side.

I struggled to a sitting position on Maple's back and looked up to find a giant vulture swooping towards us.

"Wait!" Jessamine called out in the darkness. "Wait, you can't leave!"

Castor froze. He recognized her voice. He had to.

"Castor, that's Sir Dale's sister!" I yelled desperately. "That's his *sister*!"

He might have not heard me. Or he'd heard me and couldn't credit what I'd said, as it didn't stop him from aiming at her. I screamed again, to no avail. He let the arrow loose.

Next moment, I felt all the blood fleeing my head as I heard her shriek in pain, watched her convulse before her wings folded limply and she plummeted headfirst to the ground.

A scream almost tore my throat apart. "NO!"

Before I could move, a horned figure leaped high up in the air and caught her before she hit the ground. My relief was short-lived, as Castor and his men aimed their weapons towards Clancy's silhouette as he landed with the wounded Jessamine in his arms.

I kicked the man near me in the head, taking him by the surprise as I took Maple's reins and charged towards Jessamine and Clancy, screaming for Castor and the other men to stop.

Two riders on horseback were also rushing towards them, swinging a poleaxe and a club. Only when I got closer I realized they were a centaur couple. Following them was the giant slithering mass that was Ivy the snake-woman, hissing and slamming the attackers with her tail.

It seemed horror only made the men intensify their attacks. One hunter charged the female centaur and stabbed her, while the hunter with a mace smashed it against the male centaur's leg. Both centaurs crashed into a hard kneel with agonized whinnies that distressed Maple, making her rear up and almost throwing me off.

"What are all these things?" one of the hunters bellowed.

"I told you this place was full of monsters of every sort," Castor roared back. "The sooner we're done with them, the sooner we kill their master."

"Are you sure about that?" Leander seemed to come out of nowhere, barreling into them, knocking down two men for Ivy to coil around and facing the men who'd struck the centaurs. He loomed over them, as huge and harrowing as I had first seen him. He knocked down the man with the dagger and caught the other man's swinging mace. He bent his arm farther back than naturally possible, eliciting a sickening crack and a screech of agony until he dropped his weapon.

Castor took that opportunity to attack him from behind, shooting him with an arrow. I screamed and Leander rounded on him just as the arrow ripped into his shoulder.

With a furious roar, Leander ripped the metal arrow out and bent it with one hand.

"You have a death wish," Leander growled at Castor. "Just like your father."

At the mention of his father, whatever self-preservation Castor had approached this confrontation with evaporated with a shout of rage as he pulled out a hunting knife from his belt and launched himself at Leander.

This wasn't going to end with him winning. And if it did, with Leander dead, that left every other person in here vulnerable. What Clancy feared would come to pass. Whatever happened, so many people would end up dead.

I had to stop this fight in its tracks. Any way I could. Any way at all.

I charged Maple at them, separating them and bending to pull on Castor's hair, sobbing with urgency. "Get on! Get on! Get *on*!"

"Not before I finish this!" he yelled. "Get out of my way and go home!"

Home. He wanted me in his home. Possibly as much as he wanted Leander dead.

"I'll marry you!" The promise blurted out of me, the only way I could see out of this impasse. "Come with me now and I'll marry you. I'll go to your aunts, I'll wear what you want, eat what you want—I'll do anything, if you come with me now!"

For once, Castor listened to me. After a last moment of hesitation, he swore something vicious under his breath and leaped up on Maple behind me, taking the reins. He shouted for the other men to follow us and exploded out of the gates at a hard gallop.

As the other men joined us, I tried to look back, but I

found my view blocked by Castor's body. I couldn't take one last look at the castle or see how the injured were faring. I would never know if Clancy had rescued Jessamine, or if she was beyond help. Worse, I might be unable to convince the hunters of the truth, might be unable to stop them from going back to finish the job they'd started tonight.

I might not have saved any of the castle inmates, after all. I might have paid my freedom for nothing.

CHAPTER TEN

"**I** told you not to attack any of them!"

The shrill scolding burst out of me as soon as I could draw a full breath, making Castor grunt in exasperation. "Would you shut up about this already?"

I couldn't. The idea of those poor, cursed people being hunted through no fault of their own, only because of narrow-minded superstition and unsubstantiated fear, tore at me. "I told you the flying one was Sir Dale's sister and you didn't listen to me. You could have killed her! You *might* have killed her! I thought you wanted to save her!"

"I can't save her," he gritted against my ear. "Jessamine Quill is dead, and whatever things you saw in there have clearly messed with your mind."

"I know what I saw. I was in there, I talked to them—you didn't."

"That doesn't prove anything," he dismissed. "Don't worry, you'll have a lot of time to come to your senses once we're at my family's house."

Offense and worry stormed through me, but I suddenly didn't

want to argue anymore. I was helpless to change what happened, could only hope no one had been seriously injured, that I'd bought them a chance to better defend themselves next time. For if no one believed me, I had no doubt there would be a next time.

Now all I wanted to do was find my father.

"Woodbine, one of them is following us!" yelled the man to our right.

Castor checked behind us, swearing under his breath. "It's the snake!" He turned Maple's head by her reins. "We need to lose that thing, or at least slow it down until we do. Our best option is going through the woods."

"But we never go through the woods at night!" one of the others yelled.

"And we never have monsters on our tail, either," Castor shouted back.

That seemed to end any debate on the others' part. It was clear they hated the idea of going through the woods, but were even more afraid of Ivy.

Once we reached flat ground, we took a sharp turn past the statue of Rosmerta and were soon heading into the woods. The trees had looked slim and sparse from a distance, but as we passed between them, they proved tall enough to dwarf us, close enough to block the moonlight.

The temperature dropped significantly once the woods engulfed us, and vapor puffed out with my every ragged word. "Can you see where we're going?"

Castor didn't answer me, turned Maple where a path between the trees appeared, barely lit by the pale rays that danced through gaps in the leaves above.

"You should have brought a lantern," I mumbled.

"Be quiet, I'm trying to think."

Disgruntled, I clamped my lips closed. But there was little thought in our voyage farther into the woods. We just kept going, only managing to see where the trees stood but nothing else.

Castor didn't slow our pace down the path that was now bordered by endless lines of mushrooms. With every gallop, they lit up in batches as if they were made of enchanted blue glass, surrounding us with a ghostly cyan glow.

Suddenly, one of the men yelled, "We lost the snake!"

"We should turn back now, right?" I urged, the chilling ambiance making me shiver, the bite of cold sinking into my bones. "We should ride back through the city!"

"I told you to be quiet!" he bit off. "You're the reason we're in this mess! If you had stayed at the lodge, like I told you to, we wouldn't be chased by monsters right now. The least you can do is finally start listening to me!"

"*You* should listen to me! I told you they aren't monsters! They aren't harming anyone, just staying in their place, and they did nothing to me—"

"SHUT. UP." His frustrated shout echoed in the dimness like the ringing of a tower bell, filling the freezing air and rousing things I could sense but not see in our surroundings. "The first thing you'll learn once we get back is how to listen to voices apart from your own for once in your life!"

The anger and hurt roiling through me suddenly deflated, joining the vapor curling out of my shaking lips. I was left with nothing but a suffocating sense of dread, of a danger I had no name for. A gut instinct of what lay ahead, unseen and unyielding to our oncoming stampede.

"Castor, turn back," I whimpered. "This is not a suggestion or a request. *Turn back now.*"

He lowered his head to mine, snarling through clenched teeth. "What did I just say?"

I saw them then. The sinister presence around us became white eyes above big, glowing smiles, emerging in a row right up ahead. And the moments he'd taken to scold me had led us straight among them.

Maple reared up with a distressed neigh, but it was too late.

They attacked before I could see them move.

Each creature leaped feet into the air, landing on the horses, cackling horribly.

"REDCAPS!" a man howled. "YOU LED US STRAIGHT TO THE REDCAPS!"

Before I could draw another breath, one of those redcaps descended on Castor behind me, another latched onto my leg. Terror speared through me as I saw its wide mouth up close.

The rows of jagged teeth separated, unleashing a nerve-scraping singsong screech. *Pretty fey in my way, not a good snack. Give me your human prey or hear your neck crack.*

The will to struggle slammed back into me as I kicked it in the eye with everything I had, yanking my leg free as its grip loosened—and only unseated myself off the horse.

I hit the ground with a bruising slam, and Maple galloped back along the path we'd come through after all the other horses, taking Castor with her. They disappeared before I could sit up.

The redcaps chased after the men, but before I could hope they'd forgotten about me, three fell back, turned and slowly approached me, like hunters approaching a trapped deer.

I stared back at them, feeling my heart would uproot itself within my chest at any moment. They were squat, dispropor-tionate men with barrel trunks, spindly limbs, taloned fingers and elongated heads. They all wore caps whose dark red color was blotchy and uneven, like giant bloodstains. Or was that their scalps?

Any other time, I would have laughed at the absurdity of the idea of predatory gnomes. Now they were the ones laughing, because they knew I'd be an easy prey.

But I couldn't make it that easy. I hadn't escaped the castle just to let those horrible little monsters eat me without a fight.

Ignoring the screaming pain in my side and arm, I struggled up and ran after the others with the redcaps hot on my trail, their chorus of maniac laughter pouring unknown strength into my legs.

"Wait for me!" I screamed after the retreating men.

None of them slowed down, probably unable to hear me in the midst of their frantic shouts as they fought off the flying attacks left and right.

I pushed forwards, desperate to catch up with them, to find Castor, but a sharp pain stabbed my side, worsening with every tearing breath. Soon, it would drive me to my knees—and it would be all over.

Then I found Castor. The stench of blood reached me before I saw him, and terror swallowed me whole.

Five redcaps were pinning him down, each with its teeth buried in a part of him, seeming to be drinking his blood as he screamed and struggled rabidly. I could see their caps—no, it *was* their scalps—getting darker, and nausea overwhelmed me as I realized it was with his blood.

But there was nothing I could do for him. If I stopped, the others would catch up with me, then we'd both be dead.

I had to try to stay alive. For my father. For Adelaide. And to do that, I had one last gamble. If I could stay ahead until I exited the woods, and they were confined to them, they couldn't follow me out.

I swerved off the path mid-sprint and ducked between the trees, running towards where I thought Rosemead was.

Only a few feet in, whatever hope of escape I'd had died. One landed on my back, slamming me facedown in the dirt, pouring its horrifying, rhyming giggle in my ear.

"Not so fast, pretty sprite, with the tiny head—Stay and put up a fight, now our real meal has fled."

It gripped me by the hair, its talons scraping my scalp as it lifted my spinning head. The other two gripped my ankles and dragged me back towards the path. I tried to kick, to dig my nails into the earth, but nothing stopped the inevitable.

Back on the mushroom path, I tried to throw them off but the one holding my hair slammed my head against the ground. Starbursts of white and purple flashed in the darkness behind my eyes to the rhythm of the pounding pain and swirling dizziness.

They turned me over and one sat on my chest, gripping my face while the others held my arms and legs down. Hot tears poured down the sides of my face as I feebly struggled, drowning in faintness and fear.

The redcap on my chest traced my face with its sharp thumbnails, leaving shallow scratches. *"So frail and weak, pretty pixie daughter. Your blood does reek, but you'll be fun to slaughter."*

It unlatched its jaws, descending towards my face with a smile that grew and grew until the top of its head fell back and all of its face became a gaping maw.

Heart bursting over and over at the sheer horror, of the sight, of the fate I was about to suffer, I squeezed my eyes shut, bracing for the worst pain of my life—the one that would end it.

Horrific screams broke out behind me—the other redcaps. Coming to fight over me? I wished I'd faint and be spared the ordeal—then a thunderous roar drowned all the shrieks out.

Could it be...?

My eyes snapped open to the sight of the redcap holding my hands being kicked to the side, its neck at a sharp angle, its body going limp. The one holding my face released me, its face still split in half as it launched itself up into the air, only to get punched away by the furious mass of muscle and messy hair that loomed above me.

Leander! He'd come for me!

But was it to save me, or to kill me himself?

CHAPTER ELEVEN

*T*he redcap holding my legs abandoned me for Leander.

He raised his arm to swat it like the last one, but it clung to him, biting into his flesh.

He roared in pain and flung it off, squashing it on the ground, but another two climbed his back, sinking their macabre teeth in his other arm and his shoulder.

As he roared again and blood trickled out from beneath their teeth, I realized two things in absolute clarity.

Whatever reason he was here for, I'd take my chances with him.

And I didn't want him to get hurt.

Leander spun around, snapping a redcap's neck as he flung off another who snatched a mouthful of his bloodstained sleeve. "RUN!"

His bellow was a shock that had me scrambling up on boneless legs. My disorientation tripled as I stumbled before him, at a loss. I wanted to run more than anything, to live, to find my father. But as the redcaps abandoned Castor and attacked Leander, I found myself frozen.

They were now coming at him from every direction. No matter how many he killed, more just kept appearing, clawing at him, trying to rip off chunks of his flesh.

"I SAID RUN!" he shouted again, throwing down a redcap and crushing its head underfoot.

This time, I obeyed. I staggered back along the path until I reached Castor.

I kneeled by him, holding back the urge to vomit at the sight of his blood-soaked clothes, looking like tar in the bluish light. I pressed a shaking hand beneath his jaw, whimpered when I found a pulse. He was alive, barely. But Leander could suffer a worse fate.

Patting around the ground, I found one of Castor's daggers. I could use this to fend off whatever I encountered next in these woods as I went for help.

But even if I found anyone willing to help, and we came back in time, if they found Leander, it would end in the same result: his death.

Leander let out a howl of agony and I heard his massive body hit the ground. Without a thought, I stumbled towards him, charging with a manic yell, and plunged the dagger into the redcap latched onto his shoulder. It went stiff and when I ripped out the blade it fell off him, gushing out the mouthful of blood it had just guzzled down.

With enraged screeches, others attacked me, making rhyming threats about dyeing their clothes with my foul blood.

I waved the dagger in every direction, hitting a few until one jumped up and swiped at my eyes. I instinctively ducked, squeezing my eyes, dropping the blade.

Their combined weight brought me crashing down next to Leander, who still crushed any redcap he got his hands on, even as the others ruthlessly swarmed him and tore at his body. There were too many of them, giant leeches sucking the life from him, killing him slowly right before my eyes.

Pinned again, I groped for the dagger, desperate to do anything, but it wasn't within reach and I couldn't throw any of them off.

My attempt to help him had only wasted the opportunity his arrival had afforded me. Just like my insistence on going to the Hornswoods had ended with us stranded here, with Adelaide lost, and my attempt to spare my father ruining all our futures. No matter what I did, I just made things worse.

And now I'd killed not only myself, but Leander and Castor, too...

Something whistled closer at a dizzying speed than the redcap bearing down on me convulsed, and its viscous blood sprayed my face. An arrow was protruding from its eye.

My whole being rioting in revulsion, I flailed to push his now-inert body off me, just as another arrow almost simultaneously tore another redcap off Leander. Another and another and another speared three more.

The other redcaps sprang around, babbling about new prey just as a horse leaped above us, landing by me. It was Maple!

Her rider was a man in a hooded cloak, aiming his bow down as he circled us, shooting arrow after arrow at the creatures in blinding succession, killing them instantly. Shaken as I was, I still recognized our savior at once. It was Rob!

Free of the redcaps' weight, I threw myself at the dagger. Burning blood roared in my ears and frigid air tore into my lungs as I swiped and stabbed at the ones that persisted over the now-unmoving Leander, powered beyond depletion by horror, disgust and rage.

Suddenly I noticed that everything had gone still. All the redcaps lay strewn around us, dozens of them, dead, and no more had shown themselves. I was on my knees, beside Leander, gasping for breath, shaking beyond control.

"Why am I not surprised that the idiot rode through a fairy path?" Rob dismounted, sticking his bow in his quiver as he came to stand over Castor.

Though he'd just saved our lives, I was feeling more furious than grateful. If he hadn't "sacrificed" my father to the "Beast," none of this would have happened!

Another fear burst in my pounding head, making me lunge towards Leander. I checked his pulse and almost sagged to the ground again. He was alive. But probably not for long.

As Rob approached, I put myself between him and Leander, dagger raised. "You're not going to kill him."

Rob bent at the waist to peer into my eyes. "Nice to see you too, Bonnibel."

"*Are* you going to kill him?" My voice rose hysterically.

"Why, do you want me to?"

I lowered the dagger, puzzled. "Isn't that why you're here?"

"And risk Castor's ire for stealing his noble quest of killing the Beast and rescuing the fair maiden?" he drawled, voice heavy with sarcasm. "Wouldn't dream of it."

"Then why are you here? Did Castor's friends send you?"

He snorted dismissively. "Castor's cowardly companions think you're both dead. They were debating whether it would be safe to come collect your drained bodies in the morning. *I* came to save you, and now have to collect *him*—" He pointed to Leander. "—and take him back to the castle before anyone else finds him."

That simple statement told me more than I could have imagined. This suspicious character before me knew who the Beast really was. And if he knew, then that meant...

"You knew, didn't you?" I trembled with aggravation, gripping the handle of the dagger tight enough to hurt. "That he wouldn't eat my father?"

He just nodded as he strolled around me, pulling arrows from bodies that were starting to turn into mounds of slime, before depositing them in his quiver.

"Then why did you bother taking him in the first place?"

He ignored my question as he continued retrieving his arrows, until I poked him with the dagger. He sighed. "To continue the charade. All of Rosemead believes him to be a bloodthirsty beast, but it's been years since he ate or killed a human, as they believe, and this has been increasing their urge to hunt him, like dear Castor here. I thought if everyone believes he's refusing animal sacrifices and demanding human ones, they'd leave him and the others alone."

He knew everything then, even that Jessamine was still alive. Yet her brothers still believed her dead, and Castor had shot her down.

"Don't the men from the lodge know about any of this?"

He shook his head. "Just me and Will."

"What were you going to do in the coming months when people believed they're expected to sacrifice humans?" I rubbed at the tears that had become a salt glaze from the chill of the fog. "Did you have some convoluted system for the people you would capture? What would have done with them? Was he going to pack his cells with prisoners?"

Rob cringed. "To be honest, I didn't think that far ahead. I just hoped that by next month this would all be over."

"How? How was giving him my father supposed to fix any of this?"

"It's best for him to explain it to you himself," he said. "Now I have to get him back to the castle before dawn breaks."

"You'll really return him?"

"Why the surprise?"

"I don't know what to expect from you, since you're a traitorous friend, a liar and a charlatan."

"Don't forget thief." He reached into Maple's saddlebags, took out a coin pouch and shook it. "But I resent your first statement, as I'm neither Castor's friend nor did I swear loyalty to him. Saving his hide right now is out of the goodness of my heart."

Avoiding his eyes, because I still couldn't apologize, or thank him for saving my and Leander's hide, I took hold of Maple's reins and got her to kneel. Rob pulled Leander across her back. He was limp, heavy, and still bleeding from wounds all over his body. The wounds he'd sustained to save me.

And he *had* saved me, even after I had broken our deal and destroyed his rose. He had come after me, told me to run while he let the redcaps gnaw at him.

Rob had gone to pick up Castor, throwing him across his shoulders. "Wait here, I'll go drop this one off at the nearest physician's house. He's lucky they didn't bite anything vital."

Before he walked away, I stopped him in his tracks. "My father...do you know where he is?"

He nodded. "He's being hosted by my friend, Will. We had to send him there to avoid having him run back to you. He still doesn't entirely believe that you're alive."

"Take me to him. After we return Leander, please take me to him."

He shook his head. "I can't. He's in the capital, Eglantine, a few days' ride from here, and I can't leave now. Your father's in good hands, Bonnie. I promise you that."

I groaned. "Speaking of promises, I promised Castor I'd marry him if he stopped his attack on the castle. It was the only way to save everyone."

Rob scowled at the man dangling over his shoulder. "Well, he nearly got you killed and this nullifies whatever promises you made or anything you owe him."

Though ashamed, I greedily took that excuse out of my obligation.

Then I finally exhaled, "You'll take me to my father after Leander gets better?"

"I will—as soon as our problems are resolved."

Unsure what he meant, and whether to feel sad or relieved, I exhaled. "Thank you, for everything, Robert, and sorry for the names I called you."

"Robin," he corrected, his lips, the only thing I could see of his face clearly along with his jaw, quirking. But he neither accepted my thanks and apology nor commented on them. "I'll be right back. Wait for me at the edge of the woods."

He strode ahead and I started leading Maple through the woods, retracing our earlier path in a thankfully quiet trip back beneath the fog clouds. All the way, I reeled from the harrowing experience, our needless brush with death, wondering what to do now.

I'd spent the past days wanting to escape, praying to be saved, and fearing for my father. Then my so-called savior led into mortal danger, only for the one I'd been running from to rescue me. And he'd told me the truth about my father being fine yet far away.

When Robin finally came jogging back, he motioned for me to follow him, leading us out around the town circle and back uphill.

Halfway up to the castle, I asked, "Who are you? How do know about him?"

He ignored the first question and said, "I knew him before he became the infamous Beast of Rosemead."

"Do you know how this happened?"

"It's not my story to tell."

"Why does everyone I ask tell me this?"

"Because there's hope that in telling you himself he'll figure out how to better his condition, maybe even fix it." He glanced at Leander over his shoulder and I saw his jaw clench in the shadow of his hood. "Perhaps you can help him."

"How?"

He shrugged. "I'm not sure."

He was lying. He knew, but he wasn't going to tell me.

So I went for my next burning question. "Back in the lodge, when I asked about my cousin, they said your friend's sister had been taken by fairies. Were they anything like the ones we just encountered?"

"No, Will's sister wasn't savaged by redcaps or goblins. She was carried off by members of the Wild Hunt," he said bitterly. "There are stories of people traveling to Faerie and coming back, but never of those who were kidnapped returning." He turned his head towards me, and I got a glimpse of his face beneath the hood in the moonlight. "I won't let this stop me from finding and saving my Lady Marianne, but there's so little dependable information about Faerie that my plans have been taking more effort and research than I hoped. The last thing I can afford is to end up like King Herla."

The name was familiar to me, a passing reference in one of my ancient books, but I couldn't remember what it had been about. "Who is he? And what happened to him?"

He looked ahead, exhaled. "Back when the kingdom was many smaller monarchies, Herla was the King of the Bryar, and he was said to venture into Faerie to find an ally that would help him fight the invaders from the north." I blinked at his back. He suddenly sounded like someone else, formal and polished—like a highly educated lord. "The story goes that he struck a deal with a fairy princess, his hand for the safety of his kingdom and the ensured future of his folk. But once he returned with her forces, he found that he had been gone, not for a fortnight, but for two-hundred years, and the Bryar lands had long been invaded and settled by his enemies."

That sounded terrible. To find oneself in a world where everything you knew and loved was long dead. I bit my lip. "What happened to him after that?"

He gazed ahead solemnly, shrugged. "It's said his fairy princess came to collect. Some stories say he was taken back to Faerie as her consort, others say he became the leader of the Wild Hunt. I intend to find out if he is the latter, when I find a way to track them down, that is."

Processing his story, I only reached a bleak conclusion and my heart crumpled in my chest. "So, you're saying there's no chance I'll ever see Adelaide again?"

"I'm just telling you what I've heard. Fairy stories are anything but reliable."

After that, he said nothing. I was grateful for the silence. Fearing I might have lost Adelaide where—or really *when* I could never reach her, I wept the rest of the way.

Once at the gate, Robin called out, "Sir Philip—come collect your master!"

As the gates swung open, I noticed that the fog I'd encountered the first time was thinner. Robin held out an arm, urging me to pass inside. The male centaur from earlier hobbled over to us with a lantern, a bruise on his forehead and his foreleg bandaged. I led Maple to him and Robin helped him settle Leander on his horse end.

As he trotted into the castle, Sir Philip called a boy with pale blonde hair and green scales called Oliver, who led Maple to the garden with promises of apples and water.

I stood shaking with depletion in the courtyard, replaying tonight's events, as both disappeared out of sight. Red feathers drifted around me in a gust of night wind and my throat tightened at the evidence of Jessamine's injury. Everything—from my fight with Leander by the rose tree to Castor's and his friends' attack—took on a totally different significance. What I'd planned as a harmless escape had turned into an array of near-death experiences on all sides.

Robin set a hand on my shoulder. "What are you going to do now?"

Eyes on the main castle doors, I let out a shuddering, misty breath that mingled with the fog. "All I wanted was to leave, but now—now I don't know what I'm supposed to do."

"I'm sure you'll figure it out. There's more to you than you think."

I gazed up at him for a long moment, confused by his statement. But for once, I was beyond asking questions.

As for what I'd do, I could leave. Yet—I couldn't.

I started walking. At the doors, I turned, took one last look at the gates and found Robin gone. Before I could change my mind, I stepped inside and shut the door.

It didn't matter that I despised Leander. I owed him my life now.

I wouldn't leave. Not before I made sure that he, and everyone else were all alive and well. And not before I got all the answers I needed to get my family back.

CHAPTER TWELVE

$\mathcal{U}$nlike the past few days when all of the castle occupants kept to the shadows, some showed themselves to me once Leander was whisked off to have his wounds treated.

Among those was a girl with tawny rabbit ears and reddish eyes who scurried over to me, introducing herself as Hazel. "I cannot begin to tell you how glad I am that you've decided to stay on after all!"

Whatever reasons she'd assigned my return, she looked too intensely happy for me to dispel them. I wasn't sure why any of them, starting with Leander, wanted to keep me here so badly. But one way or another, I was going to find out.

I tried to return any measure of her wiggling enthusiasm, but the muscles in my face refused to budge. Hazel didn't seem to notice my miserable condition as she bounded ahead of me towards the stairs. I went along, letting her escort me back to my room.

After I got cleaned up and treated my various cuts and lacerations the best I could, I went in search of my friends.

As I neared the servant's section of the castle, Ivy emerged from a room, Oliver the lizard-boy in tow. "Are you looking for Jessamine?"

A kindly mother's voice was the last one I'd expected to accompany her forked tongue. That prompted a deeper look at the snake-woman, searching her green-tinted face, the scales that glazed the edges of her aging skin. A layered mess of mahogany curls framed her round face and hung off her shoulders, and she had thin lips but a wide mouth to accommodate her fangs, a small nose with a flat bridge, and big, upturned yellow-green eyes.

Though I'd known that the curious creatures staffing the castle were like Clancy and Jessamine, the idea hadn't fully sunk in until now. I felt a bit ashamed it had taken me so long to think of them as people.

"Yes," I breathed through the renewed shock and belated acceptance. "Do you know where she's recovering? I'd love to visit."

"So sweet of you," Ivy cooed approvingly, slithering past me. "She's in the guest quarters. I'm afraid they're the only ones with beds big enough to accommodate her wingspan now she has to sleep with them spread."

"I don't know why she needs a bed." Oliver skipped beside me, his pale blond hair clashing with his scaly skin, his green eyes catching the brightness from the torches and shifting from human to reptilian. "Shouldn't she be on a perch by now where we can cover her with a blanket so she stays quiet."

"Ollie!" Ivy chastised. "This is not the time to joke about her state."

"Then when is it?" he complained, swinging his arms. "I can't do anything fun around here. When is it going to be over?" He turned his now lime-yellow eyes to me, elongated pupils dilating. "How long is it going to take you to fix things?"

Ivy shushed him urgently, then turned to me, laughing it off. "Children draw the silliest conclusions. Ignore him."

Telling me to ignore something was a surefire way to make me probe it. Especially considering that his question was almost as odd as the creepy rhymes the redcaps had said to me.

Though it wasn't the first time I'd been called a pixie or a sprite, those bloodthirsty little demons had definitely not been making snide remarks about my size.

"What is it that you all expect me to do here?" I asked Ivy.

"Oh, just keeping the master company." Ivy chuckled dismissively, her long, thick, glistening tail of a lower half undulating as she slithered ahead. "The gods know he needs it at this point."

Now that I'd given her a good look, that I truly considered the humanity of all these people, I had to wonder how they functioned. "How long did it take you to move?"

"Move where, dear?"

Oh, great. I'd said that out loud.

It would have been good form to brush it off with a simple "Never mind." But I had to know. The severity and mechanism of this curse they were all under.

So I said, "Your legs, when they became this tail, was it hard to move at first?"

She slowed her pace, if one could call it that, sighed, sounding sad and defeated. "It didn't happen overnight. But yes, it was difficult to navigate at first, essentially crawling on my belly. A very long, very heavy belly. Good thing is, I've grown very strong with moving requiring so much effort."

A stifling mixture of horror and pity overtook me. How

could they tolerate their transformed bodies? Not just the fact that their appearances kept them trapped here, but being covered in fur, their skin hardening to scales, horns bursting from their skulls, or their skeletons warping beyond recognition?

Needing to change the subject, I said, "Do you know Jessamine's condition?"

"It's hard to say with her. She's not much of a complainer, the sort that would walk on a broken toe. So, if you notice anything too bad, be sure to tell me, because she won't."

"Yes, ma'am."

Someone called her from below. When she called back that she was busy, Oliver piped up, "I can take her!"

Ivy looked down at him. "Do you know where she is?"

"I know everything in this castle," he bragged as he grabbed my hand. "Come, I'll show you."

I stumbled up the stairs behind him, waving back to Ivy.

He had me almost running after him up to where my room was then across the floor, before he pointed at a whitewood door that was just like mine.

"She's in there."

Before I could thank him, he was a receding dot in the distance.

Inhaling an unsteady breath, I lightly knocked before I entered. I found Jessamine sound asleep on a bed facing the door, her wings spread out, with the injured one balanced across the nightstand and wrapped in bandages. Clancy was asleep in an armchair by her side with an open book on his lap, spectacles sliding down his nose and his head lolling back so his horns hooked over the back of the chair.

Despite the terrible circumstances, it warmed my heart that he was here, watching over her. If it weren't for his timely save, Jessamine would have met the fate she'd saved me from my first night here.

Knowing she was cared for and not alone, I closed the door.

Then I went in search of Leander.

FINDING no one to direct me to "the Master's" quarters, I wandered around, familiarizing myself with the layout.

Though my body ached all over with a bonfire of bruises and lacerations, and I was deathly tired and utterly depleted, I couldn't consider sleeping yet. My mind was rioting and I knew I'd close my eyes only to relive the night's horrors. So I explored, trying to subdue my feverish thoughts, and to come to terms with everything that had happened.

But no matter how beautiful a marble vase was, or how peculiar the metal sculptures of foreign animals were, nothing could distract me. My mind now came back to those moments before the redcaps had attacked us.

By then it had been clear Castor considered me the reason for all his troubles, besides being annoying, disrespectful, and talkative. He'd dismissed everything I'd said, had been offended by my every suggestion, had led us into danger against my pleas, then blamed me for it all.

I could now see he was the handsome hunter of a hundred chivalrous stories—until things didn't go his way. Not a hero, not a villain, just a man who overestimated himself, and underestimated everyone else, with failings, and a temper.

But I couldn't tell if he'd left me behind, or if it had been yet another miscalculation that had landed him in the clutches of the redcaps. All I knew was that it had been the Beast he'd been supposed to slay who'd come for me. Leander, the gruff, volatile man who was literally turning into a beast, hadn't abandoned me when I'd transgressed against him with far worse than disobedience and criticism. He'd still chosen to brave a grisly end to spare my life.

Unable to contemplate any of those mind-scrambling realizations anymore, I went back downstairs, almost in a fugue now. I ended up following the curve of the castle to a circular, sitting hall with massive, painted double-doors at its end.

Hanging beside them was a brass frame housing a ripped painting of a family of six. It stopped me in my tracks, brought both blurring thoughts and vision back into sharp focus.

In the center, a black-haired mother sat with her youngest on her lap, a blond boy of about five. She had golden skin, high cheekbones, sharp eyes that matched her dark-green dress and an emerald tiara. Standing with his hands on her shoulders was the fair-skinned, blue-eyed father, his blond hair and beard a few shades lighter than his golden crown. To their left were two girls, one around eight, black-haired, green-eyed, skin a few shades lighter than her mother's, and one a bit younger than me, with her mother's face and dark hair, but her father's fairness and greenish-blue eyes.

The sixth figure, a taller man standing to the right of the father, had his face ripped.

Enraptured, I dragged a chair and stood on it to straighten the curled edges of canvas, and trying to approximate the slashed parts. Just as I started to make out a face, something heavy fell behind the doors, rocking my chair, followed by a pained shout.

I jumped down and tore the doors open. Bursting in, I realized at a glance that it was Leander's quarters. And he was sprawled on the floor, shirtless, covered in bandages and a lot less hair than before.

He gaped at me for long moments, as if he thought he was seeing things.

He finally shook his head, as if to clear it and snapped, "What are you still doing here?" He struggled to sit up, blood seeping through the wrappings on his shaky arm. "I keep telling you to get out."

I rushed to kneel before him, tried to help him up. "Something tells me you didn't really mean that."

Grunting, he snatched himself away from my reaching hands. "I don't need your help."

I still threw my weight against him, insubstantial as it was, doing my utmost to prop his large, heavy body until he sat on his heels. "Well, too bad, you're going to get it anyway."

When he finally pulled himself upright on his knees, he pushed his long hair off his face with his bleeding arm, and my breath stalled.

Like the rest of him, his face was less hairy than before, and the transformed, bumpy skin had softened. Not to the point that he looked human, but far closer to it than before.

I raised a hesitant hand to touch his protruding lower fangs. "How do you talk with those teeth?"

Instead of snapping at my hand as I'd half-expected, Leander stilled, stared down at me.

Then he finally opened his mouth, wide enough to swallow an apple, and moved his jaw in an improbable circle. "My face is not what it used to be."

"Is that why you ripped your side of that portrait?"

Ire hardened his eyes as he rose to his feet, bleeding arm failing to clench its fist. "Get out."

"No."

He snarled, baring every fang, wide nose wrinkling, only seeming more defensive than intimidating. Almost as if I was the one who threatened him. "I won't ask again."

"Then don't." I stood to my full height, which had me facing his midsection. "I'll do all the asking, because *Your Highness* owes me a lot of answers."

His resolve wavered then cracked as one leg buckled beneath his weight, dropping him on his massive bed with a curse and a hiss of pain.

The sight of his suffering snuffed out any confrontational mood I had, making me mumble in contrition, "I didn't come here to fight again."

"Then what do you want? You had your chance to leave like you so desperately wanted to, so why are you still here?"

"Can you stop being so difficult for a minute and show me your arm? It seems worse off than the rest of your injuries." I held out a hand, and he grudgingly sat up and showed me his arm. Carefully, I unwrapped the soaked bandage, found not just bite marks where the redcaps had fed on his blood, but deep gouges where they'd ripped at him, from which blood kept flowing.

My father had had his fair share of work injuries—including deep cuts and some burns, and I'd tended to them all. But I'd never seen anything this bad. It made me feel light-headed and queasy.

I needed to look for supplies, but when I turned away it was mainly to subdue the pity and guilt churning in my stomach. His quarters were twice the size of mine and arranged in a half-circle, with furniture mostly in black with red accents and gold-painted frames. But as I crossed to pick the roll of cloth and solution bottles off the table in the sitting area, I couldn't help being sidetracked by the huge bookcase beside it. Not just the array of interesting titles, but the pale wood that held them.

Tearing my attention back to my task, I rushed back, set the scissors, bandages and salve on the bedside table before ducking into his bathroom. Not having the time or inclination to admire its width or the pattern created by its rich marble tiles, I gathered two hand towels, emptied a soap bowl and filled it with water, then returned.

I found him literally licking his wounds!

Gagging, I moved his arm away from his mouth. "Don't do that!"

He blinked in surprise, so big he still looked down at me even sitting slouched on the bed. It seemed it wasn't only his appearance that was becoming beastly, but his instincts, too. And what was more natural to an animal than cleaning his own wounds?

Ears heating with uncertainty if those instincts were right, I changed the subject as I started working. "Is that willow?"

He watched me with suspicious eyes. "The bookcase? Yes, why?"

"Just wondering if there's a willow tree nearby." I dabbed his wounds with the damp towel and he ripped his arm from me. "Hey!"

"That hurt!"

"Cleaning your wound is supposed to hurt."

"It didn't hurt that much when I licked it."

"Well, you keep saying you're not a beast, and men don't lick their wounds." I eyed every one of his wrappings. "Did whoever bound you not clean your wounds?"

"There is no need."

"Yes, there is. Those things rabid and those cuts could become infected."

"Don't touch me!" he yelled in my face when I dabbed at the wound again, hot breath making my loose locks fly back, and my limbs shake.

I still stood my ground. "You were attacked by a pack of vicious creatures that tried to eat you, all so I could get away. You're already weakened, so stop needlessly tiring yourself out and sit still while I clean your wounds!"

He brought his face down to mine, until my view of it was all teeth. "I SAID NO!"

Every dread and worry and grievance that had been simmering within me the past week finally boiled over in a scream. "DON'T YELL AT ME!"

He sagged back on his elbows, gaping at me with stunned eyes.

I couldn't blame him. That was the loudest I had ever been. My throat burned, my face flamed and my every nerve twitched. But I'd had enough of his childish attitude. Life-debt or not, I was not going to tolerate being yelled at for helping.

"I wouldn't be yelling if you weren't bothering me," he finally mumbled sullenly, but didn't resist when I dragged his arm back, only wincing as I dabbed at it.

"I'm trying to prevent any infections, you dolt! I don't want your condition to worsen."

"I wouldn't be in this condition if you hadn't run off into the woods."

I uncapped the salve, slathering it on him, ignoring his noises of complaint. "I wouldn't have run off if you hadn't scared me!"

"You snuck out before that. And you did the same thing your father did, and expected me to not get upset?"

"Well none of this would have happened if you told me what was going on from the start!"

He avoided my eyes, gritted his fangs and said nothing more until I finished double-wrapping his arm.

"There." I set the arm over his chest with a light pat. "Was that so bad?"

"Yes, Miss Fairborn, you've killed me," he drawled sarcastically. "Is that why you asked about the willow tree? You want to bury me under one? You might soon get your chance."

Injured or not, I was not above flicking his nose in retaliation.

He bore down on me with a reflex growl, but I tested my luck by flicking him again. "I asked because willow bark can be used to relieve pain, something you and others around here could use right now."

His ire deflated, a hesitant expression entering his gaze. "There's one in the back garden. If such a remedy is true, we'd all appreciate it."

"Good." I jumped up beside him on the bed, feet dangling way off the floor. "It's bound to be better than what whoever patched you up can offer, even if I haven't tried it myself."

"Then where did you hear of such a thing?"

"Read it in a book on natural home remedies, things most households seem to have lost track of now we have apothecaries and doctors." I pointed to the bookcase. "What are those?"

"Books," he deadpanned.

I rolled my eyes at him. "What genre?"

"History, some fantastical essays and ballads I would like to believe is history, and the rest are just the journals of my ancestors."

"Other kings and princes?"

His eyes returned to me in an unblinking stare, full of dread of all things. "You know who I am?"

"I know you're not a duke. The painting outside said as much. With the tiara and the crown, and with you clearly the oldest son, it makes you a prince. A crown prince."

For some reason, my deductions seemed to somewhat relax him. "I might as well be a duke at this point. In fact, I'm more useless than a blind watchman."

"Does your whole family know about your curse?"

"Only my parents, my younger sister and my uncle know." His gaze darkened at the mention of his uncle. "Everyone thinks I'm severely ill and quarantined."

"I get the feeling your uncle isn't a favorite of yours."

His fangs flashed in a grimace. "With my father abroad, I should have been regent, ruling from the capital. But I'm stuck here, worsening by the day, while Uncle Jonquil runs the kingdom like it's his personal playground."

"There's nothing you can do?"

"What do you expect me to do? Show up at the castle, demanding my throne and getting killed on sight by my own panicked guards?"

"There must be a way to break this curse you're all under. People here seem to think I can help you. So how can I?"

Surprise softened his features, disbelief swirling in the depths of his wide-set, turquoise eyes. "You'd do that?"

If I said yes, there would be no going back. No reneging on my obligation, no escape attempts, no longing for the outside. Not until I'd repaid him and found a way to free everyone in this castle. But I'd already decided. I had to do it.

Feeling I was committing myself to something both inescapable and inexplicable, I nodded. "You nearly died trying to save me, when you had every reason not to. For that I owe you my life."

He stared at me for fraught moments, my words seeming to reverberate endlessly in his stunned silence.

Then he finally set a large, hesitant hand over mine, a few of his long nails torn off in the fight for my life, their nailbeds crusted with blood.

When he finally spoke, his voice was ragged with entreaty. "Join me for breakfast tomorrow. Join me, and I'll tell you everything you want to know."

To that, I only nodded.

I'd enter his world for real tomorrow. The world I'd just signed on to become a part of.

I could only hope I hadn't made a terrible mistake. That in trying to help him and everyone else, I didn't end up harming them even more instead.

CHAPTER THIRTEEN

*H*azel the rabbit-girl woke me up.

Taking over for Jessamine while she recovered, she came in at seven o'clock, rushed me into the bathtub and laid out fresh clothes for me, all the while twittering with excitement. Apart from her restless nose and ears, I could bet she had a wiggling cottontail under her skirt.

Whatever it was I needed to do, they all seemed to depend on me for it. I'd hate to let them down after giving them any hope of regaining normalcy and freedom.

As she styled my hair into a crown of braids, I asked Hazel about herself and the others. Her chattering kept going off on tangents, telling me about their condition instead. Rosalind, the female centaur, was resting her legs where she'd been stabbed, Jessamine was awake and taking her breakfast in bed, and everyone else was recovering in their own way from last night's attack.

I brought us back on topic again. "Were you a lady's maid before this?"

I saw her ears flatten in the hairdresser mirror. "That

would have been a good job, but no, I work in the kitchens. But I had three sisters, all married now, so I have some experience with preparing girls for important meals."

I caught her eyes in the reflection. "Can you do something for me? I was told that you have a willow tree here. Can you make tea from its bark or twigs and serve it to everyone who was hurt yesterday?"

"I've only ever made ginger tea from scratch, but yes, I can try!"

"Thank you, Hazel."

She did a double take, halting her braiding before quickly finishing up, face flushed. "You are very welcome, Miss."

A knock came at the door. Hazel made no move to answer it, so I did.

Once again, a box sat on my doorstep, peachy-pink with a carnation-like ribbon glued on its lid. "Why does he keep doing this?"

"To win your favor," said Hazel nervously. "Gifts are the way courtiers express their feelings, an incentive for you to give him your time, your attention, and a chance at winning more than that."

That was a concerning explanation. One the sender would need to elaborate on himself.

Inside the box was a set of six gold bracelets, each set with square-cut gems of different colors, citrines, rubies, emeralds, sapphires, pink diamonds and amethysts.

They were heavy, no doubt priceless—and gaudy.

Tucking the box under my arm, I made my way downstairs. Hazel hurried after me, hopping down the stairs with no fear of slipping to lead me to the dining room. We took the hall with the green Cahramani carpet, went past the room with the pegasus painting and turned left into a long and narrow room, holding a mahogany table with twenty-two matching chairs, ten on each side, and an armchair at each end. In the middle of the wall facing the door were three stained-glass windows, with cool light pouring through them and projecting their patterns and colors onto the floor and white tablecloth. It was the first time since I'd come here that the darkness enveloping the castle had parted enough to let sunlight in!

Chairs scraped against the floor as the two men stood up at my entrance. Leander, in a drawstring shirt that ought to sag on any other man but strained against his frame with his hair for once neat and pulled off his face, and Clancy, with dark circles under his eyes and his auburn curls an uncharacteristic mess.

Clancy clearly kicked Leander prompting a grumbling reply before Leander held out an awkward hand, signaling the armchair on the opposite end of the table.

"Miss Fairborn, I am pleased that you could join us this morning."

They wanted me to sit that far away? Were they upset with me for running?

Nevertheless, I sat across from him, with enough distance between us to plant a grove.

Like they'd been waiting for me to pull my chair in, Hazel and three others rushed in—another rabbit-girl, a lizard-man with a tail sticking out from his coat, and a female deer—all carrying trays. They made a quick round, placing plates, baskets and bowls and filling up glasses with water, and swiftly exited.

Peering at the variety of silverware on three sides of the porcelain plates before me, I forwent using them and reached for a bread roll. "Are they going to be joining us later?"

"No, the servants eat in their own space, at their own

time," said Leander, arms bent to accommodate his awkward grip on his cutlery, his attempt to slice his sausages futile, as they kept rolling away from him. He continued trying, making frustrated noises that escalated when the wayward meat evaded him, prompting Clancy to chuckle into his fist.

Giving up, Leander finally stabbed a sausage and stuffed it whole into his wide mouth.

"It's not funny, Lord Gestum" he hissed around his mouthful.

Clancy just laughed harder, letting out a few snorts and wheezes. "Ouch. Back to the formal titles, are we?"

Glaring at him, Leander resumed his attempt to use his utensils. "A true friend would offer a hand rather than mock me."

"Oh, grow up, you raging furball," Clancy scoffed, reaching over to steady Leander's wiggling plate.

"I'd like to see you laugh the day your hands turn to hooves."

Clancy flinched, retreating into his seat, returning his gaze to his plate as he ate.

Their mutual discomfort permeated to my end of the table, making me fidgety.

"How about instead of bickering, you tell me what's going on," I said, recapturing their attention. "What's happening to all of you exactly?" Annoyance further pinched Leander's brow as he began to speak, but I quickly added, "Don't say 'a curse.' You promised that if I came, you'd be honest."

Leander shot me an uncomfortable glance across the endless table. "This is hardly appropriate mealtime conversation."

Clancy rolled his eyes. "Because you're such a paragon of

appropriate behavior. If you'd attempted that attitude much earlier, none of us would be here."

"Not now, Clancy," Leander growled warningly.

"Then when, Leo?" Clancy hissed in frustration. "We just got attacked yesterday, I could very well be on all fours and bleating by the end of the week, so forgive me if I'm a bit bitter, and in a hurry."

I stood. "I'm going back to my room."

"Stay where you are!" Leander burst up, hand held out. Then he lowered his voice to a grudging, "Please."

Still standing, I glowered at him. "Start talking."

His face twisted in a snarl. "I'd watch my tone if I were you."

"Is that a threat?"

His aggression faltered. "No, of course not."

"Then watch *your* tone."

Swearing under his breath, Clancy got up, plate in hand. "If you'll excuse me, I need to go check on Miss Quill."

I strode towards him as he vacated his seat. "Can you tell her I wish her well?"

Though frustrated, Clancy still gave me a warm smile. "You should tell her yourself, she'd appreciate the visit."

Embarrassed, I ducked my head. "I don't know if she'd want to see me after the way I put her in danger."

"Miss Fairborn, if you're under the impression anyone here blames you for the attack, we don't." He set a hand on my shoulder, urging me to take his seat. "Now, finish your breakfast. You two have a lot to talk about." Clancy shot Leander a chastising look. "I'll know if you leave anything out."

For the second time since I'd met him, Leander rolled his eyes. It was still a too-human reaction for his face, and now that I considered it, very un-princely.

The moment Clancy closed the door behind him, I cleared my throat, reached for the butter and jam. "I assumed he was here on a formal visit when whatever happened to you hit and he got caught in it. But now I see you're more friendly."

Relaxing somewhat, Leander returned to his fruitless attempts to cut up his food. "Before he inherited his title, Lord Gestum was my tutor."

I raised my brows. "I didn't know nobility could take such jobs."

"Not officially, no. He had to come to live at my father's court with his uncle, the previous Duke of Briarfell, as part of his training as his heir." He dropped his knife and speared what had been sliced with his fork. "There was a shortage of lordlings at court, so I was encouraged to befriend him as he was closest to me in age, being only six years older. When I did, he astounded me."

"Why?"

"Every time I saw him, he'd tell me some bizarre fact. Things even my scholar tutors either didn't know themselves or didn't see fit to teach me."

"Like what?"

"I believe our first conversation went something like, 'Good morning, Lord Clarence, do you fancy a carriage ride through the city today?' To which he answered, 'Did you know that the Emperor of Zargoun has a carriage pulled by striped horses? They have the coloring of the white tigers of Opona, despite not being native to a land that snows.'"

His impression of Clancy was hilariously spot on, tone, accent and mannerisms. I couldn't help chuckling. "Speaking of Opona, what is a mammoth?"

"It is a shaggy elephant."

"I don't know what that is either."

He made what I assumed was a wince. "It's a—" He paused, standing. "You know what, let me show you."

Either I was about to meet someone who was part-elephant or be shown another painting. I didn't waste a second tailing him out to the sitting room he'd taken me to earlier, his gift box under my arm and a roll leaking butter and jam in my mouth.

He stopped over a table by the balcony window. It was spread in ornaments, the biggest of them a golden animal sculpture with a bronze saddle and silver tusks, a large, rounded mount of some sort, with big, floppy ears and thick tree-trunk-like legs, its boar-like tusks right beneath the hose-like nose it raised like a spout.

I smiled down at it. "It's kind of cute."

"Imagine that, but taller and with ruddy-brown hair, that's a mammoth." He set a large hand on the elephant's back. "In Zargoun and beyond, they're big enough to demolish homes. Ancient kings would ride them into battle, but nowadays their use is ceremonial. Many grooms ride them through the streets to the temples that perform their wedding ceremonies."

"And the hairy ones?"

"Much, much bigger. Shaped slightly different too, especially the heads, and I don't think anyone has managed riding them."

"Have you ever been to Zargoun?"

He shook his head. "Unfortunately, I've only seen illustrations of it in the books my mother brought with her to Arbore. Cahraman is a few countries to the north of Zargoun, but they have some cultural similarities. I wanted to visit both before…"

His legs buckled like last night and he stumbled back into the armchair by the dormant fireplace.

I rushed to his side, chest tight with concern. "Are you all right?"

His head lolled back, followed by his eyes before he squeezed them shut. "The blood loss is taking its toll. I'll feel weak for a few days." He gestured to the armchair by him. "Sit." He adjusted both his position and tone as he rushed to add, "Please."

I plopped down, folded my arms over the box. "You should be resting."

"I'm sitting, aren't I?"

"I mean sleeping."

"I can't honor my promise to you if I'm sleeping this off, now can I?"

I arched an eyebrow. "I've yet to see much promise honoring. Continue your story."

"Where were we? Right. Clancy's random facts." He shook his head, ironic but fond. "Needless to say, after his monologue on the fauna of distant lands, I stuck to him. I found that I learned more from him than I did from my appointed tutors, and insisted he teach me everything he knew, including the subjects we've both already studied."

"What did he add to those?"

"It wasn't adding as much as it was clarifying, and making me want to know more. Till I met him, I abhorred schooling hours at court. I had to learn so many things but retained almost none because of how tediously and convolutedly presented they were. Some days I wished I was illiterate so I wouldn't have to write those endless mock-reports for my father to review."

For some reason, I took personal offense to that statement. I would rather suffer terrible sunburn than become illiterate. My life had been an endless stretch of mind-numbing boredom before I learned how to read. I couldn't imagine an existence without an abundance of books now.

Oblivious to me reaction, he went on blithely, "But Clancy always made any subject easier and far more interesting. The way he reintroduced the most difficult concepts to me, taught me ways to bridge my understanding of all topics, made me want to know more beyond what was deemed necessary. The first gift he gave me was this old book for my birthday, along with a dare to finish it by my next one."

My eyebrows shot up. "Why would it take you a year to read a book?"

"Because it was an epic poem."

I'd heard of epic tales dubbed ballads, but never epic poem. "What makes it epic?"

"That it's hundreds of pages long, all rhymed in an archaic dialect. It was an agonizing read, but I suppose the game was to pick out the story from all the flowery stanzas."

"So, it's more like a play than a novel?"

"It's a precursor of the novel." He managed to sit up, and in the light streaming from the balcony, I saw he was paler than before. "You said you found the willow tea in a book. Were you training to work as an apothecary or to become a nurse?"

"No to both. I just read whatever I could get my hands on, even if it had no story."

"You read medicinal texts for fun?" he sounded baffled. "Why?"

"There was a limited number of books in my town, so I read whatever anyone could lend me," I said, a bit defensive. "Besides, medicinal texts are interesting."

"Yes, rambling chapters full of recipes and crude illustrations of roots and seeds and the corresponding organs they soothe," he sneered. "How *riveting*."

"Can't expect you to understand, since it seems you'd rather stare at the wall than read anything useful."

"Is it such a crime to want to enjoy your hobby?" He held the arm I'd bandaged to his chest. He seemed to be holding back the urge to tear the bandages off and lick it again. "I've had enough required reading of said 'useful' texts in my life. Now, to keep myself sane, I like to indulge in the most fantastical of tales. Those don't chain me to reality and remind me of the world I am now cut off from."

To say I was shocked would be an understatement. I'd been prepared to make some caustic retort, and for him to lose his temper again. Instead, I felt ashamed of my sensitivity about my own hang-ups, and insensitivity towards his plight. And he was upset.

Not angry, *upset*.

Worst of all, I hadn't noticed we weren't that different in our situations until now. We both wanted to escape our reality —even if my dissatisfaction with mine couldn't begin to compare to his.

The least I could do was stop criticizing him, tell him that I understood his preference, and shared it.

My throat tightened as I said, "Though I want to know as much as I can, about anything and any place, for my enjoyment and escape I'd read nothing but wondrous tales of magic and adventure if I could. There was nothing I wanted more than to leave my home, my town, to go explore, to find answers, but I was never allowed to go beyond my leash. I, too, was trapped, so the only way I could experience anything new was through a book."

His eyes locked with mine, intrigue evident in them, along

with some new intensity. "I bet you were the type to pester your teachers for answers they didn't have. Bet you asked 'why?' and 'how?' after every statement and never learned to leave well enough alone."

My jaw dropped. "How did you know?"

His mouth twisted in mockery. "You've been doing that to me since I met you, saying the first thing that comes to your mind, persisting with your invasive questions, unshakeable like a dog with a bone. You must have been a nightmare to have in class."

I sniffed in annoyance—for he was so totally right. That was what every teacher I'd ever had had more or less called me. "The point of school is to teach us. What's wrong with me wanting to know more?"

"Tell me, Miss Fairborn, did you have any friends? Or did you put off other girls with the uncomfortable situations your tactless questions and comments created? Not to mention your knowledge flaunting and judgmental attitude?"

"I am not judgmental," I snapped.

He made a humorless sound. "You behaved like my distaste for academic texts was a personal offense."

I blinked, stunned that he'd picked up on that. And though I hated to admit it, he was right about something else.

Before Adelaide had moved to town, I'd struggled to befriend others. But it wasn't my fault they weren't interesting people or good company like she was. It wasn't my fault they avoided both my questions and my company... Or was it?

I knew I could come on too strong sometimes, and miss a social cue or two, and I might have embarrassed some with some poorly-timed questions, but the fact that I showed interest in someone's life had to be flattering, right?

I slumped back in my chair, groaning.

Oh, dear. I *was* annoying.

After a squirming moment of digesting this new realization about myself, I shot up sitting straight, glaring at him. "If I'm annoying then you're off-putting. You're also putting off your explanations."

"Dog with a bone." His lips curled in what must pass for a smile as he wagged a big finger at me. "How would you like me to present my story, Miss Fairborn? As dry and droning as your factual texts or with the dramatic embellishments of your fantastical stories? I can throw in acting interludes if you like, to keep you entertained."

I suddenly found myself spluttering senselessly at his teasing.

"Just..." I wheezed. "...just don't leave anything out."

What I'd thought a smile died as he stared at me, until I too sobered.

It was only then that he sat back with an almost bleak cast over his face. But he didn't say anything until I thought he wouldn't, that he'd decided this was all a big mistake.

I was about to get up when he suddenly said, his voice a deep rasp, "Before my sister was born, Arbore celebrated only the birth of its royal heirs. But as the first princess born in seven generations, it was cause for a celebration like no other. People from all kingdoms were invited to the palace, including fairies."

I goggled at him. *"Fairies?"*

"The civilized sort." At my continued incredulity, he waved. "These do exist. And it was one of their queens who cursed us."

CHAPTER FOURTEEN

"Fairies can curse?" I exclaimed. "And that's the civilized sort?"

He shrugged. "One of the other sorts almost drained me of blood last night."

I winced as the memories bombarded me. "So the more civilized fairies get, the more elaborate and prolonged a death sentence at their hands becomes?"

His exhalation was the very sound of resignation. "We didn't have a precedent like that with that sort before." He looked out the window into the distance. "Anyway, it was custom in Arbore to invite fairies to be a princess's godmothers, as a show of good faith and unity. My parents invited seven and each came to bestow a gift on my sister. Then the Queen of the Spring Court appeared in our palace unannounced just as the seventh fairy was about to bless my sister, and demanded to know why she wasn't invited."

"And why wasn't she?"

His turned to me with a scowl. "I was getting to that part, but there you go again with the disruptive questions."

A hot flush of embarrassment engulfed my whole body. "What would you have me do? Go through life with no answers?"

"I have no problem with you asking. But you'll find that people will be more inclined to answer you if you let them finish talking first." Tilting his head, he squinted at me. "Or if your questions were phrased more like inquiries and less like impatient attacks."

"Wise words from someone so reactionary," I shot back. "You could do with a bit of that premeditation yourself."

"Well, we all have our weaknesses. Would you like to discuss my temperament or may I continue? Telling this story is hard enough, so do you think you can allow me to get it over with without interruptions?"

I disguised my mortification in a dismissive wave. "Go on."

He waited a beat, as if doubting that was all I'd say. When I forced myself to add nothing more, he exhaled. "The fairy queen stormed into the throne room, accusing my parents of insulting her when they invited courtiers from Faerie rather than the heads of the courts themselves. My father assured her no slight was intended, that he only didn't believe any royal, let alone herself, would accept an invitation, seeing as my sister was a second-born and not an heir." He stopped to let out a longsuffering sigh. "Then my mother shot all his placating diplomacy in the knee."

A question about his mother almost shot out before I swallowed it back, as it squirmed for a way out.

As he'd said earlier, his continuation answered it. "In Cahraman, my mother's homeland, they don't have any inter-action with fairies. They live too far away from the Fair-Folk's Shore, and the closest things they have to them are the *peri*, which rarely venture beyond their realm, and the djinn, which are just as wicked if not worse." He absently traced one of his fangs. "My mother did not want any fey or other inhuman creatures near her or her newborn. But after much convincing, she allowed the tradition to be implemented, but only if Father invited lower-tier fairies to attend, the sort that can be intimidated by a few guards with iron weapons."

"And she told the fairy queen that?"

I bit my tongue. What was wrong with me? Couldn't I stop asking questions for one minute?

Instead of berating me again as I'd expected, he turned to stare into nothing. "She did worse. Instead of letting my father handle the situation, she was so alarmed and offended by the fairy queen's presence and presumption that she lashed out, told the queen what she thought of her kind, that she was a queen too and she was kicking her out of her palace. Then she threatened to have our guards spear her with iron if she took one more step towards my sister."

Half a dozen questions and comments ricocheted in my mind. I gripped the arms of the chair to hold them back.

He ran big palms over his face before leaning forwards and resting his elbows on his knees. "Fairies, especially the civilized sort, are very proper. They don't tolerate slights, no matter how small. My mother having the gall to insult one of their queens, in full view of the most important people in the kingdom and beyond, called for a severe punishment."

I inched to the edge of my seat. Though I already knew how this had ended, I still dreaded hearing the details of how the Spring Queen had retaliated.

He got up and walked to the figurines on the mantelpiece, picked up his sister's. "Six fairies had already given Fairuza gifts fit for a princess, health, beauty, grace, song, wit and such. The fairy queen topped it all off by saying that, yes, she will be all manners of lovely, but before she truly has the chance to bloom, she'll be plucked. Dead before her time or her prime." He put the figurine down with a trembling hand, gestured to his. "Then she turned her sights to me, saying that if my mother's daughter would take all her hopes with her to an early grave, then I would be the embodiment of her inner ugliness behind the pretty face, the horrendous beast within that her titles make all turn blind eyes to." Leander framed the air around his face. "Now that beast has manifested, and no matter my title, no one will tolerate my existence."

Torn between being aghast and furious, I couldn't hold back my outburst. "That is—that can't—*this is not fair!*"

"Contrary to popular belief, the fair in *fair-folk*—with the meaning of just, not only beautiful—is purely euphemistic, a title given to avoid their ire."

"But you were a child, your sister a baby! How could—why would—argh!"

The sheer injustice that had shaped his life had me speechless. Something I'd never been.

But something didn't make sense. "You were cursed as a child, but you've been like this only three years. How so?"

He nodded. "I've been permanently like this for three years, yes. But my condition has ebbed and flowed since I was ten. The first time the curse hit, it covered me in hair and gave me claws." He raised his hand to me. The nails that had been broken and torn in the woods had regrown, like nothing had happened. "No amount of trimming would fix them and the hair would sprout back no matter how it was cut or shaved for the week the curse lasted. Then I went back to normal and it was dormant for months.

"But it flared up again and again, each time worse than the

time before it. Parts of me began to distort around five years ago and I'd develop fangs, new bones in my jaw and back and claws in my feet. The changes would soon subside, and my family devised excuses for the times I had to hide, once a trip abroad, another a bout of illness. Then three years ago, the curse returned with a vengeance and I was sent here to wait it out. But it only got worse then somehow caught everyone here in its malignant grip." He sat back down as if he couldn't stand anymore. "It was one thing to ruin me. But to transform my staff? Blameless people who came to take care of me, or who, like Clancy, came to check on me?"

My head spun with the new revelations. If anything, they proved what I'd heard all my life, that fairies were evil. It also turned my belief in his responsibility for this state on its head and…

My thoughts screeched to a halt, crashing into one word he'd said. Blameless.

I stared at his beastly profile. "Do I deduce you don't count yourself as a 'blameless' victim? You did do something to deserve this?"

He avoided my gaze. "After three years of thinking, I now suspect that my curse's previous fluctuating state was a warning, that I might have avoided its permanence if I hadn't done something to trigger it."

"So what did you do to turn permanently from man to beast?"

"I remain a man!" His shout sent me flying back in my seat. He stiffened, hunching further, as if to make himself appear smaller, less threatening. He gazed at his clawed hands in disgust, his jaw working. "I—apologies. As you can see, I don't know how to interact with females. At least ones who aren't nobility. I've been trained to interact with those in the ways expected in court." His eyes went to the box on my lap. "As for foreign or common women…"

Unease gripped me when he trailed off. "What did you do?"

He seemed far more uncomfortable as he faced me. "For a decade now, there's been this trend of noble families sending their sons south to work on farms rather than squire for knights. To build endurance and character, they said. I accompanied a friend who was sent to The Granary, as a minor diplomatic mission. The leader's daughter…she was unlike anything I'd ever seen before, as tall as I was, and probably as strong. I liked her. I acted on that instinct and just told her. But when she rejected me, I—persisted."

I didn't understand why he seemed so dismayed and ashamed. The persistent pursuit of one's love interest had always been shown as a good thing in my novels. The best heroes had been men who never gave up, and pursued their women until they accepted them. It had always come off as a strength, to not give up, to do your utmost to win your prized person.

But—after meeting Adelaide, who had worked and lived in all manner of places, she'd explained that maids and serving girls were frequently subjected to unwanted and uninvited interest, and it was never good, mostly insulting and oppressive and sometimes scary. It was then that persistence became something unacceptable, sinister even, turning the hero into a villain. And I realized exactly what he'd done.

"You *harassed* her!"

At my accusation, he looked away as if unable to meet my gaze anymore. "I said terrible things to her in the hopes of damaging her confidence, so she'd accept me."

"What did she do?"

He shuddered, hand reaching for his brow. "Slammed her hard head into mine. Knocked me to the ground, and threatened to disembowel me with a hayfork."

"Good," I hissed. "You deserved it."

"I know that now. And I deeply regret it. Not that it matters. It seems that moment was the final straw for the curse to take hold permanently. After that, I became what you see now, slowly and painfully."

Back to feeling conflicted about him in a heartbeat, and not knowing how to respond for the first time in memory, I sagged back when Hazel chose that moment to enter with a tea tray.

Fluffy ears turned forwards to catch whatever we said, she skittered towards us. "Hello, Master, Miss Fairborn. I believe it's time for your morning tea, since you forgot to have some with your breakfast."

She set the tray before us, excitement shining in her eyes as they flitted from me to him. The tray had two cups, each with a matching teapot, a plate of cookies and a sugar bowl.

"Here is the willow tea for your aches, Master." Hazel pointed to the teapot with gold lining, then to the other painted with green roses. "And this is the brew you requested for Miss Fairborn."

She took her sweet time exiting the room, ears turned back. Hoping to hear what, I couldn't begin to guess.

He served us both and I frowned up at him as I took the teacup. "Everyone seems really excited that I'm here, anxious even. What is it exactly that they expect me to do?

He remained quiet, making displeased expressions at his willow tea.

"How do I help you all break this curse?" I pressed.

Still no answer apart from tentative sipping sounds.

I held out a cookie. "All this food you keep inviting me to and shoving at me. Do you need to fatten me up and sacrifice me to the fairy that cursed you? Or maybe to your flesh-eating rose tree?"

Leander spluttered, spraying his mouthful everywhere. "Nothing is going to eat you! How many times do I have to say that?"

So, outrageous claims were what it took to get an answer from him?

Trying to smother my snickering into my teacup, I took a deep breath of the tea's powerful scent. It was like hot pink-rose perfume. "Oh, this smells..." I took another deep whiff, closing my eyes to savor it. "This smells—"

"It *smells*?"

"Beautiful! That's the word I was looking for. Don't think I've ever thought of a smell as beautiful."

"That's roses for you, the embodiment of beauty." He gazed out the window, possibly in the direction of the tree, looking wistful.

"Are you going to tell me about that tree? I've never heard of a rose tree before."

"That's because they don't exist." He poured himself another cup. "It's not a tree as much as it is a clock, counting down the time I have left to break this curse."

I choked on my tea, almost coughed my lungs out.

He reached over and patted me on the back, but each gentle tap of his big hand almost aided in expelling my lungs.

"Why—" I pulled away, gasping, tears springing from my eyes. "—didn't you tell me that when I came for my father?"

"You expected me to tell all of this to a complete stranger?"

"Yes! Especially when I needed an answer why a rose was

worth someone's life..." And the terrible realization hit me. "*Your* life. That rose he plucked, the one I crushed—h-how much time did it represent?"

"When your father plucked that rose for you, I felt the pain as if he'd stabbed me. From previous experience since that tree appeared, I know a rose represents a month. I hoped he only took that long off the life I—we have left. But since no one has ever plucked a rose, I feared the rest of the roses would die in consequence, and all of us with them. That was why I imprisoned him. I hadn't really intended to do so forever—I don't have that long anyway. Then I let him go, and the rest of the roses survived, so I placed it back, attempting to restore it, but the petals kept falling. Then you crushed what remained of it, and this time I—*felt* my time being cut short. And it has been. Now there are only three roses left."

CHAPTER FIFTEEN

I couldn't move. Couldn't speak. I just sat there, gaping at him, feeling the slow creep of horror and guilt cover me like frost on glass. Their cold pressure spread insidious fractures that felt would shatter me if I as much as drew breath.

After what felt like an age of muteness, I managed a whisper that scraped my throat raw. "H-how? The tree was full of roses when I last saw it. There was at least a dozen."

He dipped his huge head in melancholy defeat. "I can only speculate how it happened. When you crushed the rose in anger, another girl who hated me and wished me harm, the curse intensified. Now I—we don't have as much time as we'd thought."

He believed this curse would end up killing him, and presumably all the others. And before I'd come, even after what my father had done, they'd had a year or more to live. Then I'd crushed the rose and had cut their time down to three months.

What did I say to such a revelation? Certainly not "sorry." It would be adding insult after such an unforgiveable injury.

Now I could understand his rage and fright at the time. What I couldn't understand was how he'd stopped from lashing out at me, and how he'd let me go. How he'd still come to save me.

Maybe he had because he'd still believed I could fix what I'd done, could help save him and the others from the curse I'd accelerated?

I didn't care why he had. Before, I would have done all I could to help them. But now, I'd do anything to fix my mistake.

"Tell me how to help you break this curse!"

At my shrill outburst, he put down his teacup. "Not today."

"Why not? The sooner we start working on it the better."

"We are working on it, but that's a story for another day."

I couldn't find the words to object, to insist. Perhaps it was better for me to let it go for now. The least I could do after all I'd done was not pester him.

His gaze moved to the box on my lap. "Why are you carrying that around?"

I blinked at the change of subject. "I-I was hoping to return it personally this time?"

Offense sparked in his eyes. "Why? I've given you every possible gift worthy of a young lady and you've rebuffed them every time. Now that your freedom isn't an issue and you're here of your own free will, what more could you want?"

I handed him the box with a trembling hand. "I never had any use for jewelry, or go anywhere that calls for such extravagance. But if you insist on giving me something, though I can't think why you would, maybe something personal?"

Grudgingly, he took back the box. "Hard to be personal when I barely know you."

"Then let's get to know each other!"

My blurted out offer seemed to shock him.

He finally shook his head, as if rousing himself. "Fine. Is there anything you want to ask that's not about the curse?"

I jumped at the offer to change the subject. "Robin. Who is he? I didn't even get to properly see his face with that hood he keeps on all the time."

"I thought he'd been long gone from Rosemead, but it's fortunate he remained." He slumped back in his seat with a sigh. "He's Robin Loxley, the son of the Earl of Sherwood, and an old friend of mine."

"The one whose father hosted you?"

"The very same."

My accustomed curiosity rose from beneath the rubble of conflicting emotions. "What is an earl's son doing running around with a bunch of hunters?"

"Continuing to cause untold trouble for my uncle, I hope." He snarled as he sat forwards, poured me a second cup of tea. I took it gratefully, hoping to savor it this time, needing something to calm my nerves. "Lord Loxley contested my uncle's appointment as regent, wanted me to take over no matter my condition. When this didn't happen, the instant my father left for Avongart, our beloved regent stripped him of his title in retaliation." He sat back with his own refilled cup, seeming to be enjoying the willow now. "Robin went to war, came back and made it his life's goal to target Jon and his windbag, corrupt supporters. He robs their ill-gained fortunes, sabotages their exploitative projects and raids their embezzled trade convoys, redirecting them back to the towns they'd been extorted from or to those who've been taxed into poverty."

"He told me he's a thief. So he's a vigilante, too." That was yet another perspective of the man I'd at first hated. He was doing what Adelaide had done, if on a much larger scale. Even if he hadn't saved our lives, that alone would have made me partial to him. But I had to know something else. "How is your uncle getting away with such things?"

"The same way I used to get away with whatever I did. It's being called 'prince.'" He rested his jaw on his palm with a deep sigh, a sharp nail barely missing his eye. "But if Rob manages to prove Jon's major corruption by the time my father returns, things can go back to what they were, and Jon and his cohorts would meet the fate they inflicted on Lord Loxley or preferably worse."

All this made my head spin. I'd read so much to inflame my imagination about court intrigue and political webs in my storybooks, and here I was, sitting with someone who'd actually lived his life among them. I had a thousand questions.

It was him who asked one as he suddenly scrutinized me with renewed curiosity. "My turn to ask a question. Where did you say you were from?"

"You know I didn't. But—I'm from Ericura. What you probably know as Hericeurra."

He chuckled lightly. "Very funny. Are you from Avongart? It's fine if you are, I won't hold the war against you."

"I'm serious. I'm from the lost island of Hericeurra, or whatever you call it these days."

His amusement faded. "That's not possible. That island doesn't exist."

I flicked a hand at him. "Neither does the wicked King of the Beasts. Yet here we are, having tea."

The look of concern in his eyes grew, as if he feared I was losing my sanity.

I sighed. "You have a rose tree as a curse-clock in your garden and a giant snake as your housekeeper and you don't believe I'm from a lost island?"

He blinked, let out a ragged exhalation. "You're right. Belief in the mythical lands beyond the Forbidden Ocean should be easy at this point, but—it just feels too much." He scratched his head, making me cringe at the thought of him scraping his scalp. "All my life, the Lost Isle of Hericeurra was a very popular myth, a land that people migrated to, to venture into Faerie, before we discovered the use of fairy paths to their world."

I nodded. "That's the story of Saint Alban."

His eyes rounded in stupefaction. "Saint? Alban? You mean the story of Madman Alberic who believed he was a lost prince of the Winter Court and followed fairies that said if he brought them thousands of humans they'd lead him 'home?'"

I frowned at him. "No, Saint Alban was a hero who led his people away from persecution and some vengeful sun god, but he couldn't make it past Man's Reach so he settled in my town. It's even named after him. They called it Alban's Lair, that somehow became Aubenaire."

"What persecution?" he scoffed. "And what sun god? The man came from Ancient Arbore where our pantheon was as it is now, with a temperamental weather god. The Lower Campanians, Orestians and the folk of The Granary are the ones with the sun god!"

Now that he'd said all that, it made better sense than the story told as historical fact in Aubenaire. I'd already suspected the truth had faded into simplified myth when Adelaide had given me *The Known World*. But it still disturbed me that it appeared to be completely bogus. It went to show I couldn't trust second-hand accounts, or make them the basis of any belief.

But then I'd always questioned so-called established faiths and facts. Now I would more than ever.

"If what you say is true," he said. "That would make you a descendant of the foolish Arboreans who followed Alberic to that island before it floated into Faerie."

"It didn't. If it has ever moved, it stayed on its doorstep, from what I can tell. No one from my island has ever crossed what we call Man's Reach into Faerie—also as far as I know."

"How did you get here then?"

I gazed at my reflection in the cup, memories swamping me all over again. "It was the bonfire night when we celebrate Alban's arrival to Ericura and the founding of our town when this woman came to the tavern my friend worked in claiming her carriage broke down. She said she needed help looking for the broken part, took Ada to the woods we believe borders the fairy realm. Dad and I followed them to fix the carriage and we saw them before this portal of wind and light—then we woke up here. I think she was a fairy, and for some reason she wanted Ada, but we got sucked in by mistake and she tossed us here because we weren't of use to her."

He interrupted his absorption with my account to ask the next logical question. "Why here of all places?"

Another wave of guilt stormed through me, knotting my insides. "I'd just learned of Arbore, and wanted to come here more than anything, to see the land of my ancestors. Then I did, just not in the way I wanted. But I can't help but believe it was my desire that drew us here."

"For what it's worth, I'm glad you are here." He hesitated before he reached over and touched an uncertain hand to mine. "With me."

Since I couldn't say the same, heart heavy and blood cold, I settled for changing the subject. "Anything else you want to ask?"

He sat back, seeming disappointed. "What sort of a name is Bonnibel?"

"It's a flower."

"No, it's not."

"It is!"

He snorted in amusement. "I think I would know, considering Arbore is the flower capital of the Folkshore."

I pouted, getting cranky. "A bonnibel is a blue flower."

"Surely you mean a bluebonnet? Or a bluebell? Maybe your parents confused the two or merged them into bonnet-bell, then simplified it to bonnibel?"

I wanted to blurt out why he assumed it wasn't a flower native to Ericura, or if Bonnibel wasn't the colloquial name for either flower there? But I couldn't.

I'd never heard of it on my island, knew it was a flower only because my father once said so. The only other person who'd ever said that had been Miss Etheline, owner of the Poison Apple tavern, where Adelaide had worked since she'd come to town. The first time I'd met Etheline, she'd told me it was "A lovely flower, blue like your eyes."

So just because neither of us had heard of it, didn't mean it didn't exist!

His insistence that it didn't annoyed me more than it should have, so I fired back, "What sort of a name is Leander? It's the strangest name I've heard in Rosemead so far."

He quirked one bushy eyebrow. "How so?"

"Everyone here seems to have outdoorsy names…"

"Outdoorsy," he deadpanned. "How eloquent."

I chucked a cookie at him. "Would you let me finish?"

He caught it in his jaws, the clack of sharp teeth making me shudder. "Please, entertain me with your observations about our naming conventions."

Amazing how he'd gone from being the scariest thing I'd ever seen to a moody and morose boy. What he must be under all that hair and misshapen flesh, and for the best of reasons.

Pity and another burst of guilt pooled in my stomach like a gulp of scalding tea, softening my tone, subduing my voice. "I mean, Florian, Dale, Glenn, Robin, Jessamine, Ivy—these all come from nature, but your name and—" I eyed the figurines. "Fey-ruh-za?"

"Fay-roo-za," he corrected, wincing, as if saying her name hurt. "Fairuza is Cahramani for *'turquoise.'*"

Turquoise, like his eyes. A feature he shared with his sister, the one thing that remained human about him. At least, when he wasn't angry.

But this was the third time I'd heard of this Cahraman. The map of *The Known World* hadn't had a land by this name, so it either hadn't been discovered yet then or it had gone by a different name. I'd gathered from Clancy that it was very far away, all across the Folkshore.

"Is Leander also a Cahramani name?"

He leveled me with a fed-up stare as he sat up from his slouch. "No. My father wanted to name me Oleander for his favorite uncle, but my mother refused to name her firstborn after a poisonous plant. In the end, they compromised by shortening it to Leander, which sounds more Orestian—a middle ground, like Orestia itself is between their kingdoms."

"What is it like over there? Cahraman, I mean." I sat forwards, anxious to hear about that land, and about the story behind his parents' meeting.

"It's very hot, arid, rains a handful of times per year, and there is one major river and sand everywhere," he quoted monotonously. "It's the largest country in its region, home to many related ethnic groups and cultures and was once part of the Avestan Empire. They export most of the Folkshore's spices, a lot of the perfume and elaborate artworks, most famously their carpets."

This wasn't the description of someone who'd ever seen any of this for himself. Like me, he'd gotten all his details from secondhand accounts and books.

"How did your parents meet then?" I looked around, trying to pick out anything else that could be from Cahraman. "That must be a very interesting story."

I could see it now—a foreign prince traveling to the end of the world, for business or politics. He meets a girl in a market or in the palace where she works, and they fall in love. Then the time for him to return home comes and he asks her to go with him. Thinking he is poor, her family opposes the match, wanting to elevate their position by marrying her to a merchant. But she chooses him anyway and runs away with him from the dunes to the forests. And her soulmate turns out to be a prince, who'd since become the king.

It must have been a rare love that had united both ends of the Folkshore, must be the stuff of epic poems by now...

"It was an arranged marriage."

Leander's terse response felt like being dunked in icy water on a deep winter's day, dousing my illusions, and scribbling all over my romantic story, turning it from a thrilling fantasy to a dull footnote.

"Oh" was all I could say.

"Disappointed?"

I wanted to blurt out "YES," that everything had been one disappointment after another since I'd woken up in Arbore.

Everything I'd ever dreamed about from my secondhand knowledge of life had fallen flat onto the ground of depressing reality.

I reeled my reaction back. "A bit, yes. But why would anyone arrange a marriage to someone so far away?"

"Because the world is becoming more connected thanks to the invention of trains, and the establishment of great naval fleets, so it is wise to forge alliances far from home. My parents' marriage was a political pact between my father and hers, the late King of Cahraman."

I digested the new fact that he was royalty on both sides as I asked, "Are you arranged to marry someone from another land?"

"I was supposed to be, but even before this happened to me, the arrangement was dissolved. Once war broke out between Arbore and Avongart, and the Armoricans took Avongart's side, everything else between our lands got tossed out." His eyes flitted to the figurines. "My sister's arrangement is still intact thankfully, as all hope to save her from her curse hinges on it." After a beat he raised his pensive gaze to mine. "What about your family? Who are the Fairborns of Hericeurra?"

"Stone masons, smiths and a few carpenters, I've heard. We had relatives in the middle of the island, but I've never seen any of them." I felt myself wilting. A part of my plan for Adelaide and myself had been to seek out relatives, learn more about our history—feel less alone in the world. Now, like her, this dream was lost.

"You mention only your father—is your mother dead?" I swallowed the lump that expanded in my throat, nodded. "No other family?"

I shook my head, exhaled. "I had an uncle, Ossian, who

disappeared before I was born. And my grandparents died when he and my father were boys. As for my mother's family, I don't know anything. All my father ever said about them was that they didn't want her to marry him."

Leander's thick brows furrowed. "So, she left her family to run off with your father and was disowned?"

"That's what my father says."

"Your parents never told you anything about them? Names? Stories? Anything?"

"My mother died when I wasn't yet six, before I began to have questions, and it always seemed to pain my father when I mentioned her, so he never said much about her family, always saying the one important thing is that we had each other. That was why I was so desperate to leave home, to find answers about everything, starting with myself."

His gaze seemed to turn inwards. "Strange, that one could know so little about their own history. I know my relatives on both sides going back eight generations—who they were, what they did, and which of my heirlooms belonged to whom and what they used it for. In fact, I was required to know odd tidbits like how my great-grandmother Queen Wisteria always played the harp by plucking the strings with her nails rather than her fingertips."

He continued to list off both important and inconsequential details about his family, and the desire to fill the gaps in my own history, to put names and lives on the branches of my unknown family tree, came back with a vengeance.

When he mentioned how the dukes in his distant relatives would succeed his family should something happen to them, all known by name, age and order, it reminded me that as far as I knew, I was the last of the Fairborns. It made me yearn again to find out what had happened to my uncle Ossian or who my mother's family was. A yearning that would most probably go unfulfilled.

The rest of the morning passed uneventfully as we continued to ask each other questions, and share anecdotes from our lives.

It was shockingly pleasant, talking with him for hours on end, leaping from one topic to the next, without running out of things to discuss. I couldn't remember this ever happening, talking to someone, even my father or Adelaide, without a single awkward pause or the conversation fizzling out.

When lunchtime rolled around, and he invited me to go back to the dining room, I took my chance to broach the subject again.

"I feel we know each other better now," I said as we exited the room. "So please tell me how I can help with the curse."

His gaze swept to the end of the hall. Following it, I find silhouettes huddled together in the shadows, watching us. Among them I could pick out Clancy's horns. From the urgency in Leander's gaze, it seemed he wanted his friend to direct him like he had during our first meeting with more guiding whispers targeting his heightened hearing. But there were none this time.

Without warning, Leander turned to me and blurted out, "You can marry me."

CHAPTER SIXTEEN

I blinked at him once, twice, his words hurtling in my mind like a rock thrown through placid waters, thudding to the bottom and sending out endless ripples.

Then I burst out, *"What?"*

He began to kneel. "Bonnibel Fairborn, will you do me the honor of being my—"

"Stop!" I yelled, hands held out, pushing and pulling at him, and trying to stay upright. "Get up, please—get *up*—and explain."

When he finally stood, the spying staff scattered like startled pigeons, leaving only Clancy who appeared to have his face in his hands. Leander looked down at his bare, hairy feet, finding his overgrown, claw-like nails very interesting all of the sudden.

If I had any coordination, I would have stomped my foot. "Why on the Field Queen's green earth would you ask me that?"

"Your earth goddess is called the Field Queen?"

"Yours is Rosmerta, right—oh, no, you don't." He had the

gall to try and sidetrack me? And it had nearly worked. "You're going to answer me. Why did you ask me to marry you?"

"Because if you do, we believe that's what it will take to break the curse."

"Is that true?" I called out to Clancy.

He came out of the shadows, his clomping reluctant as he approached. "There's a lot more to it than that, but yes, essentially."

I walked towards him, stopping at the midpoint between them. "What exactly did the Spring Queen say when she cursed you? And why do both your curse and your sister's require marriage to be broken?"

Leander walked towards me. "For my sister, her curse said that only when the noblest of men pledges himself to her will her curse be broken. We never worried much about her curse, since she's been pledged almost from birth to such a man, the crown prince and future king of Cahraman. The situation changed when that prince asked for a bridal competition before he wed her, but Fairuza will surely win it. There's no one more beautiful or accomplished than her."

It was sweet that he thought that of his sister. But if she was anything like him or their mother, the woman whose temper and lack of judgment landed them all in this mess, then that prince would for sure pick someone else.

"If war broke your own arrangement," I said. "Why hasn't anyone sent you another princess to break your curse?"

"My curse wasn't as simple, because nothing ever is with fairies." He stared more in my direction than at me. "It *sounds* simple enough, but it seemed impossible—until you showed up."

"*What* exactly did the fairy queen say?"

Sighing dejectedly, he quoted:

> *"Shirk kind gallantry to favor cruelty,*
> *And lose the shelter your face provides,*
> *With roses your keeper, and no more liberty*
> *Your body baring its ugly insides,*
> *You'll live within the vileness you wove*
> *Reviled and feared from west to east*
> *Unless you're given true beauty's love*
> *You'll fleetingly live and die a beast."*

I repeated the words after him in my mind, storing them for later examination before I said, "And how did you figure the answer to this riddle is me marrying you?"

Clancy clomped closer, arms behind his back. "We believe the reason the fairy made him like this was to repel potential brides, so that prince or not, no one would ever accept him, and therefore have the curse run its course. If it does, it seems we'd all turn to our respective beasts completely. Then we either die at once, or do so after our shorter lifespans as animals end—that is, if we survive being hunted. We thought we had over a year until that happened, but now we only have three months."

My heart convulsed at the reminder of how I'd made things so much worse.

Leander came to stand beside me. "We also believe that the only way to break the curse is to have someone who only saw me as the Beast agreeing to marry me regardless."

"So when you arrived at the castle," Clancy added. "We all thought it must be a sign, that you are our only chance. Why else would a beautiful girl be delivered to our door?"

"I didn't exactly come here to visit, if you remember," I mumbled.

Clancy shrugged. "Whatever brought you here, it was fate."

Leander looked down at me, turquoise eyes glinting with hope in the torchlight. "So, what do you say?"

"I say that marriage has nothing to do with love." And even when it did, like in my parents' case, it didn't mean happily ever after. "Besides, I barely know you. We may have had a civil day, but that doesn't mean I like you, let alone love you."

His eyes suddenly reflected the firelight behind me as he gazed down at me. "So, that's a 'no?'"

"Yes. I mean, no!" I shook my head roughly. "I mean yes, that's a no."

Clancy let out a distressed bleat. "But why?"

"I just told you. The curse specified love. And marriage, even if people choose one another like they do in small towns like mine, isn't a guarantee of it." I sought out Leander's distraught eyes, feeling my heart squeeze. "You of all people should know that, considering your parents were arranged."

Leander's shoulders sagged as he exchanged a despondent glance with Clancy, before they turned their entreaty on me. Their combined hopelessness was unbearable.

According to their rationalization, all we had to do was—what? Find a priest who wouldn't be spooked by them, and would agree to marry a foreign girl to a wolfman? Or a judge who wouldn't immediately call the hunters and city guards? Though I'd never even thought of marriage until a week ago when first Castor asked me to marry him, I would marry Leander if I thought it was the answer. But it couldn't be.

The curse was very explicit. And then, how could I be the

"true beauty" it specified?

I let out a ragged exhalation. "Can I have some time to think?"

Leander advanced on me, as if to block my path, but Clancy gripped his elbow, whispering something only his ears could catch.

Leander turned and walked away, heading in the other direction, his somber voice filling the hall. "Take all the time you need."

Before following him, Clancy gave me a tentative glance. "We'll see you at dinner?"

Nodding, I headed back to the stairs, not taking my breath until I came to a wheezing stop outside Jessamine's current room. I entered with a knock to find her sitting in bed, with a tome open on her lap and a plate of fruit next to her.

Dropping her apple slice, Jessamine held out her arms. "I'm so happy you came back!"

I'd half expected her to yell at me to get out, chuck her book at me, literally anything but the joy filling her owlish eyes and spreading her bright smile.

I dove into her hug, careful to not disturb her bandaged wing, sniffling into her shoulder. "I'm so sorry, I didn't mean for any of you to get hurt."

She squeezed me back before scooting over. "I know you didn't. But what matters is that you're back and we're all alive. Maybe that battle will teach Castor not to come back here ever again."

I sat facing her, searching her tired, freckled face for any resentment, but I saw only pleasure to see me. "I tried to tell him who you were, but he wouldn't listen. He didn't listen to a single word until I said I agreed to marry him, and that was to get him away from here."

A sour expression curled the edges of her mouth. "That's Castor for you, and all men like him. They only hear what they want to hear. Anything else is just winter wind to them."

"Is it true you were going to marry him?"

She made a so-so gesture. "We hadn't really come to an agreement, but he had offered and my brother agreed, which in our social standing is as good as an engagement, and because what other offers was I going to get?"

"What do you mean? Why would you have trouble finding anyone else?"

She sighed. "Because few here would risk inflicting my red hair on their daughters."

I frowned. "What's wrong with red hair?"

Her lips twisted. "Plenty in Arbore believe it's a sign that you're a witch, and no one wants a witch for a daughter-in-law. Also, our family didn't leave us much, so I have no dowry as an incentive for any man to take me. There's also my age. And now I'm half-bird..."

"Clancy doesn't seem to mind any of that."

Jessamine started, a blush bathing all visible skin in a rosy glow. "Lord Gestum is a..." She cleared her throat with difficulty. "...personable lord. He's kind to everyone, regardless. He's a very good man."

"That he is. And I don't know how he acted so fast when you were shot down. He seemed to be able to fly in that moment, too." I watched her grow more flustered and was unable to hold back a teasing grin. "He seemed *very* worried about you, took care of you and stayed with you while you slept."

Avoiding my eyes, she cleared her throat again, but her voice remained scratchy. "He would have done that for anyone, I'm sure."

"He didn't rush to Leander's aid, his old friend and host."

"I'm sure the Master didn't need help?"

"Even if he did, I think Clancy would have rushed to help you first. I think he likes you—the way you like him."

Jessamine shook her head furiously, face as flushed as the peach on her plate. "I just admire him, as he is very admirable. He was being chivalrous and I greatly appreciate him saving me, will have to find a way to repay him somehow."

"Maybe when your wing heals you can take him for a flight around the castle," I suggested. "That might be a fun experience for both of you, maybe even an opportunity to discuss your feelings for one another."

"No!" she squeaked. "You misunderstand, I—he—it's not like that, I promise. And then as I said, I can't fly long distances by myself, I certainly can't carry someone else along."

For the life of me, I couldn't understand why she was so resistant to even discussing her feelings amongst us. "Are you sure?"

"Yes." And with that, she changed the subject. "How was your breakfast with the Master?"

"It was fine. We talked a lot. He asked me to marry him." Jessamine's eyes doubled in size, but I stifled her squeal by adding, "I said no."

Her face fell as she lamented, "Why?"

"Because I don't think it's going to do anything for the curse. There is no love between us, and then, who's going to marry us, anyway."

She worried her lips for a moment then bent her head, looking forlorn.

Feeling terrible myself, I remained silent for long minutes, and she started flipping aimlessly through the pages of her book. I suddenly stopped her, took the book and gazed at two scenes.

One was of a frail, gaunt young man writing in the sand before a girl with long wavy hair, and a bearded man that was attempting to pull her away. The second depicted the young man upright and robust, floating a few inches off the ground, and covered in shading that was either wind or a glow, in royal garb and with a handsome face.

There was a caption squished at the bottom of the last picture. *Only when the princess called him by his true name did his power return to him.*

I rushed to read the text of the story.

A Prince of Lyonesse was cursed by his stepmother to lose his name and all that came with it—his title, his magic and his appearance. Only someone recognizing him for who he truly was would break the curse. That wasn't possible since he couldn't tell anyone who he was. He was about to die when he wrote his name in the sand in front of the Princess of Cantor. He could only write it backwards, but she figured it out, said it aloud while looking directly at him, and the curse broke.

I traced the picture of the triumphant prince for another moment. Then I jumped off the bed and burst out of the room, calling over my shoulder, "I'll be right back."

I raced back downstairs in search of Leander.

I found him and Clancy sitting in a room that overlooked the rose tree.

Buzzed with determination and excitement, I barreled inside. They jumped to their feet, expectant, anxious.

Leander hobbled towards me, searching my face with wide, dilated eyes. "Yes?"

Taking a deep breath, I looked directly at him and said, "I love you, Leander Silverthorn."

CHAPTER SEVENTEEN

*N*o one moved. No one blinked.

We just stood there with bated breath, waiting for something to happen, anything.

But nothing happened.

No flash of transformative light, no fairy queen arriving to lift her curse. Nothing.

Leander's face fell as he turned to Clancy. "I don't understand. She 'gave me her love.' Why didn't it work?"

Tracing his horns sadly, Clancy looked down at the tree. "Vows, declarations, none of that matter to the fey. Not unless they're meant." He dropped his hands, closing his eyes in disappointment. "And she didn't mean what she said."

Leander let out an anguished rumble that made me shudder and struck his chair, gouging long, deep scratches in its back. "What does that matter? She said my name, said she loved me."

"Leo, let's be reasonable here. There's a reason I didn't want you to suggest marriage this soon."

I blinked up at Clancy. "What do you mean? What are you still not telling me?"

Clancy winced, and Leander hunched defensively, yet seeming ashamed, too.

Setting my hands on my hips, I tapped my foot at them. "Well?"

Clancy exhaled. "We hoped a girl would end up here as a 'sacrifice,' and that she would remain among us long enough to get to know Leander and break the curse."

I threw my hands up. "I'm here and I'm trying!"

"Yes, but you haven't been here long enough," Leander mumbled. "Clancy wanted us to wait days, weeks even, with things steadily improving between us, before I asked you. But now I no longer have time to waste."

I glanced at Clancy. "So, you wanted me to grow fond of him first?"

Clancy nodded. "Or, if it were possible, truly love him. But it's safe to say nothing has gone according to plan."

"You can say that again." I ran my hands over my face, going through the situation once again. "Wait, you said you were expecting a girl to be sacrificed. How and why?"

"It was the next logical offering," said Leander, back to avoiding my eyes. "The people of Rosemead first started circulating the tale of the King of the Beasts every time they heard me roaring in frustration or sighted me when I still went out hunting. But with the whispers of me eating everyone in the castle spreading, they started offering me cuts of meat then parts of animals, then entire ones, each animal bigger than the last. We reasoned a girl had to be next, like they used to send virgins to dragons and ogres to keep them from attacking their villages. But most of the time, the girl had to go willingly."

I stopped nodding along, gaped up at him as a realization burst in my mind.

"That faceless green bandit!" I stomped, fists stiff at my side as anger wormed through me. "That's why they took my father! That Robin in the hood knew I would come after him!"

"We'll have to thank him for that," Leander grumbled. "Quite clever, really. It's a wonder they sent him back from the frontline so early. If they'd used his talents as a tactician, he could have won them the war already."

If I had anything within reach, I would have pitched it at him. "This isn't funny!"

"Am I laughing right now?" Leander snapped, baring his fangs. "We both got our lives flipped upside down for nothing. But at least yours isn't irreversibly ruined. You can always go back. There's no going back for any of us."

Contrite again, I approached him, set a tentative hand on his wide, curved back. "I'm not going nowhere. I'll do whatever I can to help you all as I promised."

"And it wasn't for nothing, Leo," Clancy assured him. "It's just early. We should simply wait a while."

Leander grimaced. "How long is a while? The tree has three roses left."

"Then hopefully in a season we'll all feel and look a lot different than we do now." Clancy's big blue eyes sought mine. "Isn't that right, Miss Fairborn?"

I nodded warily. "I sure hope so, but how does waiting help us?"

Leander turned to me, hairy, distorted features almost too much to bear, but his blue-green eyes mirrored my own uncertainty. "It will give me time to make things up to you, change your mind about me, so when we try again, you can mean it in any sense."

"What other 'senses' are there?"

"If simple words won't do it and marriage vows are null, then that leaves us one option." He held out his broad, clawed hand, palm up. "Miss Fairborn, would you like to be my friend?"

That was an even harder request than asking me to marry him. Friendship required genuine affection and good companionship that most marriages didn't.

But—now that I knew Robin had manipulated us all to bring me here, and after the rocky start we'd had, we'd spent most of the morning together without incident. Even better, we'd had conversations I couldn't have with my father, whom I loved unconditionally, or with Adelaide, who was my best friend.

Surely friendship wasn't unthinkable between us? And then I'd already pledged to do whatever I could to save them. Becoming his friend, as unlikely as that might sound, was the least I could try.

I forced a smile on my face as I set my hand in his grasp. "I would like that very much, Leander Silverthorn."

As both men's eyes filled with wary hope, I felt the weight of all their fates press harder on my shoulders.

Here went nothing.

EARLY NEXT MORNING, Hazel came to get me ready for breakfast.

She laid out a periwinkle, lace gown that she said matched my eyes, and as she braided my hair, she babbled excitedly about what the head chef was making for dinner.

"We can no longer import anything from the market, but

the vegetable patch we have is on very fertile soil. We still have to wait till autumn to get the good vegetables." She pulled too hard on a lock of hair, making me yelp. Oblivious to my reaction, she prattled on, "I never thought I'd be looking forward to seeing turnips and carrots, but here we are. It's a relief for my mum, though. She always tried to get me to eat my vegetables, but the only thing I tolerated was potatoes. Perks of being a bunny, I guess."

I rubbed the sore spot in my scalp. "Your mother's here?"

"She *is* the head chef! If you ever need an adjustment to the menu or to request a specific dish, ask for Bryony."

"What does she—er, look like?"

Hazel pointed at her ears with the hairbrush. "Same as me, but her feet are big and flat now, she has to hop everywhere. It's kind of funny."

Somehow I doubted her mother found her legs being warped to the extent she couldn't walk funny. It amplified my sadness for them all. I'd really hoped that telling Leander I loved him would break that curse and set them free.

But how could I make myself mean it?

How long would it take for that to happen? For me to love him as I loved Adelaide, as a friend or a brother even? And if I did, would it count? Would that be enough for the wicked fairy that cursed a newborn and a toddler for their mother's arrogance?

And another such evil fairy had kidnapped Adelaide, and I had no way of knowing where she'd taken her. Even if I did, there was no way to go after her, to save her.

Eyes welling with frustrated tears again, I blinked them back as I caught Hazel's concerned eyes in the mirror. "Did I hurt you?"

"No, no! You did great!" I jumped off the chair before she

could think of adjusting the hairstyle again and ran to the door.

I kicked something on my way out, yet another box, too small for me to have tripped over. I picked it up, not bothering to look inside in my rush to check on Jessamine.

I stuck my head into her room, found her already with a tray on her lap. "Good morning, Jess! How's your wing feeling today?"

Eyes bright with pleasure at my sight, Jessamine spoke around her mouthful. "Still can't move it without hurting, but a lot better." She raised her teacup. "I asked for your willow brew thrice as strong, and it is really helping."

"Glad to hear it! I'll try to remember any other pain-killing remedies I've read about."

She swallowed and smiled. "See you after breakfast?"

"See you then!" I ducked out and headed down, straight to the dining room.

As I approached, I remembered the little box in my hand.

Inside wasn't another luxurious gift but a metal barrette with a glued-on, blue flower. I couldn't tell what kind of fabric it was made of, but it was soft and fashioned in a way that made it gleam and almost look like a living flower.

A note with Leander's shaky handwriting asked: *Is this a bonnibel?*

It looked like he'd given my words some good thought since yesterday. This wasn't a needlessly expensive gift. And it was personal.

Checking around for Hazel, hoping she wouldn't see me undoing her efforts, I unbound my braid then pulled some hair back with the barrette.

In the dining room, Leander and Clancy stood as soon as I entered. I didn't know if I should bow or curtsey, wasn't sure how people behaved in places like this beyond the passing references in stories about court and mansion life.

They were surprised when I sat across from Clancy, on Leander's right.

"What? I could barely hear you yesterday," I said, reaching for the basket of fresh rolls. They were warm and fluffy, and pulling one apart released a puff of aromatic steam. "It seems pointless for the three of us to sit in this endless room alone. Can't we eat in a smaller room or gather in one of our rooms?"

They took turns giving me odd, uncertain looks.

"That's how it always is for us," said Leander, gazing down at his piled plate, full of meats, eggs, beans and bread, still struggling with his utensils. "Everyone has their place at the table, and only the sick eat in their rooms. We only take tea in sitting rooms."

I bit into the roll. "All I'm saying is it just feels very impersonal."

"The head of the table is an honorable spot, and offering it is a show of esteem," Leander said, still dragging his knife around his plate. "That was the intention, but if you prefer to sit here, you're free to do so."

Nodding, I reached for the butter across the table, and Clancy held it out for me. "Did you check on Jessamine this morning?"

Clancy almost dropped the butter, fumbled with it before I caught it. "Yes, but she was asleep, so I couldn't ask about her condition."

"She says her wound hurts less." I tried catching his eye. "She might feel a lot better if you visited her later."

He blushed, almost as much as she had yesterday. "I will."

So, her feelings weren't one-sided. It was perplexing how

their affection, if not love, was mutual, but neither of them did anything about it. It was frustrating to see them stuck in the same place and condition and not try to act on their feelings.

A loud crack made me drop my butter knife.

His plate had split into three big shards, spilling grease and egg-yolk onto the tablecloth.

Leander dropped his cutlery and put his hand over his eyes. "Ivy is going to strangle me. It's the second time this happens."

This giant prince, afraid of upsetting his housekeeper, rather than the other way around, was quite baffling. And funny.

"Third," Clancy corrected, holding back a chuckle. "Perhaps you should spare her irreplaceable crockery and eat on tea trays. Silver might withstand your brute strength a bit better."

"Or you could eat with your hands," I suggested.

Leander gaped at me. "I can't."

"Why not? You obviously can't use a knife and fork, not unless someone welds you a larger pair." I waved my buttery roll pointedly. "Eat with your hands."

His brow furrowed, and if his fangs weren't jutting out, I believed his mouth would be downturned in unease. "It's improper."

"Are table manners really more important than twisting your wrists and shattering your dishes?"

"I can't eat like that in front of *you*."

"Why?"

"Because you're a lady, and it's rude."

"I'm a peasant, and I don't care." I stuffed the entire roll in my mouth and kept it open as I chewed loudly, looking him in the eye the whole time.

Hesitant, Leander squished some meat and eggs between two slices of bread, watching me as he slowly lifted his makeshift sandwich. Checking if I were serious or if I'd change my mind, it seems.

I made a hurrying gesture, and he spread his jaws far apart and shoved it all in his mouth.

I tried to keep quiet as he literally stuffed his face, but it was too much for me not to react. I spluttered in laughter as egg yoke dribbled into his beard.

He stopped, eyeing me again, self-conscious. I reached for another roll, heaped it with butter and two types of jam then squished it between my teeth. Jam leaked down my chin, and I tried stuffing it back in my mouth, making a mess I haven't made since I was a child.

Leander's shoulders shook as I wiped the excess jam with another roll before gobbling it, his laughter breaking out when he swallowed.

As we continued our eating match, he went a step further, piling another plate and bending to eat right off it. He wiped swathes of food in every lick before piling more and scarfing it down. One could only guess how much food it took to fuel a body that large.

Clancy shook his head at us, chuckling more from discomfort than amusement. "Disgusting."

Leander raised his face from the plate, eyes narrowed, beard soaked in food.

Clancy tutted. "Oh, don't look at me like that. Just because we look like animals doesn't mean we have to act like them."

I took a sausage out of my mouth, chewing. "He was an

animal before the curse got a hold of him. And it wasn't on account of his eating habits."

Leander choked, banging on the table as he coughed. I reached over to thump him on the back, but I might as well have been tapping him, my hand too small to make any impact.

"Is this—" He got cut off by a cough. "Is this really the time to bring that up?"

I shrugged, unrepentant. "Am I wrong?"

His coughs subsided but his rumble grew louder. "That's not the point."

Unfazed, I held his chagrined gaze. "Then what is?"

Glowering at me, he raised his plate and dumped its contents right into his gaping mouth.

It was as if he was trying to shock or revolt us. From the noises Clancy made, it worked spectacularly on him. I placidly watched him and continued my own disgusting behavior.

After that animalistic spectacle, Leander neatly wiped his mouth and hands with the splotched-beyond-recognition napkin on his lap, leaving his beard adorned in crumbs. I broke out in gales of laughter.

It was all so surreal. I was in a castle's dining room, debating past transgressions and destroying table manners with the fearsome Beast. All under the disapproval of a goat-man, who, despite what I'd seen of the indiscriminate gluttony of goats, was the most fastidious of us.

This scene reminded me of engravings in a children's book I had, one that had been in the family for years, where a little girl ventured into a forest only to find civilized animals with houses, picnics and teatime. Before my hunger for adventure and exploration had settled for traveling to other worlds in my mind, I'd always wanted to dive into that book. Now I was in a more fantastical setting, with more unimaginable companions.

Leander gestured to the box I'd put on the seat beside me, his gaze disheartened. "Are you returning today's gift, too?"

I rushed to show him the back of my head. As he exhaled in relief and poured us tea, I studied the stained-glass windows at his back for the first time.

In the first panel, Rosmerta, the equivalent of Ericura's Field Queen, stood looking at the yolk-yellow sun curved in the upper corner of the pane, her flying hair a peachy-orange and her dress grass-green, one arm cradling a warm gold cornucopia, the other extended.

The middle, bigger panel was a split depiction of night and day. In the third, there was an ominous figure swathed in deep purple and black, with an antlered head and a visible ribcage of pearlescent white, shrouded in heavily detailed clouds of smoke in shades of grey—the Horned God!

He'd never alarmed me as he did other Ericurans or Adelaide. But after we'd been whisked away through that fairy's portal at the feet of his iron sculpture—the sight of him made me shudder.

"What do you call that here?" I pointed at his panel.

Clancy self-consciously reached for his own horns, instantly uneasy. "We don't say his name, or else he'll respond and give us a personal visit and..."

Leander cut him off. "His name is Kernos. Campanians call him Orkhos, or Lucros—something like that."

"LEANDER!" Clancy yelped.

"Oh, what is he going to do to us? Drag us all to hell?" Leander reached for the crystal jug of water, filling our glasses. "He's welcome to at this point."

Clancy turned his horns on him. "If you don't stop with this attitude, I will head-butt you."

Leander scoffed a laugh. "I'm only surprised you haven't done something that goatish yet. Any day now, your eyes will grow horizontal pupils and become impossible to look into."

"Will you stop it?" I nudged him. "We're going to break the curse."

He shook his head, sighing in resignation.

"We just discussed this yesterday, what's the problem now?"

"I don't feel this will work, not with how fast I'm devolving." He raised his hands to me. They seemed bigger, hairier, his hard nails looking more like the claws than ever before.

I put my hand on his, lowering it. "If you got a grip on your temper, maybe you'd be a lot more loveable."

He exhaled, sagged in his chair. "I didn't get angry."

"By temper, I mean general temperament. You could do with some optimism." I gave him my best reassuring smile. "We have time, right?"

He only stared at his broken plate. Before I could persist, he suddenly said, "So, you *do* like the hair clip?"

I laughed softly. "Yes, it's on the right track in terms of gifts."

"It is?" His surprise had an undercurrent of relief, and disbelief.

And at this moment, I could see exactly why he'd bumbled his interactions with girls who weren't his relatives. He'd never been told how, or even worse, had been taught the wrong things, about himself and about others. A prince with every privilege this world had to offer, guided by the worst kind of example and counsel and led astray by unbridled passions.

As the conversation ebbed and flowed, my mind kept straying to the ruined family portrait outside his room.

From the example of his parents and siblings, and the bits of the slashed face I'd been able to put together, Leander must have been as handsome as he was now hideous. And I kept wondering if I would ever get to see the real him.

CHAPTER EIGHTEEN

The third morning after our new agreement, I woke up before Hazel could get a hold of me and went in search of the kitchen.

I headed where I thought it would be and was rewarded by the only sounds of life evident this early. The chatter and clanging of pots and pans. The smells soon followed as I descended the spiral stairs down one of the towers. I stopped on the last step, peering inside at the collection of girls and women, the youngest seeming to be my age and the oldest in her sixties.

The kitchen itself was a vast brownstone room with a high ceiling, full of teak cupboards and spread in orange-brown tiles. Open windows framed the sinks and counters and let in the tenuous morning light. In the center, a rectangular island dominated, its base full of cupboards, its surface black marble, with a wooden structure hanging above holding pots and pans.

A woman with rabbit ears matching her tawny hair, and big, flat, furry feet was marching back and forth like an army marshal. Hazel's mother, Bryony.

Her ears perked up as she turned my way, restless nose wrinkling. "Who's this?"

I entered, waving. "Bonnie. Hazel told me I could stop by."

Bryony narrowed her eyes at me like she was struggling to see. "Oh, hello, I've been wondering when I'd get a good look at you. I can't climb the stairs, you see." She raised her foot. "I'm stuck down here, can only take the slope in the corner up to the first floor."

If I hadn't already felt terrible for them all before, I sure felt worse now.

"Is there anything you needed, dear?"

"Yes, I was wondering if you could prepare only foods that can be eaten by hand like boiled eggs and strips of bacon and muffins?"

A heavy dragging sound announced Ivy's arrival. "Is this about the master breaking his plate again?"

"I think he needs to give up on eating like a prince. It's only making him feel worse every time he fails."

Ivy clicked her forked tongue. "I told him that. He insisted on the same food, and on breaking plates of a unique set rather than adjusting to his new condition like the rest of us."

"I have a feeling he won't object today."

I then noticed that the kitchen had gone completely silent. Everyone had stopped to stare at me, their eyes clinging to me as if waiting for me to do something, rid them of their beastly forms right now. To them, I was their only hope for normalcy and freedom.

Ivy must have sensed how unsettled I became because she bared her fangs at them. "Stop goggling at the poor girl and keep up, the firewood isn't going to last all morning."

They all turned back to their tasks, and Bryony continued

supervising. Ivy expanded up, setting a basket of bread rolls out of Oliver's leaping reach. "No, Ollie. Go help Wisteria with the cheesemaking."

"So, that's what that smell is." I sniffed the air, stomach awakening with a growl. "Do you need any help?"

"It's sweet of you to offer, but you should be getting ready for breakfast," said Ivy, trying to herd me towards the stairs.

"But I want to help," I protested.

Perplexed, Ivy blinked her yellow eyes down at me, a hint of a third lid emerging. She looked the most transformed aside from Leander. It made me wonder just how snake-like she was? Could she unhinge her jaw and gobble me up, the way they did rats?

It was a fleeting thought, but I felt ashamed to think such a thing of such a sweet woman.

"You shouldn't trouble yourself with the kitchenwork, dear."

"But I want to! My father never let me in the kitchen, either cooked himself or hired a cook, so I don't know how to do anything but serve food, and I've always wanted to bake, but the one time I tried to when he wasn't there I burned my hand because I didn't know what I was doing—"

"Breathe!" Ivy shook me by the shoulders. "By Rosmerta, it's a wonder you haven't bitten your own tongue talking so fast."

I hung my head, embarrassed. "I wanted to say what I could while I had your attention."

Ivy frowned. "Unless something starts burning, you have my full attention. Why would you think otherwise?"

"Well..."

"Now you're at a loss for words?" She chuckled, flattening

more of her tail, so she became shorter, and looked me in the eye. "What's the matter, really?"

"I'm used to people losing patience quickly as soon as I start to speak," I said, again in a rush. "Most cut me off, or tell me to go do something else, or in my father's case *not* do something. I couldn't go out alone, couldn't go with him to his forge, couldn't go to others' homes, and at home, I wasn't allowed to mend my own clothes or make my own food, and I couldn't even talk about certain things."

Ivy's frown deepened, pulling the scattered scales bordering her green-tinged face inwards. "That's an oddly coddled upbringing for a common girl. Where was your mother, aunts, or grandmother to knock some sense into your father?"

"They're all dead or estranged," I said, suddenly feeling more forlorn than ever about the fact. It had to be Ivy herself. I didn't remember much of my mother, and since her, I'd never had someone look at me in such a motherly way. "I thought my father believed girls should only worry about schoolwork and shouldn't be troubled with housework, but when my friend moved in with us, he had no issue with taking her to his forge, and letting her do the cooking or shopping."

"Was that friend bigger than you?" said an amused voice from behind us. Jessamine was taking the steps one at a time as she made her way down. "That could be the reason. No risk of her dumping hot soup all over herself as she took the pot off the stove."

I was too happy to see her up and about to complain about the height jokes.

Though I got to her first, catching her middle in a hug, the rest quickly huddled around us, asking questions, offering seats and food, or in Bryony's case, telling her to get back to bed.

"I'm fine!" she protested. "Please don't send me back to bed. I'm going mad with idleness up there, and lying down is not fun with wings to start with, and when one is injured, it's agony. I'll sit if you insist, but let me do something. I can't keep reading picture-books all day!"

Ivy contemplated us both. "We could use some help with the bakeries, especially since there's a change to the menu this morning." At that, she smiled down at me. "You two can make the muffins."

I yelped in glee and jumped to hug her.

In a minute, Jessamine and I settled at the island beside a girl making the dough. I watched her mix the ingredients, committing every detail to memory. It was one thing to read a cookbook, and something else entirely to see the method for myself.

The girl let me knead the dough, and I discovered that making the mixture not look like clay was a lot more taxing on the arms than I'd thought. A steady practice of this and I'd have muscles. Now I understood why my local baker and his employees were built closer to my father and his apprentices than the cooks at the tavern.

When I felt my arms about to fall off, I left the dough to her, feeling very accomplished when she complimented my efforts.

I turned to making the muffins, and after the struggle with the dough and with my arms aching, mixing the batter wasn't as easy as I'd hoped.

I grunted as I poked Jessamine, "So, those picture books you read. Do you prefer them to novels?"

Jessamine paused crushing the walnuts with a knife.

"They're just easier. I never finished school and over the years I've mostly forgotten how to read. Lord Gestum offered to teach me the language properly, but said I had to start small, hence the children's books."

"That's sweet of him, helping you learn. It seems he likes teaching people things."

"He's very kind, very humble." She peered at my bowl, wincing at the mixture. "You missed some flour at the bottom, scrape it from the edges. That's it. Maybe add some milk?"

I did as she said, mixing harder. "So how did he come to offer to teach you?"

Her ears turned bright pink as she dumped the walnut into the batter. "He caught me squinting at the title of a book he was reading and realized I couldn't read it. I thought he'd mock me, like others I worked for did. But he only said he'd make me as well-read as a duchess. When I didn't progress as fast as he hoped, I thought he'd get give up, but he said 'you're stuck with me.' I know he meant we're all stuck here, but still..." She trailed off, blushing deeply. "No one has ever wanted what's best for me, or expected nothing from me in return."

That statement made me realize how opposite our lives had been. My father and Adelaide had only wanted what was best for me, and they, and everyone else had expected nothing from me. And the two extremes had made us equally discontented.

I sighed. "Clancy seems pretty lovable that way."

Jessamine cleared her throat, taking the muffin mixture from me. "I think that's enough. Let's put them in the pan, shall we?"

I stayed by the oven, watching the muffins slowly rise and take shape, all the while thinking: I did this!

Then my mind turned back to Leander, and I wondered.

When was the last time someone wanted the best for him, unrelated to who he was, or what they had to gain from it, but just for his sake?

CHAPTER NINETEEN

By the time Leander and Clancy arrived for breakfast, I'd been examining the stained-glass windows for what felt like an eternity.

"You're early." Leander approached with heavy footfalls. "Couldn't sleep?"

"I just wanted to get to know everyone else here," I said absently, still admiring the windows. From the way Rosmerta and the Horned God were positioned, I could almost see them becoming animated, see him stalking her, ready to pluck her from her fields and off to his dark lair beneath the earth.

If my experience with a half-man, half-beast had been this tumultuous, what would it be like for a girl to be carried off by Death Himself?

A muffled slam pulled me out of my thoughts, making me nearly tip my chair back.

I threw my weight forwards, facing Leander in disapproval. "What was that?"

"You weren't listening to me," he said gruffly.

"I didn't hear you to begin with."

He made an irritated noise, a low, internal growl like a defensive dog. "It figures that when you tell me to lower my voice you don't hear it at all."

"So, it's either you're louder than a temple bell or you're quieter than a mouse, there's no in-between?"

"Can you two please *not* start?" Clancy begged, pouring himself a glass of water. "Can we talk about something else? Like the change in the menu this morning?"

Leander finally looked away, quirking an eyebrow at the food displayed. "What's all this?"

"Finger food, mostly, so we can dig in without making too much of a mess and sickening Clancy." I slid the basket of muffins forwards, proud of myself. "I helped make these."

"Did you now?" There was something unreadable in his eyes, but slowly, the corners of his fanged mouth curled up. Rather than taking a bite of one muffin, he stuffed two whole ones in his mouth. I supposed that counted as a "bite" when you had a jaw that extendable. "Did you remember the recipe from a cookbook you found in an ancient, haunted house or whatever else you have on your weird, forgotten island?"

"Yes, it was buried in the midpoint between our exorcism parlor and our cemetery, *A Witch's Guide to Frightful Food*. An exquisite find! Full of the most inventive recipes on incorporating every bit of the human body! But since I had no children to bake into gingerbread, I had to settle for hair and toenails, so if you feel anything crunch..."

Leander gagged, choking on his chewed up food, spraying still-dry crumbs onto his plate.

I watched him as he pounded his chest and his eyes watered, thinking it would end in some kind of wrathful reaction. Instead, in between barking coughs, he broke out in raucous laughter.

"You—" he wheezed, still laughing. "—had me for a second there."

I hadn't expected he'd appreciate my goading humor. But he did, and the sound of his big, rumbling laughter infected Clancy, who snickered politely into his teacup, and spawned a fit of giggles I at first covered with my hand before abandoning the attempt and letting go in all-out cackles.

Leander watched me, eyes in a squint as his chest and shoulders shook with fading laughter. He looked younger, more human now, with such a carefree expression. It loosened the tension I'd been feeling pulling on my heartstrings since I'd arrived here. In its place, a tentative warmth spread.

"What other macabre recipes did this book have?" he asked in mock-curiosity, picking a bunch of eggs.

"Oh, plenty your bloodthirsty, beastly self should enjoy." I put some fruit slices in my oatmeal, mixing it up so the sugar and cinnamon aroma rose with the released steam. "The next human they sacrifice to you will suffice for all thirteen dishes."

"Any blood soup? I had Orestian pig's blood soup while visiting Lower Campania. It was to die for."

"Yes, there are even some gelatinous desserts we can use that for, and once we've used up all the meat and organs, we can make a bone broth with the skeleton."

"I reiterate—you're both disgusting—and ghoulish!" Though Clancy sounded appalled, the excitement dancing in his blue eyes said otherwise.

Leander ignored him, still focused on me. "What if I acquire a taste for it? What will we do then?"

"You can eat Castor then, like you did his father."

That sucked the humor from his eyes, rendering him tense. "You know I didn't eat him."

I groaned inwardly. Some things you just *didn't* joke about.

But since I'd already put my two feet in my mouth, there was another thing I wanted an answer for. "But you killed him?"

He said nothing, which sounded like a confirmation that created a lump in my throat, like I'd failed to swallow one of those boiled eggs.

Clancy picked up his plate, stood up and tried to slip out of the room, but being quiet was impossible with his hooves. He muttered, "I'll go ask Bryony if I can have fried eggs instead."

When the door shut, I set down my spoon, facing Leander. "So—what happened?"

"What do you think happened?" He wasn't being sarcastic, or cranky, he was earnest, and dare I say, anxious.

So what did I think? I had at first thought that his beast had taken over and he'd killed the man in a fit of rage. But my view of him had changed drastically since the night I'd crushed his rose and cut short his very life. Instead of hurting me, he'd risked his life to save me. I no longer believed him capable of losing control to that extent.

Swallowing, I vocalized my deductions. "I think Lord Woodbine was stalking you, maybe injured you, almost trapped you and you lashed out and mauled him, by accident?"

He watched me with an intense stare, pupils dilated, irises a thin, bluish ring around them. "Not exactly."

"Please, tell me."

"What if you don't believe me? I don't want to erase whatever progress we've made, have you look at me the way you did before."

I reached a tentative hand, hovering it over his arm. "I have no reason to doubt you anymore. Just don't leave out any details, unless you want me to nag you to the end of time."

His lips twitched. "But that would keep you around for that long."

"Leander!"

He raised a hand as he pushed up, almost tipping the table then began that trapped pacing in front of me. "That day was supposed to be the day my sister would be shipped off to Cahraman to marry their crown prince, before he had the gall to ask her to compete for his hand among fifty others instead. I knew that once she left, it was unlikely I would ever see her again. I wanted to say goodbye, not with a letter, but in person."

"I didn't think you two would be so..."

"So what?"

Attached? Affectionate? Considerate? "Close, I suppose."

He faced me as he turned back. "With our father always preoccupied, and our mother seeing us as already dead —'doomed investments' as she'd once said, to the point she'd convinced our father to have two more children to replace us in case the curses came true—and with no other relatives at court but one overgrown, destructive brat of an uncle, Fairuza and I had only each other as family. It was my job since child-hood to be there for her. We were also the only ones who could understand each other's situation, being cursed by the same vile, vicious, pointy-eared harpy of a—"

He threw his hands down, as if shaking off water, body tight, vibe anxious. "Anyway, that day I needed to see her, hug her one last time and wish her luck in breaking her curse. But I only got so far before Amos Woodbine and his hunting party spotted me. He'd made it his mission to be the hero of Rose-mead, to rid it of its resident monster that minds its own business up in its castle. His son shot me with an arrow to slow me down, and though I was in great pain, I still managed to run. They chased me towards a trap they'd set for me, as I discovered a bit later, when I barely escaped it. I stopped a couple of feet from it, to catch my breath, and Woodbine descended on me with an axe."

A full-body shudder had me wrapping my arms around myself, rubbing the painful goosebumps. "What happened next?"

"I grabbed the handle at the last moment before the axe lodged in my chest. I tried to reason with him, even told him who I was. But he was so insistent on killing me, he refused to listen." A clawed hand pressed to his side, as if talking about it sparked the old pain of his injury. "He ripped out the arrow from my flesh to distract me, and once he did, he pulled the axe out of my grip so violently, he slammed the blade into his own skull."

I squeezed my eyes and tried to visualize anything but a man smashing his own skull.

Argh! I just visualized it. The horrifying mental image made me nearly dunk my face into the oatmeal.

He returned to his seat, stood stiffly beside it. "He stumbled back into his own trap and fell there, dead. I took the axe out of his face—I don't know why, but I couldn't bear that sight, even if he'd just tried to kill me. It was then the rest showed up, and what they saw was the man dead at my feet in the trap they'd set for me, with his head cleaved almost in two, looking like I'd brutally mauled him. Knowing it was pointless to try to explain, and that they lost me my chance of seeing my sister one last time, I could only run back to the castle. I never left it again."

After a long moment of oppressive silence, I let out a shaking exhalation. "But you left it and risked being attacked again to come after me."

"They'd already attacked me on my own turf that night."

"Yes, on your own turf with your fearful 'monsters'—which, come to think of it ought to have intimidated anyone with half a brain."

"From what I've seen, the Woodbines did split one brain amongst themselves," he grumbled.

I snorted a terribly inappropriate laugh, considering he'd just told me Lord Woodbine had split his own brain. I pursed my lips, quashing the gruesome humor. "Still. It was one thing to fight here, and another to do it alone out in the woods, with hunters, redcaps and who knows what else…"

I stopped, stared up at him. What I'd accepted at face value before, suddenly made no sense now.

I shook my head in confusion. "I'd just crushed your rose and cost you most of what remained of your life. You must have given up on me being the answer to breaking the curse at that point, so much so you told me to get out. And when I did, I ran off with your enemy. So why *did* you come after me?"

His hands curled into fists only for the long nails to dig into his palms. He unfurled them with a grimace. "Because whatever you did, I knew you didn't mean to harm me. And even if you did, I wasn't letting you get eaten by the redcaps."

I shook my head, bewilderment deepening. "But when I left, you had every reason to believe I'd go back to Rosemead with Castor. How did you know I was in the woods and that there were redcaps who were about to eat me?"

He rolled his shoulders, clearly uncomfortable telling me those details. "Unknown to me, Ivy went after you, to try to convince you to come back. It seemed they thought she was pursuing them, because she saw your group veer into the woods to escape her. She came rushing back to tell me and I came after you then, because I knew these woods have a fairy path infested by redcaps. I only hoped I wasn't too late." His gaze went down to his bare, hairy feet in a gloomy frown. "Not that I did you much good. It was Robin who saved us both in the end."

I gaped at him. Not only wasn't he taking credit for saving me, he considered he'd failed me.

I burst up to my feet. "You risked your life for mine, after everything I'd done! But instead of running, and letting you run after me, I foolishly stayed around, thinking I could help, costing you your escape window, until we were both overpowered. It was I who spoiled your rescue. As far as I'm concerned, you did save me. Then Robin saved me again, and you, from the consequences of my actions."

He stared at me, looking flabbergasted.

He finally tore his gaze from mine, looked at his feet again, tapping a nervous rhythm on the back of his chair. "Regardless, that's what happened that day I killed Lord Woodbine."

"You didn't kill him!" I bobbed my head into his line of vision, trying to catch his gaze. "Leander. Leander, look at me. It wasn't your fault!"

He exhaled, more awkward than ever. "I was expecting you to say it was, that it was his right to hunt me down, that maybe I deserve to be on their wall."

I threw my hands up in frustration. "Why would I say any of that?"

"Because you said I deserved this!" He motioned his hand over his entire body.

"That was before I knew the curse would get worse then kill you. I certainly never meant you should die, not even for killing Lord Woodbine, even before I thought it was an accident, since *they* were hunting you. But it wasn't even an accident. He chose to pursue you, *hound* you. He put killing you over his own self-preservation and ended up killing himself. It's abundantly clear you didn't do *anything*."

His eyebrows descended until they almost covered his eyes. "You probably don't have the experience to judge such situations."

"Being fair doesn't need experience, it only needs an open mind and all the details."

Neither of which I'd had until now.

Even after pledging to help him, because he'd helped me, and because I'd worsened his curse and everyone else's, I'd retained a degree of my earlier opinion of him.

But now, any lingering belief in his savagery had been erased. Now I knew him to be someone who'd shouldered the burden of his curse since childhood, and now seemed to care more about his sister's, whom he loved, and everyone else's, whom he felt responsible for.

It seemed that half of Leander's curse had been having a spoiled rotten shell at odds with its caring if confused core. Now all that was needed was to wrench open the giant clam to get to the gem it had formed under pressure.

Maybe that was where loving him as a friend came, what would be the key to undoing the curse for them all. Because that was what *he* needed. What he deserved.

I tried again. "Whatever you are, Leander, you're not a killer. And whatever you did, you don't deserve that extreme punishment."

Still avoiding my gaze, he let out a trapped breath. "I'm thankful you think so."

He didn't sound too convinced that I did. But I decided to let it go. "Now, I have another question for you." I saw him tense up again, and quickly added, "What was that slam earlier?"

"It was this." He picked something off his chair and dropped it on the table, recreating the thud. "I was offering it to you, but you found the windows far more interesting."

I peered over the belted tome with a stiff painted cover of a badly-rendered forest with even worse-drawn monks in brown robes, set beneath an uneven, golden, black-lettered title: *Apothecairie's Gyde to Banes and Remedys*.

I unfastened the book, checking the browned, bumpy pages beneath its heavy binding, flipping through the crude drawings. There were illustrations of people with ailments from morning sickness to gangrene, and poisons, from flora like hemlock and mushrooms, to fauna like black widows and salamanders. All came with recommended cures.

It was also written in the worst spelling I'd ever seen outside a primary education classroom. Or maybe it was just that old. Reading this would be a challenge.

I loved it nonetheless. Back home, I'd lived in hope of finding something like this. A puzzle to occupy my constantly buzzing mind. And I was excited to begin.

I told him so, and he seemed equally incapable of accepting my thanks as he had my rejection.

I chuckled at his reaction, and at the abundance of y's and archaic letters. "Where did you find this?"

"I can show you." As my eyes widened in expectation, excitement seeped into his as he jerked his head towards the door. "Follow me."

CHAPTER TWENTY

On our way past the entrance, we spotted Clancy and Jessamine walking ahead.

Their bashful tiptoeing around each other was apparent even from that distance, as Clancy delicately stroked her feathers, checking her injured wing. They were so engrossed in each other they didn't notice us coming up behind them.

Leander slowed his pace so we wouldn't overtake them as we heard Jessamine insisting, "It's a flesh wound. The arrow hit any vital structure. I should be flying again by next week."

"I should hope not," Clancy said, alarmed. "Not so soon. And then, the hunters might be lying in wait outside, and they'll stop at nothing to kill as many of us as they can."

"No one can shoot an arrow from over the wall!"

"Arrows no, but they might bring in catapults."

"Catapults?" she squeaked. "Where would they get those? And why would they use them now if they do get them, when we've been here for three years?"

"For the same reason they dared such a direct attack,"

211

Clancy said. "They now know it's survivable. The Woodbine boy must have told them he survived his encounter with the Beast after all, when he came to rescue one of his fair maidens and avenge the other."

"I was never his," Jessamine said urgently. "Neither was Bonnie."

I could feel Leander getting stiffer with each word.

Clancy sighed. "I have a feeling it's not the last we've seen of them. And as if that's not enough trouble to look forward to, I feel myself getting worse. My body is stiffening, and my horns are getting so long I can't lie in my bed."

"Can't you bend your legs?" she asked tentatively.

He snorted humorlessly. "Goat legs have kneeling or standing positions, no adjustments."

"If it makes you feel any better, I don't think I'll have knees soon."

"Of course, it doesn't! Even if it didn't mean we're all doomed."

Leander chose that moment to let them know we were behind them. "Lord Gestum, Miss Quill, if you need us we'll be through there."

As if they had been burned, Clancy and Jessamine jumped apart.

"Right behind you," Clancy said.

Avoiding each other's eyes, they followed us, Clancy on Leander's side and Jessamine on mine, piquing my frustration. If they had mutual feelings for each other, then what was the problem?

I wanted to ask them every "what" and "why" that crossed my mind, but they seemed uncomfortable enough, with us ruining their moment.

Leander led us beneath a massive skylight and up one of the two slopes framing an extensive hallway. After passing through many consecutive doorways, we entered a space paved with bluish-white marble leading up to a set of half-moon stairs.

I linked my arm through Jessamine's as we climbed up. "So, what was that you two were saying about your knees?"

She ducked her head, blushing fiercely, seeming more concerned about me mentioning Clancy than the further transformation of her body. "It was a mutual concern. After the initial curse hit us, we changed slowly, but our conditions seems to be escalating lately."

A deep chill settled over me. "Is...is this because of me?"

"No!" Her protest echoed faintly as she hopped onto each step rather than climb them like the rest of us. "It started a bit before you arrived. It was scary actually, that's why your arrival was such a godsend, like the Fates were finally showing us some mercy."

That awful guilt stabbed me in the pit of my stomach again.

A godsend. That's how she saw me. That was why she'd been devastated when Leander and I had gotten off on the wrong foot, why she'd risked herself to stop me from leaving.

If only I could control how I felt for all their sakes.

But if things were getting worse for them all so quickly, after years of gradual changes, then maybe they didn't even have three months before the curse reached its full effect. And even if the escalation had started before I'd arrived, crushing that rose could have only made things worse.

The thought made me feel sick.

"Are you feeling well?"

"I'm so sorry," I blurted out, feeling even worse at her concern. "I hate that you've all been subjected to this. I want to release you all from this, but what if I can't? What if we don't have time?"

Her yellow eyes watched me unblinkingly. They looked a little bigger than before, her lashes uncomfortably longer, and her delicate nose was harder, pointier, taking up more space. Almost like it was making way for a beak sometime soon.

"I don't know what to tell you," she whispered, looking at Clancy's and Leander's backs. "I hate to put this pressure on you, but you truly are our last hope. But we still have some time."

"We're here!" Leander announced, ending our distressing conversation, pushing open a set of tall white doors, their edges decorated with a pastel design of curling vines, thorny stems and blooming blossoms.

A few steps into the room and I forgot how to breathe.

Between a ceiling the height of two of the castle floors, and a vast, ornate green-marble floor, gigantic bookcases soared. Mezzanines split their enormous sections between towering windows into levels, and spiral ladders connected them and framed their ends.

A massive, extensive library. A place out of my wildest dreams.

Books of every size and color crowded every shelf, all baring their spines to me, beckoning. And I ran to answer their siren call.

The endless variety made my head spin, the excitement getting too much to be contained in my small body. Everything was labeled by genre or subject then by alphabetical order in an ingenious system. Everything from storybooks to compendiums filled the chamber that was twenty times as big as my house. A fathomless selection of knowledge and enter-tainment that would take decades to go through, and that was not accounting for rereads.

I found Leander beside me, and I turned to him, wide-eyed and speechless. He was looking down at me, smiling as gently as his brutal mouth would allow.

When he met my eyes, he snapped out of it, comically serious as he pointed to the wall behind me. "The apothecary texts are that way."

I laughed. "Is that the only section I'm allowed in?"

"If you will spend hours chasing your tail over which section to start with, then yes."

"Is that what you do? Do you have a tail yet?"

I groaned. I really needed to think over what I said before it left my mouth.

"You recently said my hands would turn into hooves," Clancy reminded as he stopped before a ladder, seemed to be debating whether he could climb it. "So it's not hard to assume you'd have a tail soon. But watch that one, Miss Fair-born. He doesn't take jokes in stride."

Before I could say I hadn't been joking, just being tactless, Leander said, "I'm actually beginning to." He looked down at me with an unreadable expression in his brilliant eyes, and I for some reason felt faint for a moment. Then he sighed. "But to answer your questions, no, I don't have a tail, and yes, I sometimes find myself chasing my proverbial one for ages."

Relieved that I hadn't offended him by stepping all over such a sensitive subject, if still ashamed, and confused about those strange sensations coming over me, I blinked up at him. "Why, when you have so much to choose from?"

"Well, that's the issue. It's like being a mouse in a cheese-maker's shop. Which type do I nibble on first?"

That analogy made me think that should I ever be infected by his curse, I would turn into a mouse, as I was small, and evidently, a bit of a pest.

"As someone who's sampled the whole shop, which cheese do you recommend?" I smiled, hoping to soothe the jitters in the pit of my stomach.

He still gazed down at me with this unusual quiet intensity. "Would you like me to choose for you?"

"Are you going to surprise me with another archaic tome?"

He didn't answer for a beat, before words left him in a rush. "I was thinking more along the lines of giving you one of my favorites."

"Oh, I'd love that!"

Surprise lit up his face. "You would?"

"Yes, I can't wait to critique your terrible taste in reading material," I teased, trying to get back into an easier to handle bantering mood.

"I will not be shamed for my preferences, Miss Fairborn." He started walking away, looking over his shoulder, eyes glinting with something I hadn't seen there before—mischief? "Regardless, I will find you a book and by all the gods in heaven, you will like it!"

"And if I don't?"

"Then you'll read it again with a keener eye!" His voice blasted through the room as he stopped before one section, startling Jessamine and echoing loudly before fading.

"I can hear you in this silence even if you whisper," I groaned. "Use your indoor voice, please."

"It is my voice, and we are indoors, therefore it is my indoor voice," he tossed back.

It was intriguing how that very tone and expression had gone from terrifying to funny. Even more so when I envisioned him as the spoiled prince he used to be. I told him so.

He gazed back at me with—fondness? "You may be disrespectful, and more than a little thoughtless, but I do appreciate your honesty. It makes for stimulating conversation."

Before, this would have warranted a huff, but now his sincerity made me smile. "And you may be loud and aggressive, but I too appreciate that you're an open book. Those unbridled reactions could just use a little restraint."

"Then that's something we both need to work on."

"You more than me."

"No, we either share this burden or I want no part of it," he joked.

I couldn't resist snorting. "What do I do until you find that book then?"

He pointed where Clancy and Jessamine were doing a terrible job of pretending to be browsing a shelf while surreptitiously chatting. "There's an array of books on flowers. Maybe one can tell us if there is such a thing as a bonnibel."

I narrowed my eyes at him. "When I find it, I will rub it in your face."

"To do that, you'd need to reach my face first," he teased.

I didn't know which was worse, that I hadn't seen that joke coming, or that I didn't have a comeback.

Not giving me a chance to think of one, he turned away. Harrumphing, I headed over to my friends.

Clancy's wide smile shrank as soon as I approached them. It seemed to tip Jessamine off as she retreated out of the library with a hurried excuse. "I will get tea right away!"

I raised an eyebrow at him, an unmistakable "Explain yourself."

Clancy was so flustered he took the bait, spluttering a

defense, "She asked me which bird I thought she resembles, so I was searching for a book to guide me to an answer."

"You sure that was all?"

His fair skin flushed. "Yes, well, we have every right to worry about what we might soon turn into, and to learn what we can about them."

That was a blow of misdirection. But my guilty sympathy wasn't yielding the conversation. "You two didn't seem upset at all, until I showed up."

"I do enjoy talking to Miss Quill. She is a very personable young woman."

"She's very pretty as well," I pointed out.

Clancy took out a handkerchief and dabbed at his forehead, where his curls were suddenly drenched. "Objectively speaking, yes, she is."

I elbow poked him. "You like her, admit it."

"We're just friendly," he said in a rush.

Just what was the issue here? Could this be about the disparity in their social standings? Or did he think it pointless to pursue his passion for Jessamine with the curse hanging over their heads? I would have thought it should have done the opposite, making him throw all cautions and considerations to the winds.

But I'd done enough matchmaking, and though I hated seeing them torment themselves needlessly, I had to step back.

"So, what is it you're looking for?" he asked, tucking the handkerchief away. "Perhaps an old cartography book, to investigate your lost isle?"

"I'll hold off on the really ancient stuff for now that I've seen how some were written." I waved a hand around the shelves by us. "I'm looking for a flower book actually."

"Native or exotic?"

"I suppose native, assuming my island is similar to Arbore."

He headed in the other direction. "I'll help you look!"

I followed him until I stood facing a shelf, eyes roaming over book spines, some with beveled titles, some a blank mystery. There really was a daunting number.

I started sampling some and from the variety, it seemed they'd been collected from around the continent, originals or copies, handwritten or printed. There must be rarities here, too, full of one-of-a-kind information, probably most lost to my people. From the little I read, I felt it put Ericura in one century and Arbore in another.

The concept of lost knowledge dug up thoughts of my mother, my uncle Ossian and, strangely, the redcaps. I didn't even know what my mother's maiden name had been or anything about the circumstances of my uncle's disappearance. I knew my father was hiding some things, possibly the whereabouts of his brother and why we never visited other Fairborns. But whatever they were, terrible truths, shameful secrets or even a silly family feud, he intended to take the knowledge to the grave.

Then there were the redcaps and their morbid rhyming, and the things they'd called me.

It must have been my size. Adelaide had jokingly compared me to gnomes that last day together, and I'd told her I'd seen shorter trees. And to think she was somewhere in Faerie now, seeing actual gnomes, sprites and sylphs and who knew what else.

I missed her terribly, and the gnawing loss was made even worse by not knowing how to start looking for her. When or if I broke the curse.

An odd noise crackled behind me. Thinking it must be Leander's rummaging, I continued my search until my gaze snagged on a blue book.

FÆRIE FLORA & FAUNA.

I reached for it on my toes, arm stretched to its limit. The noise behind me continued, now sounding like an open window on a windy night.

I started to turn to investigate, and Clancy came over, got the book down for me. I smiled my thanks up at him and....

"WATCH OUT!"

Leander's thundering shout had us both jumping around.

Behind us, blocking out the entrance, a hole in the air was hovering in the middle of the room. Its edges spun with light and color until an image started to form within it.

The memory surged, so clear it blinded me. That was *exactly* like what I'd seen back in the Hornswoods. What had sucked us in and spat us here. A magic portal!

Next heartbeat, the image inside it sharpened, and my heart almost burst in shock.

On the other side, with long, rioting hair, strange, ornate clothes and a sky-high gate behind her, Adelaide stood in a sea of sand.

Not caring how or why this was happening, I dropped the book and barreled towards her, hands desperately reaching, a scream for her ripping from my depths. *"ADA!"*

She ran, too, mimicking my movements, her expression, urgent, anxious, overjoyed, her mouth moving but no sound leaving it. She seemed to be screaming my name, too.

As I got closer, I saw three people behind her. One who seemed to be the fairy woman who'd kidnapped her, another younger woman who was even taller than Adelaide, and a hulk of a man in dark clothes, with everything else about him totally white.

I was almost touching her when the portal suddenly collapsed on itself, winked out of existence with a harrowing snap of wind and an eye-searing flash.

CHAPTER TWENTY-ONE

"*A*da!" My scream echoed in the library long after the portal disappeared.

Nothing moved. Not even my heart, it seemed. Everything seemed to be bating its breath along with me as I stared into the nothingness where Adelaide had just been standing.

Adelaide! I'd seen her. She'd been right there. I'd almost touched her.

Suddenly everything exploded within me, my heartbeats tripping over each other as my heart seemed to try to ram out of my chest.

"D-did you see that?" I finally rasped, throat feeling gashed with my screams for her.

"I did." Leander stopped beside me, panting, his eyes, stunned, anxious. "That was why I yelled. I thought...I don't know—I just thought it was a threat."

He'd seen it too. It had been real. And now I wished it hadn't been.

It would have been better if it had been my mind playing a

trick on me, fueled by my intense yearning to find her. Better than knowing she'd been within reach, right across from me, then, like a ribbon in the wind, she'd slipped through my fingers.

Gone into the unknown—*again.*

Clancy gently touched my shoulder, concern lacing his voice. "You don't look so good, perhaps you should lie down."

I shook my head frantically. "I can't! It might open again! I need to be close enough this time to reach her—can't risk losing her—" I couldn't finish, refused to blink, remained fixed to the spot, everything inside me winding tighter with dreadful hope.

They talked to me. Talked *at* me, for what felt like ages. At some point Jessamine returned with a tea trolley, and Clancy filled her in, and told Leander off for something.

My feet began to hurt and my barely blinking eyes dried, stung, wetting themselves with a burning precursor of the desperate tears I couldn't yet shed. She might still come back.

I started begging, and kept on begging. "Please—*please* do it again—come back. Ada, come back."

But nothing happened.

"Surely if it were to happen again it would have done so by now." Clancy again tried to nudge me away. I swayed on aching feet but didn't budge. He sighed. "Have you seen that —that portal before, Miss Fairborn?"

"That's what brought me here," I choked. "I saw my friend on the other side!"

Leander bent down to face me, eyes grim. "The one that was taken by fairies?"

A sob tore from my chest. *"Yes."*

He shook his head, straightening as much as was able to

now. "Then you should stop waiting for it to happen again. It's unlikely it would any time today."

"Don't say that! Why do you say that?"

His gaze grew apologetic. "I do because time works differently in Faerie. Even if she tries to contact you again at once, it could be days or even weeks from now in our realm."

I hated to hear it, but he wasn't the first one to tell me that terrible concept. Robin had said the same thing about his Marianne, who'd been carried off by fairies, and about the king who'd gone there for days, returning to find centuries had passed.

The thought that she might return for me days from now, only to find my tomb instead was horrifying.

Abruptly, Leander swept me off my feet. "You need to sit."

I didn't struggle. Enervated by despair, I let him carry me to the seating arrangement in the center of the library. He tried to place me gently on the crimson sofa, but with his clumsy hands and my uncoordinated body, I plopped on it in an ungainly mass.

He dropped in the chair next to me, and its legs groaned under his weight. "Tell us everything you saw exactly. I couldn't see anything inside the vortex from my vantage."

"I saw Adelaide with three others, two women, the one who kidnapped us, and another—she was *huge*—with long, pale hair..." I stopped as the significance hit me. "Ada herself had long hair!"

"Is that bad?" Jessamine set a teacup before me, sounding confused.

"The last time I saw her, a couple of weeks ago, it was almost as short as a boy's!"

"Months must have passed on her end then." Leander exhaled heavily. "If not years."

My heart squeezed even harder. To think she'd been lost and alone and trying to find me for that long! "I thought it was the other way around, that time was slower there?"

"There are theories it swings to and fro," said Clancy. "Or that in some courts it's slow, in others fast, depending on the climate, or the flow of magic."

I let out a whimpering keen, everything inside me muffled by deepening shock.

A frown of concentration pleated Leander's brow. "Did you see her surroundings?"

I pounced on his question. "Why? Can we find out where she is, depending on those? Do we have a map of Faerie?"

"Nothing accurate, I'm sure…" Clancy stopped when Leander batted a hand at him. "But do describe what you saw."

"Sh-she was standing before a massive gate, attached to a towering, white wall, and there was sand everywhere."

Jessamine stopped pouring the tea. "Sand? Where in Faerie do they have sand?"

"The Summer Court, presumably." Leander tapped his nails on the arm of his chair, a nerve-wracking noise in my state. "From what I've heard, the days are longer there while the opposite is true for Winter, where time moves faster."

I sat up, hope flaring in my chest. "I need to get there!"

"NO!" The sharp objection made me jump. Not a growl from Leander or a bleat from Clancy, but a squawk from Jessamine. "You can't leave again! You promised!"

"Miss Quill."

At Leander's gruff warning, Jessamine ducked her head, avoiding all our eyes. "Sorry. It's just…" She trailed off, raised a glass bowl in shaking hands. "Would anyone like cookies?"

Clancy jumped at the chance to break the tension, took one, then turned to me. "Now, what were we saying?"

Not wanting to upset her further by discussing leaving, I shook my head.

Leander watched me as he brought his cup to his lips. Visibly irritated with his loud slurping, he clattered his cup down. "Would you have gone?"

"What?"

"Had that portal stayed open longer, would you have gone through it?"

I was at a loss how to answer him. I'd be lying if I said I wouldn't have, because I'd been about to leap through it when it had shut in my face. The truth was, the thought of them all had fled my mind the moment I'd seen Adelaide—different, yet alive and well and within reach.

I finally said, "I just want her back. All I could think was to reach her, to pull her through."

"Or you would have leaped through and gotten stuck on the other side." I expected Leander to get worked up as usual, that I would have left them to their doom without a second thought, but he only exhaled dejectedly. "But you're still here."

Yes, I was. Only because I didn't get the chance to leave. And Adelaide was who knew where or when, in the Summer Court, all by herself, at that fairy woman's mercy.

Leander set an uncertain hand by mine, as if he wanted to console me. His nails were becoming the translucent silver of claws.

I shook my head at his silent question. I couldn't talk about Adelaide anymore now.

So I pointed at the book he'd dropped on the table. "What did you pick for me?"

Blinking, as if he couldn't process the switch in topic, he picked it up, handed it to me. A smooth, teal hardcover with an embossed pearlescent title framed by a circle of rose thorns. There was no subtitle, no brief description on the first page, just the names *Amadeus & Gratia* and in a much smaller font *Translated by Lady Mullein.*

It was a new book. Something a few years old and only ever owned by one person. Him.

I looked up at him. "What's it about?"

"I wouldn't want to spoil anything for you, so I'll only say it's an old Orestian tale that was recently translated by a former lady-in-waiting of my mother's, Lady Crisanta Sorley."

I grasped at the distraction. "Her name here is Lady Mullein."

"Yes, she's the Countess of Mullein, but she is a Sorley by marriage. In general terms, she is Lady Sorley, but professionally she is Lady Mullein. The same goes for her husband."

That only confused me more, which I welcomed now, but Clancy elaborated. "Titles can come from the land or castle one inherits, and inheritance can go sideways if a bloodline dies out. I believe that was how the last Prince of Almaskham came about?"

Leander nodded, something heavy in his eyes. "Yes, Prince Faisal was sixth or seventh-in-line. It's why he was allowed to marry a common woman. A few disasters and abdications later, he and his Orestian peasant girl found themselves on the throne."

Clancy grew visibly uncomfortable. "Yes, it was their luck that he ascended after they had several sons. If his succession had happened a few years earlier, he would have been forced to put her aside for a more suitable wife."

Jessamine clattered the cup she handed him.

I exhaled, shock and disappointment making me unable to read or worry about what was happening between them.

I still said, "Theirs must be an interesting story. A prince marrying a girl from another land, with no expectations or pressures, since he was considered disposable and she was considered no one, only for them to end up being the most important ones."

"I haven't thought about it that way before." Leander seemed pleased with my input. "The most interesting thing was, you'd expect a man unprepared for ruling and his common wife would have been disastrous rulers. But they elevated Almaskham into what we, centuries from now, might call its Golden Age."

"Did you ever meet them?" I asked, only because he seemed to be expecting more interaction from me.

"Faisal has been dead for over a decade, but I did meet his wife in a diplomatic summit, when I was touring nearby nations to learn foreign politics firsthand."

"And?" I prodded.

He huffed a reminiscent laugh. "She was a viper, I'll tell you that. The first thing she said when she walked into our meeting was that we were little boys with wooden swords play-acting at being lords and leaders. Anyone who tried to flatter Dowager Princess Aurelia got ripped to shreds. You either truly engaged her or she tore into you. She was inordinately shrewd and unlike anyone I'd ever met."

His oddly fond recollection of someone who'd been apparently mean and offensive to him lifted my spirits a little. "So, Faisal chose well?"

"That he did. I wouldn't be surprised if she was the one in charge during their reign. She reads people so well, knows how to make them do her bidding." He frowned as he gazed at his warped hands. "If I wasn't so offended by what she said about me, I would have heeded her judgment, and adjusted my behavior, and I wouldn't have fully unleashed the curse."

"I recall you said she was unfairly hostile towards you," Clancy pointed out. "So you think it was justified now?"

Leander nodded, grimacing at his hands. "Most of it probably was, but once she realized who my mother was, she stopped acknowledging me at all. I felt worse when she ignored me."

"How many people has your mother offended?" The words were out before I could stop them.

Leander didn't seem to mind, sighed. "Plenty. But this time, Aurelia's rancor was more about my maternal uncle than my mother. King Darius of Cahraman married her niece Jumana, who I understand was the daughter she never had. When Jumana died after she gave birth to Cahraman's heir— the prince pledged to Fairuza—the old woman grew to hate all of us, seeing us as complicit in her death somehow."

I put down my untouched cup. "How is that fair?"

He slumped with a deflating sigh. "Grief is too strong an emotion to be reasonable. Sometimes people need someone to blame in order to feel better. That's how my mother is, I suppose."

"Who is your mother grieving for?"

"Myself and Fairuza. I told you that since the first time my curse manifested, showing her the Spring Queen had been serious, she considered us as good as dead."

Though he was sort of excusing his mother's behavior, I didn't. For a mother to give up on her children like that, to have "replacements," because she considered them damaged and hopeless, was unthinkably callous.

That was the last discussion of the morning, as we spent

the rest of it in near-silence in the library. At lunch and dinner, they attempted to talk to me, but my mind was elsewhere, wherever the Summer Court was.

All my life, I'd fantasized about leaving Aubenaire to travel. But it had been just that, a fantasy, with no consequences. I hadn't thought how my father would feel, how long I'd be gone, if I'd be in any danger, and how I'd ever return. When the possibility of having that fantasy realized had presented itself, it had taken my first, and now only, argument with Adelaide to realize that my choices and actions could affect others' lives.

Travel had only represented insecurity and danger to Adelaide, and my father was a simple man with no aspirations beyond me and his job, and taking on apprentices, in hope of having one succeeding him as town smith and handyman. He would have likely wanted me to marry his successor and live in our stone house, and have the big family I'd always yearned for. Adelaide would have been happy with any local boy, just to make his family, their history and traditions hers. My desire to leave, to wander anywhere, had rocked the boat of the peaceful future together that they'd both coveted.

Then my wish had come true, ending with us scattered, and with me staring down a new reality. Not the one where the Folkshore existed, but where I had something I'd never had.

A duty.

To my father, to Adelaide, to Leander and to the people of Rosemead Castle.

But I didn't know how to save them all, give them back the lives they'd had. And I couldn't bear not knowing. I'd always needed answers. It was why I'd spent my life within the pages of books that could give me those.

Now I wanted to skip to the end of this story and read the ending. But it was only half-written. And for the first time, I wasn't the reader, but the writer. And it was up to me to write the next chapter.

It now remained to be seen whether I resolved our complicated plot, or rocked the boat harder and knocked us all overboard.

CHAPTER TWENTY-TWO

J couldn't shake the feeling that the portal had reopened somewhere in the castle, and I had missed Adelaide again.

It had made sleep impossible. Giving up after hours of tossing and turning, I sat up in bed, lit a candle, and began reading Leander's book.

Whatever expectations I'd had for it faded as I was sucked into the story, barely registering the increasing brightness of my surroundings as I turned page after page.

A knock made me jump, and Jessamine entered. "I'd say good morning, but you look like you had a hard night."

I rubbed my swollen eyes, nodded.

I was about to bend a page when I remembered the book was new and belonged in that phenomenal library. I patted around, searching for something to mark where I'd stopped, and a crimson feather fluttered before me on the duvet.

"Use this," Jessamine said.

I picked up her amazing feather and reverently used it as a

bookmark. "Thank you. But hasn't your wing suffered enough?"

"It was falling off, and another one was already pushing it out." Her face pinched in unease. "It's not like hair that falls off and more grows back without you feeling it."

"Is it painful?"

Her feathers twitched along her uneven wings, the injured one not folded neatly as the other. "Not really, just itches, like a scab."

"I never got to ask, but what was it like growing wings?"

She shuddered. "Now *that* was painful, like I was teething but on a wide scale, and, well, on my back."

I cringed, feeling a phantom pressure between my own shoulder blades. "I'm so sorry."

She waved dismissively. "They're not so bad once I got used to them. The most inconvenience was refashioning all my dresses for them. My legs are the real bother."

I resisted looking at her gnarled, taloned feet. "Do you like flying, then?"

Her yellow eyes brightened. "That's the one good thing about it. I used to watch birds and think they were so free, could go anywhere they wanted." She gazed out my window and down at the city. "Ironic, isn't it? I get the chance to finally go anywhere, and I can't, because someone might shoot me down."

The blood-chilling fear I'd felt when I'd watched her plummet washed over me all over again. I shivered. "But if you could fly anywhere, where would you go?"

She checked behind her, as if she was afraid someone would hear her. "Since this all started, I've had this dream of touring the fairy courts."

That was strange, considering her panicked reaction when I mentioned going to Faerie yesterday. But then she'd thought I'd be the one to go, alone.

I sighed. "I used to have a similar dream. I grew up in a town where the path to Faerie was supposedly through the woods. The more people tried to scare me about going there, the more I wanted to go take a look."

"And did you?"

My shoulders slumped, heavy with guilt and gloom. "I did. And that was where the fairy that took my friend saw us. If I hadn't insisted on going in, none of this would have happened."

"But we also wouldn't have gotten to know you!"

I couldn't agree on the silver lining, since I'd done nothing for them so far. So I said, "By 'we,' do you mean all of you or yourself and Clancy?"

She moved away, uneasy. "Bonnie, I told you, there's nothing between us."

"Regardless of what's going on, just answer me this: do you love him?"

Her lips trembled as she nodded. "But it can't go anywhere."

Knowing she'd evade my questions if I asked why, I went for something else that had been bothering me. "What about Castor?"

Disapproval pressed her mouth into a thin line. "What about him?"

"Was he horrible to you?"

She shook her head. "No, nothing like that. I just couldn't be the focus of his obsession."

"What do you mean?"

"You must have noticed how naive he is?" Jessamine rolled her shoulders, unfurling her injured wing. "He thinks life is a children's book, where he, the noble hero, chooses the fair maiden and goes around saving her from everything, starting with having a mind of her own. He will take her home, dress her in his mother's clothes, and keep her there forever, having his children, listening to what he says, doing what he wants and receiving his stifling attention without complaint. The instant you show signs of being a real person, he falls apart."

I nodded. That was exactly my experience with him. "How is he like that?"

"Like all minor nobles, he was raised in boarding schools, and never talked to a female who wasn't his mother or relative. The only ideas such men have about us are from stories." She tapped my book. "But *this* story would shock the socks off Castor, my brothers and every other young man in Rosemead."

I'd stopped midway, where something very exciting was about to happen. The story of Amadeus and Gratia, as the forward claimed, was that of a god and the mortal woman he fell in love with. Hounded by suitors for her incredible beauty, Gratia tried everything to rebuff them, from cutting off her hair to chucking firewood at them from her window. But some even started worshipping her, considering her the living extension of Aglaea, their goddess of love and beauty. The town's women then banded together to be rid of her, fearing she would take their husbands or had an evil hold on their sons. Summoning Aglaea, they told her Gratia boasted that she was more beautiful than her and was trying to usurp the goddess.

Enraged, Aglaea sent her son Amadeus, who carried out her mandated love matches, to make Gratia fall in love with a satyr. Unexpectedly, Amadeus fell in love with her himself, and devised a plan to hide her from his mother. Under the guise of an eccentric foreign lord who never showed his face, he promised he'd pay off her father's debts if she married him and lived with him in his palace on a mountain plateau.

But on that first night, she tried to escape. He stopped her and invited her to a dim-lit dinner, telling her he wanted her to grow comfortable with him first, as the sight of his face could scare her off. This continued until she fell in love with him.

Then one night, a servant played on her insecurity, told her that her husband would never trust her enough to show her who he was. Overwhelmed by her need to see his face, she entered his room with a candle. But to her shock, he was the most beautiful man she had ever seen. Shaken, she spilled the melted candlewax, burning his arm, waking him.

It was then the servant shirked her mortal form, revealing herself to be Aglaea. She bound her son in adamantine shackles for disobeying her, and dumped Gratia back in her town, where she was at the mercy of lecherous men and envious women yet again.

Infuriated, Gratia found a temple of Aglaea and vandalized it to get her attention. She demanded to have Amadeus back, but Aglaea told her she wasn't worthy of her son, let alone of being compared to her. Gratia insisted she would prove she was worthy of both.

That was where I'd stopped.

I was dying to know what happened next. I'd hate for it to be that Aglaea turned Gratia into a pillar of salt or something for her arrogance, with the rest of the book being Amadeus's widower grief and his vengeance for her death. There were enough dead-wife stories as it was.

I cocked my head at Jessamine. "You've read this story?"

She shrugged. "I've heard it. Stories travel by mouth for years before somebody finally puts them to paper. It's why so many take place centuries ago."

"How does it end?"

Jessamine grinned with a headshake. "Master would have me boiled into chicken soup if I ruined the story for you."

I smiled back. "All right then—tell me something else. Why have you been thinking about going to Faerie so much, if fairies are so scary?"

She bit her lip. "I figure they wouldn't harm us, since we don't look human anymore. We'd be nothing of note in Faerie, so we could live there and be free of this world and its expectations and prejudices."

So her goal for escape made my previous desire for travel, for curiosity and adventure, feel childish in comparison, if not flat out stupid and irresponsible.

"Why did you come here?" I rose up on my knees, seeking out her eyes. "I sense it wasn't to escape or spite Castor, and surely the distance you keep between Clancy and yourself has nothing to do with him, either."

She shook her head, then after a tense pause, she said, "His name was Yewan. And he was the first thing I ever wanted for myself."

That admission was the last thing I'd expected.

It wasn't like I didn't know people had first loves. Those were usually *first* for a good reason, but not *only* for a bad one. I just hadn't expected one to be behind her reticence.

"But this story began long before I met him, after my mother succumbed to a fever." She threw her hands up and her wings followed. "I was seven! I could barely braid my own hair or read, but overnight, I was shoved into her role. It

237

became my job to mind the younger Glenn, and keep the older Dale out of trouble, while doing everything around the house —and trying to attend school, which I soon had to leave. My father worked me to the bone, but didn't even give me an allowance. I had to eventually go begging people for their dirtiest laundry and dustiest cellars for whatever price, to have any money of my own."

I gaped at her in suffocating dismay. A fraction of this was enough to make me eternally grateful I didn't have brothers, and to kick myself for every time I got impatient or petulant over my father's coddling.

"Then, I met him. Sir Yewan Rowntree." She sighed, a heavy, miserable sound. "He was a competitive jouster, a prime candidate for His Majesty's cavalry, so another knight honored him with the title. He was charged with training all young men in Rosemead in riding horses and wielding swords, in case they were called to war. Then one day, he was knocked off his horse and Dale told him I could fix his shirt. He gave me a job at his family mansion that day.

"It was a relief from the chores I used to scrounge, freeing me from my family and forcing them to look after themselves. I sent them money still, but I kept most of my generous wages. And at the end of every day, Yewan would return from training boneheaded boys like Castor and my brothers and talk to me in the kitchen while I served him leftovers."

I bit my lip, my heart fluttering at the melancholy in her voice. "You fell in love?"

Her nod made a tear escape down her cheek. "When his family found out, it was a disaster. He was to make a name for himself in the army and marry a noblewoman at court, to lift the whole family up. Wanting to waste their future on a maid made his father and brother beating him senseless. They threw me out in a scandal, but my father was only angry that I ruined such a high-paying job, saying we'd starve with him retired and my brothers too busy training to work. But when I said I had money saved, he realized I've been giving him only a portion of my wages and he—he…"

I couldn't ask what her father had done to her. But I knew that haunted look. It was what I'd seen in Ornella Dufreyne's eyes ever since her stepmother and her daughters had moved into her home.

"I told him he could have the money, and the venomous women who never worked a day in their lives could trash my honor, I no longer cared. It was then that Castor asked for my hand, and it should have been a perfect escape from my situation. But I couldn't escape one prison and enter another. So I came up here and asked for a job, where no one wanted one no matter the pay. Everyone believed our duke had a contagious illness at the time, but I said I'd do anything, even clean his rashes. Ivy asked if I had family in town, and I said I had no one. She hired me on the spot, certain I wouldn't talk about what I saw."

"What did you see then?"

"The Master, just smaller, with less hair and only fangs. Then Lord Gestum came to visit. Not three days later the curse took hold of the castle, catching us all in its noose. And you know something?" Looking more defiant than unhappy, she waved over her whole body. "I would rather morph into a phoenix and burst into flames than see downtown Rosemead again."

I nodded, understanding completely, but still compelled to say, "I met your brothers, and they seemed very angry and sad thinking the Beast killed you. And Dale became a knight."

"Looks like my absence has done wonders for them," she

said bitterly. "With me gone, and our father dragged to the abyss by the Horned God, they've been forced to finally grow up." She wrapped her arms around herself, glowering down at the city. "It figures it took me 'dying' for them to start caring about me. Why not start while I was there with them every day?"

"They probably thought you'd always be there, and when you weren't, the shock woke them up." I got up to hug her, setting my head on her arm. "I never thought of my father when I was dreaming of traveling, only thought I'd return to find him where I left him. But being separated from him made me realize that I miss him every minute, that I had so much to say to him and do with him, and would do anything to see him again—and that's when I now know he's nearby, and safe." I turned my face up to her, trying to smile through the emotion sealing my throat. "They may not have appreciated you before, but I bet you anything they do now. And anyway, you don't have no one. You have everyone in this castle, and now you have me, too."

Jessamine gave me a watery smile. "I really am sorry for the circumstances that brought you here, but I am still glad that they did."

I now understood her hesitance about Clancy. Her first brush with love had burned her, leaving her afraid of trying again. If only I could show her it wouldn't happen again, have Clancy prove to her that their situation was different.

And it wasn't only for their sakes. If I could see them happy together, I might understand what love beyond family was like. Only then could I free us all from this castle, and give them the possibility of a long life together.

But she would never take the first step. It had to be Clancy who did. And since he was as adamant as her that there was nothing between them, I had to find out his reason for keeping *his* distance.

But I doubted he would tell me, so I needed to talk to the one person who knew him best.

Leander.

CHAPTER TWENTY-THREE

*H*azel burst into the room, bunny ears perking in surprise when she found Jessamine.

"Back to work already?" She pouted at her. "You could have warned me."

Jessamine's lips twisted as she detached from me and went to prepare today's clothes. "Why? It's not like you had anything better to do." She wiggled her eyebrows at Hazel. "Unless you call mooning over Sir Philip from the first floor windows that.'"

Hazel stuck out her tongue between buckteeth as she skipped out. "Just don't make her late to breakfast now, Birdie."

"About that, when do you all eat?" I said. "Do you have to wait for us to be done?"

"In any other household, we would have, but the Master is easygoing, so we eat while you do, then clear everything in one go."

Only one thing stuck out at me in that statement. "Leander is *easygoing*?"

Jessamine nodded as she came back with an emerald-green dress. "For someone who grew up as a crown prince, he doesn't expect us to wait on him hand and foot, or to remain on our feet till he sleeps. Far, *far* lesser people expect their servants to wait on them every single second they're awake."

"If so, why don't we set up the dining room for everyone today?"

Her already huge eyes grew enormous. "You mean have us eat with you?"

I nodded vigorously. "Yes, it should save us all time, and it'd be nice, all of us together."

"That's not appropriate, impossible! We can't overstep our boundaries!"

"Didn't you say he was easygoing?"

"As an employer, he is, but having the servants crash his dining room isn't the same as washing his silk shirt in hot water."

"*Please*. It's so awkward for just the three of us to sit at such a big table alone."

Jessamine worried her lip, clearly tempted to be wherever Clancy was. Then she said, "It's Ivy you have to ask."

At that, I was bursting out the door, still in my nightgown, messy hair and robe flying behind me.

IT TOOK a lot of convincing and begging and not a little whining, but Ivy ended up indulging me.

People quickly filled the dining room and more chairs were brought in to accommodate everyone. A variety of food crowded the table from one end to the other, taking into account carnivores, herbivores and those who couldn't use cutlery, among heaps of mouthwatering bakeries.

Now the hustle and bustle of set up paused as everyone stared at the door, expectant and anxious.

Leander finally stuck his head into the room, thick brows rising over wide eyes in confusion. "Is it someone's birthday?"

Oliver leaped into the air with his arm up, yelling, "ME!" only to be shushed by his mother.

A wave of relief went through the room as Leander walked in without further comment, avoiding everyone's eyes, hunching self-consciously.

He took his seat beside me and before he could utter a word, I launched into my prepared defense. "This dining room is too big and too quiet, and it has enough room for us all."

"I know that."

"Then what's the problem?"

"Did I say there was an problem?" His lips twisted over his fangs. "Did I say *anything*?"

"You gave me a 'we have an problem' look!"

"Maybe you thought that, because *you* know we do, that it's not appropriate to fraternize with your employees. Being friendly tends to make them uncomfortable."

"Is that a universal wisdom or just your experience?"

He shrugged his massive shoulders. "My experience." Then noticing they all remained standing, he gestured at them hurriedly. "Sit."

Most were as unsure how to proceed as Leander was. He made eye contact with a select few before nodding at them to start eating. Given permission, they dug in, some making the civilized effort to eat with cutlery, others not bothering, encouraging him not to try keeping up appearances today.

Clancy joined us last, going from being surprised at the company, to startled at finding Jessamine seated next to him.

"What's the occasion?" Clancy asked us as he accepted the bread basket from her. "Not that I'm complaining. It's truly nice to finally have other company."

"Bored with me already?" I teased.

He shook his head chidingly. "How could I, when you keep managing to surprise us?"

I checked to see if Leander was bothered now that the room was full of loud chatter, but he seemed more intrigued than anything, turning from one side of the table to the other, chewing as he listened intently. That hearing of his!

"I've never seen this many of them in one room," he mused, as if to himself. "I thought they might have staff parties or something after finishing their chores. Not that there's much to celebrate, but I hoped they did."

"You sound like you wanted a gathering like this yourself."

He simply said, "Yes."

My eyes almost bugged out. "Then why didn't you say so before?"

His voice, usually booming, was so hushed I had to lean over to hear him. "I thought that, unless I made it an order, no one would show up."

I blinked up at him. "How could you think that?"

"I can because I am the reason they're all cursed and stuck here."

I reached out to urgently touch his hairy, clawed hand. "I don't think anyone blames you. It's not like you did this."

His brilliant turquoise eyes filled with guilt. "Not directly, no. But I can't help but be glad I'm not alone in this. I keep wondering if this was the reason the curse extended to them." When I couldn't say anything reassuring to that, he exhaled.

"I've been wanting to talk to them, to discuss our experiences and trials with our transformations. But I always felt they didn't want to be around me, so I let them be."

"Well, now you have your answer." I waved my arm out to the table. "No one blames you, no one hates you, no one is avoiding you. The truth is, when I asked them to come, they all wanted to jump at the chance. They just didn't want to overstep any boundaries. Sticklers for rules, even in the wholly unconventional situation we're in."

Something I'd never thought I'd see from him shone in his eyes. Delight. "Good thing you don't care for rules."

"Not if they get in the way of good things."

Keeping his mouth from spreading to hide his fangs, he lifted his porridge bowl to me. "Words to live by."

Deeply relieved, and thrilled, I clinked my bowl against his.

Then we both proceeded to eat, making absolute messes of ourselves.

Breakfast continued for almost two hours, with Leander and I engaging different people in conversation. This was the most social he'd been in years, he'd said. It was the most *I'd* ever been. Apart from Adelaide, all my prior attempts at socializing had been unsuccessful, with people considering me a strange nuisance, and avoiding or ignoring me. But no one in this room considered me odd, and if they did, it didn't matter to them.

Maybe it was because they'd given me a chance, gotten to know me a little. Or because I hadn't met the right people before. The right people for me.

I focused back on the two closest to me—and caught Leander watching me.

He snapped his gaze back to Clancy, diving back into their

conversation, leaving me filled with—that uncertain, light-headed sensation I'd first felt in the library.

It unsettled me, but it had to be a positive one, right? After all, I could already see he was like no one I'd ever known, and I could see us becoming the friends we'd hoped to become.

But I also already had a feeling loving him as a friend wouldn't be enough to help save everyone in this room. I needed to love him, period.

I looked at Jessamine and Clancy, my one example of romantic love. They'd been smiling giddily at each other just a minute ago. Now they'd retreated to their proverbial corners, pretending to find others as interesting as each other.

I turned to Leander, thinking how I'd ask him about them. And I found him watching me again.

CHAPTER TWENTY-FOUR

*A*fter the last platter had been wiped clean, everyone left, taking everything back to the kitchen. Jessamine said she'd help the others, while Clancy said he needed to change his shirt after staining it with egg yolk. Leander and I said we'd head to the library and Jessamine asked me to pick a picture story for her.

"Wouldn't you like to try a different sort of book, Miss Quill?" Leander suggested, elbowing Clancy. "Perhaps Lord Gestum can get you started on some novels."

Jessamine gave him an appreciative smile. "I'd very much like that, Master."

"There are plenty that are timeless favorites of maidens from all backgrounds, what even one as old as you would appre…" Leander stopped, lips stretching to bare big, sharp teeth in a grimace. "Forgive me."

Jessamine hung her head, cheeks pink with embarrassment. "You're not wrong, though, I am old for a maiden."

"You'll have to excuse him," said Clancy as he escorted her

away. "Beyond spouting rehearsed pleasantries to women, anything else has him stumbling into an insult."

Leander mumbled something incoherent as he led me away. I looked back at them before falling into step with him, trying to rethink my view of them.

After Jessamine's doomed relationship with the knight, *would* things be even worse for her with a proper lord? As the Duke of Briarfell, had he not been caught in Leander's curse, Clancy would have been married by now, likely to some other lord's daughter. He didn't have a betrothed out there somewhere, did he? And even if he didn't, what would happen once the curse lifted and the real world intruded once more? Was expecting it to tear them apart why they were being so guarded about their affection for one another?

"So..." I focused on Leander once we settled down in the library after he picked me some books. "Jessamine and Clancy are..."

"...not fooling anyone," he finished for me.

"Why do they try?"

He raised his thick brows at me. "You mean you don't have theories?"

"I do. I need something more solid than those."

He sighed. "To put it simply, Clancy is a lord, Jessamine is a maid."

"A lady's maid," I corrected. "And her brother is a knight! That must count for something."

He shook his head, looking regretful. "Her brother being knighted during the war doesn't make them noble, only means he's an esteemed soldier. Even if he's granted land, and makes an advantageous marriage, and his line becomes members of the gentry, only he would have the title Sir. It wouldn't afford Jessamine a title, or a chance at a lord like

Clancy. The only lord a common girl can get is an impoverished one, with a title, a castle, but no money, and that's only if that girl is from new money, whose dowry will be given in exchange of being called 'Lady.'"

This was not how it went in my novels. Marriages in such tales didn't have so many impossible requirements, just minor conflicts.

"Lords must marry common girls all the time," I argued. "Folktales are full of not just lords, but princes marrying girls they stumbled upon in woods or ruins or balls. I even read one where a prince married an inhuman being from the sea!"

"Ericura really is an Arborean colony, isn't it?" he hummed interestedly. "You've even kept our stories about men marrying creatures like selkies, it seems. A bizarre concept, really."

"Why?"

"What if the children came out a completely different creature?" He waved his hands around his face. "It's one thing to become this, but to be *born* like this? They'd live as outcasts from both their parents' people. You'd have to be pretty selfish to risk that with your children."

I gave a surprised huff. "That's a good point. I've never thought about that."

He raised his brows in mock-shock. "You're telling me you didn't think of every possible theory how such marriages would work and what they would produce?"

I lightly smacked his arm. "I would have come to that conclusion if I thought about it. You just beat me to it."

He began to grin but immediately covered his mouth, hiding his fangs.

I wanted to reach out and remove his hand, tell him not to be self-conscious, at all and especially around me, when he dropped his hand, no longer smiling. "It really is something to think about, marrying someone you just happened upon. What if there is a secret in their bloodline that blindsides you, showing up in your children?"

"Like red hair?" I joked.

He shrugged. "If you're among the superstitious crowd that considers them signs of witchcraft, that could prove a major problem indeed. But I meant inhuman traits. The idea is that this woman who showed up in a seaside town one day would be revealed as a mermaid, or a man found wandering the side of the road is a werewolf, and you have no idea until your child is born with webbed hands or fur."

I shuddered at the image. "It can't be too common though?"

He exhaled. "More common than nobles marrying peasants, that's for sure. There are rumors of men who marry fairy women here in Arbore, and along the Northland Kingdoms. Robin's mother was rumored to be a fairy herself, as her family came from Nexia."

At that point, I could believe anything. And I wouldn't put it past Robin with his infallible aim.

But now I remembered a map of the Folkshroe showing an island called Nexia between Faerie and Armorica, one of the lands Arbore was fighting. That could be a place with a fairy population living alongside humans, intermarrying over generations. One had to wonder what such offspring would look like. And if that was the reason Robin was always shrouding his face in that hood.

The mad, rhyming threats of the vicious redcaps wormed their way back into my thoughts.

I shook my head as if to clear it of the terrible memory and asked, "Do people keep track of such things? Who might be part fairy or part witch?"

"They do. In some lands they're proud of such crazy couplings. I heard that Orestian men marry nymphs and that Oponans have wizard noble families. I'm not sure what is real and what is folktales in that, though."

"If it's real, then those people must lead very interesting lives, full of magic and things we could only guess at."

His eyes roamed the library, as if checking for eavesdroppers, before reluctantly agreeing. "If anything, they must be living the stuff of our fantasies."

"There's a 'but' in there somewhere."

"But, as I said, you might not know what you're getting yourself into, especially once it comes to becoming a family." He suddenly coughed a laugh. "Imagine having a witch for a mother-in-law."

"She might be very useful to have around," I said, liking it a bit more each time I saw him smile or heard him laugh. "As long as you keep your wife happy."

The mirth in his gaze fled as he sighed. "Maybe. But it's a huge risk, more so for nobility and royalty. A common man can choose his path, since his actions would only affect him and his line, not a whole city, or even a kingdom." He picked a book from the pile before us, flipped to a page, and showed me a detailed family tree of an ancient dynasty. His. "This is why marriage matches are made with such care, with both sides having everything in their lines documented, from history, to relatives, to prior conflicts and diseases, so we can take all things into account."

"It sounds so cold, like a business deal."

"It is." He frowned down at the book then at me. "What did you think marriage was for?"

I couldn't say love, since I'd already said the two things didn't necessarily mix. "I don't know, having common interests, values and goals and wanting to build a life together? Liking and trusting a person enough you want to have them as the other parent of your children? And I do know people marry for love. My parents did."

"That's not why most get married, let alone nobles and royals. Marrying for love or even personal preference is a luxury few can afford." Sad notes permeated his words, scraping an aching tune on heartstrings already wound tight enough to snap. "As for true love, that is even more difficult to come by. Why do you think we love hearing about it in stories so much?" He looked at his hands, failing to fully clench his fists. "And why it's the key to unlocking curses such as mine?"

"I thought the fairy queen made it a stipulation because she knew you'd grow to be unlovable..." I cringed immediately. "I meant you were, in the past tense and..." I stopped, tried again. "I mean..."

He let out a tired, rumbling chuckle. "Don't worry. I understand. At this point, mine is a face not even my mother can love."

"Oh, I don't know, I've grown quite used to it." I reached over, pushing a chunk of his long hair off his face and behind his angular ear. He maintained some of what must have been his original bone structure—high cheekbones, a strong jaw and a sloping forehead. His nose and mouth didn't look too odd from a side view, so he retained a powerful profile.

I couldn't decide if his looks had improved with his behavior lately, or if I'd gotten over the shock of his appearance, or if it was starting to appeal to me the more I enjoyed his company.

In the span of two weeks, I'd gone from wanting to run

from him to wanting to talk to him all the time. From finding him a monstrous sight to seeking out his eyes and watching his peculiar face to see the explicit way his expressions matched his words.

Whatever I felt when I was with him, it was a whole new feeling, one I didn't have a word for. It felt different from the fondness I had for Jessamine, the love I had for my father and Adelaide, or even the friendship I had with Clancy. It had elements of each, mixed with—something else.

The slashed painting by his room flashed in my mind. At first, it had been an unnerving fact that he'd once been a normal person. But now it was a maddening curiosity. I wanted to one day look at the real him, and see how his disparate parents intersected on his face.

I wanted to see a face fully capable of smiling at me.

Finding him staring at me, blue-green eyes wide with surprise brought me back to the moment. I had my fingertips on his jaw, under the ear I'd just tucked his hair behind.

A sudden heat flared up to my face, no doubt making it match the pink dress I'd ended up wearing. "Um, what were we saying?"

"The politics of marriage and importance of genealogy?" he said, voice tight.

I rose and settled down on the couch beside him, blindly reaching for one of my books on the table. "Tedious topic, isn't it?"

"I suppose it is, for someone who doesn't know her own grandparents' names."

"I know their names!" I protested. "Keenan Fairborn and Fiona Teagarden." He raised his eyebrows when I didn't name my mother's parents, and I said, "What about you?"

"King Florent the Tenth of Arbore and Princess

Marguerite of Lyonesse, and King Xerxes the Second of Cahraman and Lady Morgana Makhzan of Anbur. I can list their parents and grandparents going back eight hundred years."

I made a face at him. "No wonder you're grumpy, having to learn and remember hundreds of pompous names like that."

He boomed a laugh as he rose, saying he'd fetch more books.

I cracked open the one on my lap, unable to help being bothered by how lacking my answers had been compared to his. They would be compared to most everyone's.

After a few absent page flips in, I went back and read the book's title. It was the one I'd picked right before Adelaide's portal had opened. *Færie Flora & Fauna*.

Short, handwritten paragraphs were arranged around beautifully detailed watercolor plants or strange animals. My eyes roamed over the neat script, noting odd facts about giant birds or man-eating flowers as I went through the alphabetical order.

Halfway through the B-section, my breath caught in my throat.

Under a tall stalk covered in blue flowers shaped like sleigh bells with bright centers and darker outlines, the name struck me like a blow to the gut.

Bonnibel.

Heart stuttering, clutching the volume with shaking hands, I snapped up straight, unable to read fast enough.

~ BONNIBEL ~

A perennial bright-blue flower typically found in the woods of the Spring Court. It drinks in the sunlight during the day to emit a glow at night, creating bright swaths of woodland roads that lead directly to fairy paths.

Its scent is bittersweet, and culinary uses include jam and tea made from its petals, which are tart and are believed to stimulate the third eye, and a paste made from its pollen that transfers its glow to the skin and eyes of its consumer.

It is used by travelers in place of torches and lamps, and given as a crib-toy to fairy children, specifically changelings, as the soft blue light lulls them while they are being swapped for human babies. This practice is so common that fairies have come to name their changeling girls after the flower.

CHAPTER TWENTY-FIVE

I dropped the book as if it burned me.

It thudded to the floor, still open on that page.

Unable to tear my eyes away, I slumped back, trembling all over, unable to manage a full breath.

No wonder I'd never seen or heard of my namesake flower in Ericura, and neither did Leander in Arbore. We didn't because it didn't exist on the Folkshore.

Bonnibel was a fairy flower.

But the rest—it couldn't—couldn't be what I thought it was, could it?

I felt I'd choke on my heart as I kicked the book closed, as if it would stop the doubts, erase them. But it was too late. A slew of facts about myself tangled with recent and half-formed memories, all slotting into place, framing an awful context.

My size and the intense color of my eyes. The monstrous fairies calling me "pretty fey" and "pixie" and "sprite", calling Castor my "human prey," and not attempting to drink my blood, saying it was foul. My father never allowing me to do kitchen work or taking me to his forge. The pain I'd felt as a small child holding an iron pan, even when it hadn't been on the fire. Trying to bake behind his back and getting burned inexplicably...

Everything gathered, cutting off my breathing, coalescing into one crushing suspicion.

Was I a changeling?

Was I a fairy weakling who'd been unable to survive in Faerie, and had been swapped for a healthy human girl? Had I been sent to the human world, while she'd been taken to the Spring Court in my place? Was that why I had that name, like the book suggested?

My father had once told me he'd wanted to name me Fionula after his mother Fiona, but had never given a reason why he hadn't. Had it been mind-altering magic the fairies had worked on my parents, after swapping their human child for me? To make them blindly accept the changeling found in their crib? But had they learned the truth eventually?

No one had known what had killed my mother in her prime. What if it had been the shock of discovering I wasn't hers, and her heart had broken beyond repair?

And my father? If he'd been overprotective because he knew what I was, when had he found out? Before or after my mother's death? Was that the reason he'd cut us from both his and my mother's families? So no one would suspect, and harm me? Even kill me? Was that why he hadn't wanted me to leave the house, or work or travel, so I wouldn't be exposed to people and materials deadly to my—kind? Had it all been to protect me, and to stop me from learning my truth?

Was my whole life a lie?

Leander startled me by setting a hand on my shoulder. "Are you feeling unwell?"

There was no point in saying I was fine, because I burst into overwhelmed tears.

"What is it?" Leander dropped beside me, sounding panicked. "Tell me how I can help."

I opened my mouth, ready to vomit out the terrible conclusion I'd reached, but a primal tug of fear for once tethered my tongue.

Leander, and everyone in this castle, hated fairies, and they had the best reason to. If I suspected I was one, I had to keep that to myself, or else it could ruin all the progress we'd made.

Leander arms hovered around me, hesitant. Needing his nearness even when I couldn't test his understanding, I leaned towards him and with a forceful exhalation of what sounded like relief, he pulled me into his hulking, warm embrace.

His massive, clawed hands patted my back with shocking gentleness, and his fanged lips roamed over my hair and forehead. "Whatever it is, stress, worry for your friend or for us— it's all going to be fine, eventually."

"Wh-what makes you say that all of the sudden?" I blubbered pitifully into his chest, staining his shirt. "You're the one who always believes the worst in any situation."

A sound reverberated in his chest below my cheek, the rumble so oddly comforting. "I'll admit I am not the biggest proponent of hope, but I am starting to believe that our situation won't have a grim end."

"Why not?"

He began to gently stroke my hair, another unexpected gesture that had my blurry eyes sliding shut, savoring the affection. "Because you promised."

I barely held back a wet snort. "That's what you built your belief on? My word?"

"Yes, I…." He paused as his claws snagged on some hairs

and he disentangled them as carefully as he could. "I know you better now, know that you'd stick through with any choice or promise you made. So, when you said you'd see us free of this curse, I believe you will."

"But what if I can't? What if I'm the wrong person for this job?"

What if I'm not a person at all?

"I'd say it's far too late for you to have applicant anxiety." A smile entered his voice, calming me even further. "You've already signed on and been unanimously accepted."

He was right. I'd made a promise, and I was seeing it through. As for my bout of mindless panic—I could be overreacting.

It was just a name in an old book. It could have been carried down from Faerie to Arbore to Ericura, and my parents had just thought it pretty.

Deciding I'd been jumpy, and jumping to all the wrong conclusions, I looked up at him. Feeling so pleasantly swamped within his arms, I attempted to lighten the mood. "So—does that mean I get a salary like the staff?"

He chuckled, the deep rumble buzzing pleasurably along my every nerve. "If you'd like, though you won't be able to make much use of it for a while."

"Then I'll be saving up for a shopping spree."

He quirked a bushy eyebrow at me. "And what would Miss Bonnibel Fairborn, the serial rejecter of expensive gifts, splurge on?"

"Buy my father new tools for his forge, and a tavern or inn for Adelaide," I said without hesitation. "Owning her own business was something she dreamed of."

"Here or on Hericeurra?"

"Wherever." And I believed Adelaide wouldn't mind where, as long as she had us, her family, with her.

"If you stayed here, wouldn't you miss your home?"

While Aubenaire was the only place I'd ever known, I certainly wasn't homesick for it. I'd spent my life wanting to see beyond its borders, my plans anchored to it only for my father's sake. But if we broke the curse, rescued Adelaide and reunited with my father, we could settle here. There were far more people, bringing more opportunities and customers for both of them, and answers and discoveries for me. As a reward for saving the crown prince, I could request a job as a royal librarian—if there were such a position.

"Home is not a place to me." I breathed out, washing away the last of my distress. "It's wherever my family is."

Hesitation gone, he pulled me deeper into his embrace. "I understand completely."

He paused his strokes to roll a lock of my hair around his fingers, watching it reflect the light in an undulating gleam. I supposed fairies, even the weaklings they cast away, wouldn't have my split ends, would they?

Letting myself sink into the comforting warmth and strength of his arms, I felt my heartbeat steady as I listened to his own, and that new feeling I felt for him surged.

But was this warm, intensifying affection enough, for him, for them all?

It clearly wasn't since nothing changed about him.

So what would it take if not what I now felt? What was that true love that persisted in timeworn tales and locked fairy curses? And how could one recognize it?

Leander tensed around me, dispersing my fuzzy thoughts. "Did you hear that?"

I blinked up at him. "Hear what?"

As if in response, a loud slam came from outside, followed by another and another, then the screech of stressed metal hinges.

The gates! We were under attack again!

Leander surged to his feet, still pressing me to his side, defensive and territorial as he took us to the nearest window, peering over its edge and down at the grounds, just as the gates gave way.

My blood froze as they screamed open, and our attackers poured in, their chorus of rabid shouts carrying the threat ahead of their torches and weapons.

Not a handful of men like last time, but *dozens*. This time, they'd come in force, intent of wiping everyone out.

And this time, I could see no way they wouldn't succeed.

CHAPTER TWENTY-SIX

*C*ursing viciously under his breath, Leander sprinted out of the library.

I felt like a ragdoll in his arms, tried to make him put me down. His protective hold only tightened as we reached the entrance and he panted, "You will stay in the highest chamber of the East Tower until this is resolved!"

Before I could choke out a question how he thought it could be, or a refusal to leave him, a rock crashed through one of the windows by the main doors. The battering ram slammed into them almost simultaneously, the boom deafening, winding the barbed wires of brutal fear into my bones.

Leander had barely started on the stairs when the doors burst open. Against the faint light coming from outside, I saw only ominous silhouettes and the menacing glint of weapons in their torches' orange light—lances, poleaxes, hayforks, hammers and even butcher's knives.

Throwing a roar back at our attackers, he chucked me at the stairs, hissing urgently, "East Tower—*now!* Take whoever you find on your way with you!"

Remembering how I'd hindered him and almost gotten him killed by the redcaps when I hadn't run when he'd told me to, I whirled around and bounded up the stairs.

But once I was high enough, I threw a glance over my shoulder and saw just how many people were attempting to fight their way in. Far more than the staff who rushed out to intercept them. Among the latter I saw the centaurs, Sir Philip and his sister Rosalind, galloping with clubs, Ivy trying to get Oliver to stop following her, and Clancy, brandishing a suit of armor's sword.

The moment the first men came face to face with the "creatures" they'd come to hunt, I could see the shock, disgust and horror shifting across their faces, darker than their shadows in the firelight. Then everything gave way to aggression as they exploded in attack.

I let out a piercing scream as the closest man swung his axe at Leander. It made the man jerk and look up, providing Leander with the crucial instant of distraction. He snatched the axe away, picked the man up with the other hand and hurled him into the men behind him, knocking half a dozen off their feet.

That warning display of strength didn't work, as more men replaced the ones who'd fallen, coming at Leander from all angles. Blood chilling, feeling like cold molasses trudging through my veins, I had a terrible flashback to those moments when the bloodsuckers had taken him down.

I had to do something. Anything. But I couldn't think what as the centaurs charged, allowing Leander to duck and dodge while knocking out more and more men. But more just kept coming through the doors. Then I heard one man's voice over the cacophony of violent shouts.

"Leave the Beast to me!" Castor Woodbine emerged out of

the mass of angry men, crossbow armed. "There are more monsters hiding all over the castle! Go after those!"

It was only then I snapped out of my paralysis, remembered what Leander had said.

The others! The smaller, weaker animals without fangs, horns or claws, like Hazel and Bryony, or the injured like Jessamine. Those would be easy kills for the mob!

Panic washed over me in a wave of heat as I ran back down the stairs, ignoring Leander's shout for me to run away, and half-deaf to the exclamations bursting around me.

"Is that a girl?"

"The girl!"

"Bonnie?"

The too-familiar voice shouting my name almost made me tumble down the stairs.

Unable to slow down, heart doubling its speed, I barely spotted the last person I'd expected to see here, before I reached ground level.

My father.

He'd been standing at the front of the mob, directing them with more authority than Castor. But I couldn't even think what he was doing here, or of going to him. If I couldn't help fight, I had to lead the others to safety.

I rushed past Ivy, who was hissing and spitting venom at apprehensive men with smith tools, and caught Oliver around his waist. He was almost as big as I was and I wheezed under his weight as he struggled, crying for his mother.

"I have to help my mum!"

"Ollie, listen to me," I gasped, trudging away from the mob, heart thundering as the hall seemed to go on forever. I could now discern two more voices shouting my name, getting closer behind me, Sir Dale and Glenn Quill, Jessamine's brothers. I didn't have time to reason with them, and I couldn't let them carry me away thinking they were saving me. "Ollie, listen! You'll help her if you let her fight without worrying about you. And we need to help the others hide. This place is your playground, and you said you know everything about it. Is there a place that no one can find?"

Still looking conflicted, he stopped struggling. "I know a secret way to the servants' quarters. I use it to sneak down to the kitchen at night. And there's another secret passage down to a cellar no one knows about. At least mum never found me when I hide there."

"Good boy! Now take me to the servants' quarters so we can get everyone," I wheezed as I ran after him towards the West Tower.

In one of the hard turns, I nearly crashed into a wall with dozens of odd artisanal items. Among them were blue glass eyes, some set within hands, small paintings of winged, bearded men and a robed woman with a peacock crown and a water lily in her hand. Things Queen Zomoroda must have brought with her from Cahraman.

"Now what?" I whispered urgently as the pursuing shadows entered the hall beyond.

Oliver jumped to push the frame of the peacock goddess aside and press a brick behind it.

A teeth-gnashing scrape erupted as half the wall moved, revealing a stairwell beyond. I burst inside after Oliver as the men shouted my name.

I wanted to run back to them, tell them to make everyone stop. But I couldn't risk failing to convince them quickly enough or at all, and waste my chance of reaching the others before the mob found them.

Trying not to trip in the dimness of the hidden stairwell, I looked down and my blood froze. "Why didn't the wall close again?"

Oliver let out a startled squeak. "I forgot to close it!"

But now he had, they'd follow us up here. All I could do was keep going, and hope we'd be able to lose them somehow.

As we stumbled out of the second moving wall, I almost sank to my knees in relief when he pushed another brick from inside and it started closing behind us. I turned away from it and found myself beside a window directly above the rose tree. There were masses of people near it, still trying to push their way into the castle, and a horrifying thought struck me. If they knocked it over, by accident or by vindictive destruction, and crushed the roses underfoot, it would kill all my friends in one go.

But there was nothing I could do about it now. After I got my friends to safety, I'd find a way to go down there and preserve the roses.

We reached the servants' quarters and my heart sank further when I found the rooms I could see open and empty. Everyone must be hiding, probably in one place, what they believed the farthest and safest. But this would be giving the enemy exactly what they wanted. I'd heard enough stories of villagers dealing with suspected witches, locking whole families in their homes and setting them on fire. It was a matter of time before the mob found their way here, and finding their quarry already locked in one place would make this option easy. My friends would be smoked out, or burned alive. They'd die either way.

We must get to that secret cellar before they found us. It was their one chance of survival.

"EVERYONE OUT! We know a better place to hide!"

At my frantic yelling, heavy furniture scraped a lament on

stone ground, then a variety of footfalls stomped closer, coming around the corner. Hazel was the first one I saw, sprinting ahead of the crowd, rabbit ears flying back with her hair.

The moment she reached me she grabbed me by the arms, eyes wide with panic. "Have you seen my mother?"

"Why isn't she with you?"

"She can't climb the stairs!" Oh. Oh, no. Bryony, like the centaurs, was stuck downstairs. Hazel let go of me and started running. "I have to get to her!"

Whatever reasonable protest or plan I could have come up with flew out my head with a scream as a shout exploded from behind me, just as an arrow whistled past.

It barely missed Hazel and impacted the wall behind her, chipping off a chunk of stone before clattering to the ground. Hazel and two others, the deer-legged laundress and the dish-washer with a squirrel tail ran back, screaming warnings to the others.

The wall hadn't closed behind us as I'd thought! A huge hammer was keeping it open, and I found the men from the Woodbine hunting lodge, Glenn, Dale, Will and Robin at the end of the corridor. They seemed to be arguing heatedly about something.

Caring only that it held them up from pursuing the others, I swirled around and ran after them. If we could get to this last secret passageway and to the cellar...

Someone caught me around the waist, lifting me off the floor with ease.

I shrieked and kicked my feet to no avail as Dale turned me in his grip, shaking me. "Why do you keep running from us?"

"Put me down!" I kicked at his shins with all I had. "And call off your mob!"

It was clearly surprise not pain that made him put me down. "Call them off? Are you out of your mind?"

I pummeled his chest, frustration almost bursting my heart. "Call them off before they kill someone!"

"Killing them's the point!" Glenn joined us, aiming his crossbow behind me.

"I told you to put that down, you idiot." That was Robin, smacking the crossbow down.

Glenn frowned at Robin. "I thought you were afraid I'd hit Bonnie."

"I said call your mob off," I shrieked.

"They're not our mob," Dale said. "We're not leading this mission."

I stomped my foot. "Then who is? Castor?"

"Your father, mostly," said Robin, his face still mostly obscured, with his lips twisting in an apologetic cringe. "By the time Will told me he'd escaped, he was already back in Rosemead and rallying the people, and Castor wasted no opportunity in lending his support."

"But why did the people follow them? Why risk an attack after all these years?"

"Because they think both men faced the Beast and survived, making them experts," said Robin, exasperatedly lowering Glenn's crossbow again. "People joined the cause when they knew the creatures here could be harmed, and that one man's daughter and the other's beloved might still be alive." He patted his chest. "Nothing gets men's courage invigorated more than a low-risk chance to be chivalrous, saving a kidnapped lady and whatnot."

"Why are you talking to her like this isn't serious?" Dale shouted at Robin. "That Beast killed our sister!"

"If this is the afterlife, then I'm going to haunt every

priestess who promised me paradise!" said an infuriated voice behind me.

Glenn dropped his crossbow, Dale released me abruptly, mouth dropping open.

Robin merely chuckled. "Hi, Jessie."

Jessamine stood behind us, wings folded, hands on her hips, displeasure brimming in her lowered gaze, the glare of a giant vulture. "If one of you shoots at me, I swear I will stuff you with all my molted feathers like one of those fancy pillows you've always wanted."

Dale let out a horrified shout, arm lifted over his paling face as if he couldn't bear the sight of her.

Glenn retrieved his weapon and aimed it at her, blue eyes wet, voice shaking. "Don't taunt me, demon! Change your form or I'll make your regret ever thinking of my sister."

Unfazed, Jessamine came closer until she nudged the tip of the crossbow, looking like she was about to throttle him. "Dimwit, I *am* your sister."

"No," Dale choked, looking and sounding haunted. "Castor told us about you, about how the things here take on the faces of our loved ones to manipulate us."

"You think if I were capable of changing shape I'd chose to be a cross between your sister and a red cardinal? How would that help manipulate you?"

"How else would you have brainwashed this girl so that she runs away from her saviors?" Dale protested, gesturing at me.

I put myself between them, before Glenn accidentally shot her or Jessamine provoked them by giving in to the urge to smack them. "I'm *not* brainwashed! And this *is* Jessamine! Robin, tell them!"

Dale's confusion deepened, while Glenn grew angrier. "Rob? What would he know?"

"A lot more than either of you," Jessamine snapped. "Which isn't saying much, considering Glenn kept trying to eat soap until he was thirteen."

Glenn grew defensive. "You told me it was made of animal fat, and my favorite part of whatever meat we got was the fatty part!"

Jessamine got equally worked up, waving her arms around. "It was full of scented oils and I was using it to wash our clothes! Why would you consider it food?"

"It smelled better than any food we had, I wanted to know if would taste the same!"

She crossed her arms over her chest. "And after the first half dozen times you realized it didn't?"

"I kept hoping..." Glenn stopped, swallowed, gaze wavering towards Dale, who looked as flabbergasted as he was. I could see the moment it finally fell into place, as matching looks of realization dawned on their faces. Then Glenn finally rasped, "J-Jessie—it *is* you!"

She threw her arms up in mock-praise. "Congratulations, you found me. You know, it's a wonder you didn't get yourself killed, because you two are so dumb, I can't believe—"

Glenn let his crossbow clatter to the ground again and pulled her into a shaky hug, breaking into sobs. "It's you. I can't believe it's you."

Dale joined them, an arm around each, pulling them closer. "We thought you were dead. For three years, we thought we had lost you forever, and you've been here the whole time, as one of these..." He trailed off, wide-eyed as he gaped at Robin. "You knew. You knew the whole time, you weasel!"

Robin waved. "Excuse you, I'm a robin."

"This isn't funny!" Dale shouted. "Why didn't you tell us?"

"Would you have believed me?" Robin tutted. "I had to bring you here, to see it all for yourselves."

Glenn pulled back to tentatively touch Jessamine's smaller feathers with a look of awe. Then he blinked, as if coming out of a trance. "Wait—if you were never slaughtered, then is everyone else here like you? And if no one died, does that mean the Beast is our duke?"

"Yes, he is," Robin said, clearly thinking Leander's real identity should be kept secret.

Dale let out the most undignified gasp, like he was about to faint. "B-but Castor, and everyone else—we all came here to *kill* the Beast."

Like a coiled spring, I sprung up to pull Dale down by the collar. "And if you don't call this all off now you're going to kill your duke and dozens of innocent people!"

Dale went ashen. "Why me? Why not Robin, the one who knows everything?"

"Because I'm a conman," Robin snapped. "And the son of a disgraced lord. While you're a knight sent back from the frontline to keep the city safe. Who do you think they're going to listen to? They didn't even consider listening to me when I tried to stop them from charging the castle."

"Then we need to act fast," I said, head almost bursting with urgency. "Do you think they're all where we left them?"

Oliver jumped as if out of nowhere. "I heard the Master tell my mum to help him herd the attackers somewhere! I didn't hear where, but he said it would be a dead end."

I whirled around to Jessamine. "Where would that be?"

She shook her head. "I-I don't know."

Oliver jumped, hand held up. "I do! Follow me!"

I sprinted in his wake as he scurried ahead, the sight of his lizard tail hanging behind him like an untucked shirt eliciting ridiculous noises from the Quill men.

We were heading down the nearest staircase to a deserted floor packed with echoes of the fight coming from below, when a slam rattled the ground beneath our feet.

"What was that?" I jumped down the last few steps, ignoring the pop of my knees.

"A chandelier?" Jessamine caught up with me in a swoop that earned an impressed whoop from Will. It seemed her injury had mended as she'd told Clancy.

Robin tsked. "That's not what a crashing chandelier sounds like. I would know as I cut one loose over my county sheriff."

Dale shot him a disapproving look. "I don't even want to know."

"Then what could it be?" I asked, trepidation creeping up my spine.

Robin shrugged. "Something tall and heavy, but not a door —maybe a cupboard?"

"A bookcase!" I yelled, stumbling as I abruptly changed my direction. "His quarters! Leander has led them to his quarters."

Jessamine's earlier ire gave way to squawking panic. "Why would he do that?"

I knew why. He was again doing what he'd done in the woods. Gathering the enemy in one place to center their focus on him, and him alone, to give us a chance to escape.

To spare us all, like he'd spared me before, Leander was going to get himself killed.

CHAPTER TWENTY-SEVEN

*A*ll senses dulled by overwhelming dread, I ran faster than I ever had.

I was soon forcing my way through the cacophonous throng milling around Leander's quarters. Once I shoved out of their arc, I saw what was keeping them back. Ivy, who had a cut on her cheek, splitting her scales, was hissing and snapping her jaws at them, and Clancy, who'd lost his glasses, but looked ready to run someone through with his horns. From the numbers, I could tell most attackers had backed off, maybe even given up and fled the castle. But too many still remained.

Among those at the front, enraged and brandishing a hammer, was my father.

I tackled him sideways, making him narrowly miss Ivy's head. "Dad, don't!"

With a gasp, he dropped the hammer, barely missing our feet as he let me push him away from the crowd.

A moment after he stumbled to a stunned halt, he scooped me up in the same bear hug he'd frequently had me in, in the months after my mother's death. *"Bonnie!"*

After weeks of worry, the first time we'd ever been separated, it took all I could not to burst out in tears. At this moment, I just wanted to be a child again, when a distraction and a hug had chased off whatever had made me sad or frightened.

But I wasn't six and crying in our living room because I couldn't grasp Mum was never coming back. I was eighteen in a castle under attack, and I couldn't let any more people mourn!

I squiggled in his hold. "Dad, put me down—you must stop them—and it's not good for your back!"

He squeezed me tighter against him, his voice shaking. "I thought I'd never see you again."

"You were going to, soon. I was fine, and was going to remain fine. Didn't Will and Robin tell you?"

"You mean that Scarlet boy who held me hostage in his town house and his hood of a friend?" He set me down, still hugging me. "You expected me to believe their cock and bull story about that monster being a hideous, hairy man?"

"Yes! Yes, you should have, because he is. It's just a fairy curse!"

He abruptly let go, glanced back at the two guarding the door then to the others who'd just caught up with me.

His pale eyes went back and forth between Sir Dale, Glenn and Jessamine before he finally shook his head, as if coming a realization. "Ah. I take it this is your missing sister."

Strange. He didn't seem shocked. If anything, it was his reaction that shocked me. He didn't even try to argue that it was impossible, just accepted it.

Jessamine gave him an uneasy smile. "Pleased to meet you, Mr. Fairborn."

"Oh, I bet you aren't too happy with me," he said, guilt

creeping into his posture as he looked down at me. "Neither will you be when you know what I did."

I grabbed his arms. "What do you mean? What did you do?"

He swallowed as he glanced over at the door. "I—I was so desperate to get you back in one piece, I went to the one person I knew here after my escape. We bonded over the Beast taking people we loved and about getting rid of it once and for all." He fidgeted, conflicted, apologetic. "I promised that if he helped me save you, I'd take him on as an apprentice, leave him my shop one day and give him my blessing for your marriage."

Though I wanted to rave and rant, that he'd again taken unilateral major decisions about my life, it wasn't the time. Only Leander mattered now. "There's more, isn't there?"

He gave a difficult nod, seeming as distressed as I was. "When our efforts to get through the monsters' defenses didn't go as planned, I told Castor we needed to kill the King of the Beasts first, rationalizing that the others would either all die, too, or be easy prey without him."

"He isn't a beast, Dad!"

"I know that now, but when he lead us to this chamber, Castor slipped inside before those two stopped the rest of us from entering. It seems my offer made Castor even more determined to kill him himself."

I swallowed a jagged lump in my throat. At least Leander wasn't cornered in there with dozens of men bound on killing him. Leander could overpower Castor easily and...

My father's next words made me break out in cold sweat. "Before the doors closed, I saw Castor gaining the upper hand. He seemed to be drawing the fight out only to play with his prey. But he'd get tired of that soon and finally exact his revenge."

Bile flushed up my throat as every mounted kill in the Woodbine lodge flashed behind my eyes.

Without another word or thought, I dashed away, ducking all attempts to stop me, from my father, the people in the crowd, Ivy and Clancy, and slammed myself against the doors, caring nothing for the dozen bruises it would spawn as I fell into the room.

The first thing I saw amidst the trashed room was the massive bookcase lying sideways on the ground with all of its books scattered—and Leander was beneath it. Castor stood over him, crossbow loaded, ready to shoot him in the throat.

There were no thoughts left in my head as I scrambled up and ran to ram into Castor. "NO!"

Both men's shouts clashed together, crashed in my pounding head.

I pushed against Castor, chest barely containing the booming beat of my heart. "Castor, listen to me, you're making a terrible mistake."

"A mistake? Saving you, avenging my father and Jessamine and releasing the entire city from a life of fear is a mistake?" he seethed, teeth gritted, eyes bulging. "I suspected you were bewitched last time, but now I am certain."

I shoved at Castor's crossbow with all my strength. "I am not bewitched!"

"Why didn't you take the others and run as I told you?" Leander groaned, voice heavy with pain as he lay inertly beneath the case.

"And leave you to die?"

"I know what I'm doing, Miss Fairborn."

The way he said that! It made the realization burst in my

mind and almost my head with it. He hadn't only put himself in danger of death to save us, but he'd actually decided to *let* Castor kill him. That was why he'd let him overpower him, why he was lying there, not putting up a fight.

"How many times do I have to tell you to get out?" Leander rumbled.

"You can say whatever you want. I don't take orders from you!"

"It seems you do," said Castor venomously.

"I'm not, I'm telling you the truth, and I am *living* proof of it." My arms trembled along with my voice as I pushed as hard as I could against Castor's chest.

"I don't know why that monster left you alive…"

"He's not a monster!"

At my protest, I could see whatever affection Castor had for me going up in flames as disgust warped his handsome features, as fury and frustration broke his voice and wet his eyes. "That thing ripped my life apart. It orphaned me, and ended my hope for a new family when it seized this castle, slaughtering everyone who came here to work. It caused dozens of people endless pain and you tell me it's not a monster? Either you're not in your right mind, or you're a monster like them."

I fought off untimely thoughts of changelings and bonnibels and what I might really be. Of my mother's death and the fairy that had kidnapped Adelaide, and the one that had cursed Leander and his sister, causing me and everyone else the desperation and fury Castor felt now.

But though he believed Leander was speaking through me, manipulating us both, it was he who wasn't in control, anguish and vengeance blinding him. And I wasn't helping, hadn't said anything to influence him yet. I had to calm down, try to reason with him.

"I can explain everything to you," I said as gently and patiently as I could. "Just please, put the weapon down and listen to me."

Tears falling down his twisted face, he shook his head, lifted the crossbow. "I don't need to understand anything. I only need is to kill it."

Insides quivering, I put myself between the arrow and Leander. "Then you'll need to go through me."

Castor's eyes widened in shock, before they glazed over with a rabid gleam. "You're trying to distract me until it can overpower and kill me. Maybe you're some magical illusion and if I shoot this arrow it would only go through your image and right into its heart."

"I'm not budging, so if you want to get to him, you can risk being wrong and killing me!"

"You are not risking dying for me!" Leander ripped out an anguished roar, throwing off the massive bookcase as if it weighed nothing, rising in one move and pulling me behind him.

"No one is ever dying because of you ever again," Castor hissed, aiming the arrow up towards Leander's chest. "Avert your eyes, Bonnie."

I pushed at Leander, trying to get him to duck, but there was nothing I could do as Castor's finger curled around the trigger.

"*Castor!*"

The shriek made Castor's aim swerve, shooting his arrow at the wall.

It was Jessamine, struggling against Clancy as he held her

back at the door, hissing to her, "Stop! He'll shoot you —again!"

A haunted look gripped Castor's face as he limply aimed his weapon at Jessamine. "It's a trick. It has to be."

Jessamine broke free from Clancy, advancing into the chamber followed by her brothers, Robin and Will. "It's not a trick, it's really me."

"It *is* her," Glenn assured Castor.

Castor shook his head, looking like he was about to vomit from the sight of her. "No, no, it's a trick, this castle, it's cursed—it's playing with our minds."

"The castle isn't cursed," Jessamine told him. "We are!"

I hurried to add, "But there is a way to break the curse, and we've been working on that since I came here."

Castor still aimed at Jessamine, eyes growing more horrified. "I've heard stories about fairies and ghosts who impersonate loved ones to lure in prey, but you're neither—and you're not doing a good job of wearing her face."

I stared up at him in stymied frustration. Like Jessamine had said, he was trying to force everything to fit into his simplistic black and white view of the world. He was the handsome, righteous hero who would save us all from the hideous beast who must have us under some magical compulsion. Now that nothing was going according to his accepted scenario, he could snap at any moment, and his next arrow would be in someone's heart.

I had to find something he would listen to. For once, I had to carefully choose my words, and think about their impact, because the wrong phrase could end with one of us or more dead.

Dreading I'd set him off, but knowing it was a matter of

moments before he did anyway, I exhaled. "If she isn't who she says she is, how do I know who she's supposed to be?"

Castor blinked at me dazedly. "What does that even mean?"

I ventured a step closer, forcing calmness into my voice. "It means that none of you mentioned the name of the girl you all lost. But I don't only know it's Jessamine, but that she worked in people's homes and that you met when you were receiving battle training with her brothers from a knight called Yewan. How could I know all these things?"

His face went lax as his tears stopped, dripping off his lashes as he stared ahead blankly, lowering his crossbow. "She told you."

"And if she told me, that makes the harpy before you, and everyone else here…"

"People," he finally rasped in answer to my prompting, his voice a horrified tremolo. "They're all people."

CHAPTER TWENTY-EIGHT

"I told you that!" Leander rumbled. "As I told your father. But neither of you would listen to me!"

Castor stumbled back, his grip on his weapon loosening, his eyes glazing over. "Jessie. Jessie." His stunned gaze went to her wings then to her face. "I thought you were dead, I thought this thing ate you, wore your face, I thought—" The crossbow hit the floor with a hard clatter. "If you were all never slaughtered, if you are the staff of this castle, then that means you're..." His eyes widened at Leander above me. "You're our *duke!*"

Castor spun around, chest rising and falling, his breathing labored as he glanced at each face in the room, then at the doors where the commotion of the mob continued unabated.

Castor rounded back on Leander, sweating and shaking. "But my father—you killed him."

Leander's beastly face scrunched in a grimace. I knew how guilty he felt about Woodbine's death, feared he'd say something that would set Castor off again.

Thankfully, he only said, "I didn't."

"But I found him clawed to death!" Castor cried.

Leander looked away, probably seeking Clancy, to tell him how to proceed.

I nudged him. "Just tell him the truth."

"He won't believe me." I nudged him again, and he let out a heavy breath. "It was an accident."

Castor surged towards him with an incredulous shout. "An accident? You expect me to believe that?"

"Would you let him finish?" I pushed Castor back, with no real strength, but he let me stop him. "Would you for once let *anyone* finish?"

Glaring at both of us, Castor still clamped his mouth shut.

After all this effort to let him say his piece, Leander said nothing more.

I threw my hands up in frustration at both of them. "Your father came at him with an axe, and Leander stopped the blow. But in the attempt to rip the weapon back, your father ended up hitting himself with the blade."

Castor dropped Leander's gaze to gape at me, growing even paler.

"Castor, you're a hunter," I persisted. "You must know what claw marks look like and that your father's head was cleaved. There must have been blood on the axe and—"

Castor let out a keen that made his entire body spasm as he stumbled back. It was an agonized sound, an outburst fueled by a sudden slam of life-changing realizations.

"Why didn't anyone say anything?" he wheezed shakily. "Why didn't you tell us who you were, and what happened here?"

"Would you have listened?" Leander snapped. "I told your father and it made no difference whatsoever. I only wanted to be left alone, but you made this whole story about me being the Beast and started sending me tributes, and at the same time it became your obsession to hunt me."

Castor lowered his gaze, avoiding Leander's and seeking mine. "That day I came to save you, you already knew the truth already. Why didn't you say anything?"

I gritted my teeth, feeling the hot breath of my bubbling anger whistle through them like steam. "I *did*. Over and over. And you called me delusional and ignored me. Whatever I said, about anything, that night and before it, you ignored me!"

Castor looked like he was about to collapse. I could almost see consciousness fleeing his eyes as he grabbed his hair in spastic fingers, mumbling sluggishly, "All this time, everything I thought happened—and it was all a lie."

"More of a misunderstanding, really..."

He cut me off by suddenly straightened up, wiping at his eyes roughly. "I put you all in danger. I wanted to save people but I nearly got so many killed. I'm an idiot."

"No one is contesting that," Jessamine said, taking the words out of my mouth, gentler than I thought she could be with him.

But actually, he deserved it. He was being more account-able and mature about this than I'd thought him capable of.

Leander faced him. "You can stop this, Woodbine. If they listened to you once they'll do it again, whether it's to convince them of the truth or just to spare us. It's not too late for you to be a hero."

Pained and enraged as I felt he was, Leander had his tone and words under control, sounding calm and comforting, and it had an immediate effect on Castor.

"You said you were trying to break this curse?" Castor asked us. "How soon will you do it?"

I rushed to answer him, hoping I sounded as confident as I totally wasn't. "Within the next season, we hope, if not sooner."

"There's no guarantee they'll believe us," Dale said. "They might just think what we thought of Bonnie—that we were compelled."

"Then make them believe you killed me."

Leander's words made us all gasp in shock.

"It's for the best." He set a large, gentle hand on my shoulder stopping my protest before facing Castor. "Make them believe that with the King of the Beasts dead, the rest would die right after. But say that the castle would be haunted, so no one comes back to loot it, so my people can stop living in fear. Then from now on suppress our story so it never goes beyond local legend or travel beyond our borders, causing unnecessary trouble for our—monarchs."

Castor appeared to be considering the suggestion. "What happens if anyone doesn't believe me, or come back to loot the castle anyway, and find out you're still here?"

"It won't make a difference, because either we are spared from the curse and would resurface in a miraculous return, saying we were lost in Faerie the whole time, or—" He stopped, reluctant to say the alternative out loud. That if the curse didn't break, they would all die for real. "Either way, as Miss Fairborn said, we have a season. What happens after that won't matter."

This was a new side of Leander I hadn't thought I'd ever see. Though he didn't look the part of a prince, he now embodied it. The way he held himself and spoke, issuing reasoned strategies and commands to resolve the crisis and deal with its aftermath, thinking of his people first and himself last—it was awe-inspiring.

This was a glimpse into what he could have done for Arbore as regent in his father's absence, if not for the curse. Instead the kingdom was now in the grip of his corrupt uncle. And should King Florent die at war, and Leander not survive the curse, the rule of this nation would fall to his child brother, Florian, who would be solely steered by said uncle.

But Leander was stuck here, devolving into something that inflamed his people's superstition and aggression, when he could have been ruling them with the firmness and wisdom he'd just given Castor.

Appearing to make up his mind, Castor nodded vigorously and rushed to the door. Robin and the Quill brothers helped him open it, saying they'd herd people away from the quarters, while instructing whichever staff members they found to play dead.

I asked Leander and my friends to hide until everyone had left and followed them as they burst outside.

"It's over!" Castor booming voice drowned even the cacophony. "I killed it! All of its fellow monsters should drop dead now. No need to fight any of them anymore. We're done here! Everyone out! Out!"

Voices rose, relaying the news from one to the other, until I could hear victorious shouts coming from every direction.

Rushing them along, I directed everyone I passed out of the castle while I searched every face for my father, calling for him over the stampede.

Failing to find him, and with the last of the mob disappearing into the distance, I ran back inside. He was probably hiding, too, so no one would see him and think it strange that he wasn't leaving with them.

I found Leander calling for everyone to stop playing dead or emerge from hiding and gather in the main entrance for a headcount. Everyone gradually shuffled in, filling the area, checking each other's injuries and tearfully reuniting with those they'd feared losing. Some asked him what to do now.

"First, we search for those unaccounted for and treat injuries," he said, booming voice for once working in his favor. "Second, we put the doors back in place. After that's dealt with, I want you all to retire for the night." More distressed questions overlapped, becoming a garbled mass of frantic voices. He held up his hands, silencing them. "This won't happen again, I swear to you, on my life."

A long moment of absolute silence reigned. Then everyone started moving and murmuring as they shuffled away to do as their master bade them. They believed him.

Hazel and Bryony led the injured to the kitchen for first aid and medicinal teas, and Ivy and the centaurs helped Leander with the doors. I went in search of my father, calling for him from the stairs on every floor.

By the time I returned to the entrance, to find them having trouble with aligning the hinges, I was beside myself with worry. Where could he have gone?

Will Scarlet popped up behind me, spiking my nervousness, pointing at the doors. "Where is your father when we need him?"

Glaring up at him, I ran to search the halls on either side of the entrance again, finding only the Quill brothers lingering with their sister and Clancy.

I ran back to Leander, anxiety consuming me nerve by nerve. I found him testing one door to see if it would close. Before it did, Robin strode back in.

Upon seeing me, the hooded man approached me, his face semi shrouded, his voice uneasy, even pained as he muttered, "You and I have the worst luck."

Apprehension shot up my spine as I froze. "What do you mean?"

"Fairies seem to have it out for us." He paused, before addressing Will. "Well, and you, too, seeing as it was your sister they took. But Bonnie's luck is now twice as bad as ours."

I stiffened, not wanting to get what he was saying, heart pounding with painful pumps. "What makes you say that?"

"Because as your father led people away from the castle, I saw a fairy woman grab him and disappear into thin air."

I stared up at him for one more second, then my legs buckled beneath me.

I hit the cold floor before either of them could catch me.

CHAPTER TWENTY-NINE

*L*eander hurtled to my side with an alarmed shout, crashing to his knees and pulling me into his arms. "What happened?"

I could do no more than blink, breath shallow, body limp and head heavy as the helplessness I'd been feeling since I'd been tossed in this land deepened to paralysis.

Jessamine tried to kneel by me but her legs wouldn't allow it, so her brothers helped her to sit by me, while Robin discussed something with Leander I couldn't entirely grasp. He seemed to be telling him about my father. I only got that from Leander's tightening hold and the look of absolute horror and pity that gripped his face as he looked down at me.

I could understand the pity. Leander was reunited with his friend and Jessamine with her family, whereas I had lost my best friend and my father one after the other, to the same kind of creature. The kind that might have swapped me for another baby at birth, and that had inflicted this ordeal on us all to begin with.

I tried to even my breathing and forced my thoughts away from the too-fresh wound of my father's abduction to Leander.

In his handling of the attack and Castor, Leander had made it clearer to me that I didn't need to help him just because he and the castle's inhabitants were victims and my friends, but because he was the future of Arbore, the evergreen kingdom, my ancestral home.

A whole kingdom now depended on how I *felt*.

But under the multiplied weight of responsibility, my confusion deepened. I hadn't thought about the implications of my action at the time, but I'd put myself between Leander and an almost crazed hunter. Didn't risking my life to spare his say that I loved him?

So why hasn't the curse been broken?

There could be one answer. The Spring Queen didn't consider what I'd done an act of love.

But if putting someone's life ahead of your own wasn't love, then what was?

NEXT MORNING CAME after the bleakest night I'd ever suffered through.

I dragged myself down to the dining room, hoping to find the others, if not cured of their curse, then at least improved. My hopes were in vain. No one showed up to breakfast.

A sense of defeat filled the castle like trapped smoke that no open windows or cold drafts could clear. By now everyone must be certain if the curse was to be broken, it would have been already.

So what had I done so totally wrong that I couldn't even slow it down?

I couldn't figure that out. There *had* been a complete overhaul of my feelings towards Leander. I'd gone from wanting the hunters to get him to blocking an arrow meant for him with my own body. What else was there?

Still finding no answer, I headed for his quarters. As I approached the ruined family portrait by his door, his booming shout carried to me through the closed door.

"You can't!" He sounded panicked, not angry. "You can't leave!"

For moments I thought he was talking to me, until I heard Clancy's heated response. "I'm not going to die without saying goodbye to my sisters. And without explaining to Lobelia what happened."

"Did you forget what happened when I tried saying goodbye to my sister?" Leander gritted. "As for Lobelia, she must be married off to some other lord by now."

Clancy was engaged?

I leaned against the door as Clancy's hooves clomped past. "Even if so, I must explain why I didn't honor our arrangement. I'll also need to choose an heir. Hopefully either Lucasta or Sorcha have married and had children since I've last seen them. If not, I'll have to search for a relative to marry either of them, so they can keep the castle, and leave it to their children."

The door disappeared from beneath my cheek and I fell into the room with a yelp.

Clancy caught me before my head could meet the carpet. "Miss Fairborn, good morning."

Though it was dark outside like it had been when I'd first come, the curtains were drawn and bedside lamps were lit, casting the messy room in a sinister amber glow. Leander was in his sleep-clothes, the legs of his pants riding up his calves, the shirt stretching across his curving back, and his hair bound at the back of his head, baring bruises on his cheekbone and forehead.

He came over to pull us both deeper into the room, ignoring Clancy's protests. "Perfect timing, Miss Fairborn. Help me talk some sense into the man."

It was only then I realized that Clancy was fully dressed. Not just in his usual shirt and waistcoat, but he wore boots that fitted awkwardly over his goat's legs and hooves, riding pants and a woolen coat, with a tall top hat in his hand.

He really was ready to leave.

Residual terror from the night before came rolling back, making me choke, "If anyone spots you, they'll know the rest of the castle's inmates didn't die as Castor told them, and they'll kill you and come back for the rest again."

He shook his head. "I can still pass for human with some effort. To be honest, I should have left far sooner, long before my legs changed, when I would have only needed to file my growing horns. I don't know why I stuck around so long."

"For the same reason you came here in the first place," Leander said grouchily. "It was a good excuse to avoid Lobelia."

That ticked Clancy off. "I came to check on you. I thought you were dying!"

"I am now!" Leander threw down arms that looked thicker. "We all are!"

His hopeless declaration made me feel even sicker.

Clancy brought his hands together in a silencing clap. "This is why I have to leave. I've waited this long for this to end, and it won't, so I need to wrap up my life before it's too late."

I caught Clancy's arm, partially to steady myself. "You won't make it to Briarfell, and even if you do, who's to say your sisters won't react horribly to you?"

Clancy gave me an exasperated look. "It's not like I'll barge in and say 'I can eat paper, want to see?' I'll talk to them first, explain everything."

Leander felt up his bruised jaw. "They think you're dead, Clancy. So when you show up at all, then they realize you have horns and hooves, they'll think you're some fairy creature trying to lure them into a trap and have the guards spear you."

"I'll prove it, like Miss Quill did with her brothers," Clancy insisted. "With knowledge only I could have."

"I don't think they'll give you time to talk," I argued. "You take off that hat and you're dead."

He gave me a puzzled look. "Why are you so certain of that?"

"Because you look like a satyr!" I yelled, matching Leander's urgency. "The embodiment of evil lechery! No woman would let you near her!"

Leander pointed to me triumphantly. "See? It's not just me."

Clancy crossed his arms, shaking his head at me. "Of all the times for you two to not argue…"

"You're leaving?" We all turned around to find Jessamine clinging to the doorframe, feathers ruffled, matching the climbing alarm in her yellow eyes.

It was Clancy's turn to panic, but he didn't attempt to lie, his mouth twitching wordlessly.

She moved as if to block the doorway, gaze seeking mine out. "Are you leaving too?"

I could only shake my head. "I don't know what I'm going to do anymore."

Clancy faced her. "If I don't leave, tell me, what do I do?"

"Wait for the curse to break," she pleaded.

Clancy threw his hands up in the air. "It won't break! I wouldn't be surprised if this whole thing about a way to break it was an extra cruelty from the fairy queen, to torment us with hope."

Her wings spread out as he made to move. "There are still three roses left!"

"And one is already wilting." His voice cracked, sparking a sharp pain in my chest. "That's not enough time for me to get my affairs in order! I can't die here, none of us should, but after we came so close yesterday..." Suddenly he reached out to her, breathing rapid, eyes desperate. "Come with me. We can hide your wings in a coat, and we'll find a way to disguise your feet." He squeezed her hands fervently. "I've been telling you all about Briarfell for months, and you deserve to see it."

She shook her head, still blocking the door, her voice strangled as she whispered, "Please stay. We'll figure something out!"

I sensed Leander's gaze on me, turned to find him watching me with something ache-inducing. Was it—longing?

He tore his gaze away from my scrutiny and said, "It seems our only option is to wait to be free or wait to die. There's no other way around it."

Like a startled deer, a random thought galloped through my mind, scattering words out my mouth. "There might be a way around it!" My outburst made them swing startled gazes to me. I elaborated, mind racing, "Sitting around this castle for three years hasn't done anything before or after my arrival, so we need a new strategy. We all need to leave!"

Leander frowned down at me in confusion. "We both just finished convincing Clancy he can't leave. Now you want us all to?"

I scrunched up my face at him. "May I finish?"

He raised large hands in a placating gesture, their skin looking harder, as if preparing for the time when he would walk on all fours. "Continue."

"My idea comes from feeling that we're missing a few pages in this story—that there might be another condition to this curse that we don't know about. Is there anything else your parents told you about it? Anything at all, even if it sounds insignificant?"

Leander's thick brows lowered in concentration, shadowing his eyes. "No, but there might be something they haven't told me. Looking back as an adult, the story never made much sense. There does seem to be some parts they left out."

Content that Clancy wasn't about to escape, Jessamine folded her wings and entered. "Forgive me, Master, but I always wondered if Her Majesty provoked the Spring Queen by violating a fairy's revered guest rites, why wasn't she the one transformed into a beast, or given a death sentence like Princess Fairuza?"

I looked up at Leander. "Why indeed? Especially since the reason they gave you, that punishing you instead would hurt her more doesn't seem true. She only had more children to replace you, and went on with her life without incident."

"It's likely the same reason witches and demons ask for one's firstborn as payment or as a sacrifice," Clancy said, giving up on his departure plans and dropping into an armchair.

"Which is?" I prompted.

"Because it *does* hurt more." Clancy took off his glasses to massage the spot between his brows. "In a different way for everyone. For some the worst thing is being parted from their child, but in your case, Leo, your parents were robbed of an heir. Even if the Spring Queen didn't hurt your parents personally as much as desired, she hurt them as rulers. She took away the only reasons they were pushed together in the first place, you, the future king that bound the West and the East of the Folkshore, and Fairuza, a rare princess nations would have gone to war over."

Leander shook his head. "My parents now have another future king and princess."

Clancy reached up to rub the base of his horns as if they ached. "But they'll be no good to them for years to come, when it would probably be too late for them to be of any use. Take the war for instance. I doubt that the peace treaty with Avongart will go through, or if it does, that it would last. But a lasting one could have come about if Fairuza married their crown prince."

I raised my hand in question, baffled. "Why couldn't she have done that already, instead of wasting her precious time on the demanding Crown Prince of Cahraman?"

Clancy shook his head sadly. "Because Prince Laurent is nine-years-old. Although you can arrange marriages for children, they remain betrothals until a boy's twenty-first birthday, when he becomes a man of marriageable age."

"Even if she is eight years older, it could have been arranged." Leander's voice was stifled, as if he was being choked. "But such a wait was out of the question, for the peace, and for her survival. Cyaxares is her only option, since Fairuza is meant to succumb to her own curse on her eighteenth birthday next spring."

Clancy exhaled heavily. "So whatever gaps in your parents' story there might be, finding them out won't stop the clock."

"Not here it won't," I said. "But we can go where time does slow down. I'm saying we go to Faerie."

Three voices rose at once, filling the room with clashing exclamations.

I raised my hands. "One at a time!"

They stopped then Leander went first. "How is going there supposed to help any of us?"

Clancy followed. "Please tell me you're joking."

Jessamine only looked at me, something like hope, tentative and terrible flaring in her yellow eyes.

"I'm serious," I insisted. "*Don't* give me that face, Leander. It was you who said time moves slower in some courts than it does here. And assuming everyone is tied to you, then if your condition stalls, so should everyone else's, giving us more time to find a solution."

After a long moment of staring at me, Leander exhaled. "Any theories what that might be?"

"Yes. We seek out the Spring Queen and convince her to lift the curse."

Leander continued staring at me, like he was waiting for me to add, "Ha! Joking!"

But the longer I stayed silent the more incredulous he looked.

His massive shoulders finally slumped. "She would never do such a thing."

I reached out, gripped his arm urgently. "Just consider it, Leander. Fairies are all about courtesy, and if we go to her court, the Spring Queen will have to hear out your case. I'll vouch for you—we'll all vouch for you, prove to her that you've changed, that you are someone worth loving, if not as a suitor, then as a friend, brother, and master."

At that, looking conflicted and something more—disappointed? Leander turned to Clancy. "Would that be enough?"

When he found all three pairs of eyes on him, Clancy shoved his glasses back up his nose. "Why are you all looking at me?"

"You're the eldest and most experienced," said Leander. "Not to mention the wisest."

Clancy's eyes brimmed with annoyance. "Honestly? *Now* you defer to me?"

Leander made a hurrying gesture. "Speak, sage."

"Of all the times to decide to take my advice, you choose now?"

A low growl echoed deep in Leander's chest. "This isn't the time to bring up the past."

"Why not?"

Leander's voice became a heavy-hearted rasp. "Because I want to ensure that we all have a future instead!"

"It's..." Clancy stopped, swallowed. "...it's an unprecedented decision to consider. Going to Faerie, negotiating with one of its queens for your release—it goes against all we know about solving magical problems! It's unheard of, really. We have no prior example to measure our odds against!"

"Clarence," Leander demanded, both firmly and agitatedly. "Yes or no?"

Clancy slouched in his chair. Then he gazed at Jessamine, who was hovering anxiously by him, and exhaled loudly. "Why not? It's not like anyone else has a better idea."

I clutched Leander's arm, hope surging within me. "We can solve so many problems by going to Faerie. All of them, actually!"

Images began to form in my mind, of the chance to save my family and lift the curse among the backdrop of the fairy courts. I could already see everyone reverting to their old selves among a glitter of magic and the lushness of the Spring Queen's domain, imagine formally reintroducing Leander the prince to my father...

Clancy doused my fantastical imaginings with the cold splash of his worry. "We may have maps of the courts, and ideas on how each realm functions, but we don't know if any of that is accurate. And negotiating a curse? That is uncharted and certainly perilous territory."

"It actually sounds exciting," Jessamine protested. "Who knows, maybe our quest being unique will appease the queen, at least convince her to give us a hint or two, or an extension? And things should be fine as long as we all stick together, right?"

Clancy forgot his usual reticence, gripping her hand. "You can't think of coming! You're still healing—and it's too dangerous!"

She squeezed his hand back, gazing down at him with fervent intensity. "No one there could mean me more harm than the hunters here. I also want the chance to fly in an open space. If I can't do that over our green fields, I want to do it over their blue ones."

Leander looked at me, and I nodded. Jessamine had dreamed of going to Faerie, and whether this would be her salvation or the last thing she did, she deserved to get the chance to fulfill that dream.

Leander finally exhaled. "Then it's settled. We'll go, all four of us. We'll leave Ivy in charge."

Clancy protested again that we should leave Jessamine behind, and she poked him in the chest with a wing tip. "You expect me to stay and keep your rooms clean while you're gone?"

"Of course not," Clancy spluttered in chagrined indignation. "I just want you to be safe."

"What *I* want is to take control of where my life is heading, of what happens to me," she said, taking his hand again. "Let me have this."

Visibly moved, he gazed up at her with suspiciously bright eyes as he squeezed her hand, placing it over his heaving chest. "I suppose you joining us would help me keep an eye on you."

Exhaling in relief, Jessamine grinned as she pulled him up to his feet. "Then we best get ready for our trip. I'll go pack us all travel essentials."

"And I'll go fetch the maps of Faerie and any books that can guide us there."

"Wait." Leander stopped them at the door. "If the passage of time does fluctuate between courts, then we have no way of keeping track of how long we'll be gone. What if once there, my time is no longer connected to that of everyone else's here, and time runs out for them before we even reach the Spring Court?"

That was a concern that had slipped past us all.

I could see him retreating into defeated apathy, giving up the effort to straighten, hunching, arms hanging limply. "I realize I just ruined the one hope we had, but we can't risk going in blind. We might only manage to get lost in time, literally, and cost everyone any chance of resolving the curse during our remaining time here."

No! This couldn't be it. There had to be something we could do, rather than leave it up to the whims of time or magic, or to a specific kind of love that I might never feel.

Suddenly, in the darkest depths of my thoughts, an idea sparked, tiny and tenuous yet lighting up the gloom.

I reached up a trembling hand to his face, sought his despondent eyes, determined to see them full of the rare ease and humor I'd sparked within them again. "I think I might have a solution for our problem."

CHAPTER THIRTY

I looked down at the city from its highest point, taking in our immediate empty surroundings, and the raucous crowds in the distance.

Believing the Beast was defeated, the people of Rosemead had gathered into the biggest town square to hold their triumphant parade, full of food stalls, dancing rings and singing stages.

Leander had said it would occupy them all in one place, making it possible for us to leave the castle. He also thought anyone who wandered off would have had enough mead to dull their senses. His and the others' disguises should suffice for a quick, drunken glimpse from afar.

Now we headed for the woods, escorted by Robin and Will Scarlet. They'd decided our venture was their best bet to find the kidnapped Marianne, too. The Quill brothers had stayed behind to keep an eye on the castle. Sir Dale had been tasked with keeping track of our absence, and given letters by both Leander and Clancy to deliver to their families if we didn't succeed.

Clancy led our procession with Jessamine who held up a lantern for him as he read the map for directions to Nexia, our layover to the Summer Court, where I hoped to find Ada. Our closest shortcut to the island was the fairy path in the woods. It was risky, considering what lived around the path. But the other option, crossing into Armorican territory during a war was as dangerous, with the added disadvantage of wasting days traveling by land and sea. And this time, we were ready for whatever we'd find in there, and armed.

But what had made it possible for us to take the trip in the first place was what I now held in my hand. One of the enchanted roses.

That had been my idea, to take one with us to tell the passage of time, as its lifespan marked one month in the Folkshore. Leander had dismissed the idea at first, fearing it would die rapidly like the one my father had plucked, or worse, cause the remaining two roses to die right along. But I'd suggested that if he were the one to pluck it, as his own life was tied to it, it would live out its natural span. Once in Faerie, if time did pass slower there, we hoped a month would be enough time to get everything done.

After much deliberation and hesitation, Leander had plucked the rose.

So far, it appeared my rationalization held true. The blue rose now hovered in the glass jar, emitting a faint glow that grew brighter as dusk settled around us. I'd been checking on it in my bag every minute and it still showed no signs of wilting.

Forcing myself to close the bag and think of something else apart from obsessively checking the rose, my mind turned back to *Amadeus & Gratia*. I'd finished the book last night.

To my relief, Gratia didn't die as I'd dreaded. Instead, after she'd tricked the goddess Aglaea into showing herself, she'd struck a deal with her to perform tasks to prove herself worthy of Amadeus. Each test the wrathful goddess gave her was grueling and designed to rid her of the girl. But Gratia passed each, through sheer ingenuity and determination. Outraged, Aglaea broke their deal, smiting Gratia for not only defying her but also for winning.

But instead of ending her problem, killing her only back-fired, causing Amadeus to find the strength to escape his shackles and attack her. During the fight, Orcus, a skeletal antlered god rose from the underworld and dragged Aglaea bodily down to the hell-pit of Erevor to serve punishment for breaking an oath and killing the girl.

Amadeus cried over Gratia's body, declaring to all the gods that he would bind himself to her and rot along with her. Moved by his undying loyalty to Gratia, the gods took mercy on them both and brought her back to life, no-longer a battered, burnt husk, but a minor goddess he could take up to the heavens with him. In time, Gratia took over his mother's place as goddess of love and beauty.

We were now passing by another goddess's statue as we approached the woods.

Rosmerta was looming over us when Leander suddenly said, "If it weren't for your bizarre ideas Miss Fairborn, we wouldn't be here."

I snapped my head up to him. He was huddling over me protectively, disguised as best as we could get him in case we stumbled on anyone. "A bizarre idea is better than no idea."

"Normally, I'd say that's debatable, but not when it comes to you. You continue to do the unthinkable."

At detecting the smile permeating his voice, I relaxed. "Like what?"

"Like saving us all by managing to reason with that most unreasonable hunter who's made it his life's ambition to kill me." I waved his statement away as I opened the bag. I couldn't resist not checking again. He peered down at the rose through the glass and its glow played over his sobering face. "I never got to thank you. For everything. For coming back when I got injured, for leaving your father behind so you could help us, for offering your very life for mine by putting yourself between me and a crazed man. If it weren't for you, it would have been a gruesome ending for us all."

No response formed in my mind. I didn't view my actions with the significance and nobility he ascribed to them.

Suddenly, a recollection pricked behind my eyes, making me glare up at him. "Mentioning that, I never got to scold you for lying there and intending to let Castor kill you. Why did you do that?"

He tore his gaze away from mine, was silent for moments before he exhaled. "I hoped if I died, the curse would break. And that once it did, the hunters would spare the others."

I'd already suspected he'd let Castor overpower him on purpose, but had thought he'd just given up, no longer wanted to fight. But to discover he'd done it in hope of saving the others...

His quietly intense words interrupted my seething thoughts. "I now know it was wrong not to fight to my last breath for all our lives. So I have you to thank for being alive, for having another chance to save us all."

I blinked back tears. "The best thanks would have been all of you turning back into humans. I don't understand why everything I did wasn't enough for that fairy queen."

"Maybe she didn't consider that love."

"Then what is?" I hissed in frustration.

"I wish I knew." He stared down at me, his eyes brimming with emotions I couldn't fathom, but that made the whole world spin around me. "If it depended on feelings from my end, we would have been free already."

A flush crept up my neck, burning my face. My heart buzzed inside me like a hummingbird. I again couldn't think of a single thing to say.

What *did* one say when someone basically said they loved you? Especially when it was the last thing you could have expected?

All through, I'd only been thinking of my feelings, and how they would impact his and everyone else's fates. I hadn't even considered it was possible for him, in his situation, to feel anything for me.

But if he did love me, what was I supposed to say? Thanks? And what was I supposed to feel? Flattered? Shocked? Pitying? Delighted?

"Conflicted" won out over all other emotions.

As if realizing what he'd said and regretting it, he attempted to straighten his back and avoided my eyes as we walked on.

Still speechless, I busied myself with adjusting the padding around the rose jar. We'd packed everything we could, food, water, first-aid, clothes, and the required reading for our destination. I'd taken *Færie Flora & Fauna*, in case we needed to sample the local fruits or fungi.

We entered the woods, and soon found ourselves on the fairy path, bordered by lines of those blue, glowing mushrooms. I'd hoped that Leander and Robin had killed all of the redcaps, but they'd assured me there'd be more of them. I bated my breath, ready for them to pop out.

But they didn't.

Robin had his bow out, arrow drawn, Will had his throwing knives, and I had a hunting blade left behind after yesterday's attack, with etchings of vines and leaves on the handle. Leander had his brute strength and claws, and Clancy and Jessamine had their own beastly defenses.

We remained on alert as we continued along the path, watching the mushrooms' glow intensifying as the remnants of the day fell beyond the trees, and the leaves above cast inky shadows. Vapor clouds began to form between the trunks, thickening into fog that completed the eerie atmosphere.

Where could these creatures have gone? Did they just pop out at deep night? Were we due for a belated ambush once all traces of dusk had vanished into darkness?

Deeper and deeper into the woods we went, until the landscape around us started changing with an undulating shimmer, like sunlight on rippling water, shifting our surroundings in a dizzying yet smooth transition.

The woodland territory changed into the cold, windy one of an open field overlooking a seashore. Tall, greenish-blue grass covered the land, dotted with purplish weeds and fist-sized dandelions pulsating with a warm, golden glow. Large, antlered rabbits hopped in the distance, chasing giant blue moths, all to the tune of the crashing waves beneath a cloudy, twilit sky.

We had arrived in Nexia!

After a few miles' walk, we arrived at the threshold of a town. It bore a combination of Rosemead's beautiful architecture along with stunning fairy influences; abstract, colorful wall paintings, intricately carved greenwood doors and golden carriages pulled by white stags.

It was so beautiful and peculiar, but not yet overwhelming in its difference as Faerie itself ought to be.

"Now that we're here," said Clancy, folding the map back into its book. "Should we ask for directions?"

"Maybe another fairy path will show up to guide us there?" Jessamine said hopefully.

Robin put his weapons back in his quiver. "I'd rather the second option. Interacting with the natives is a bad idea."

I trudged to his side though the improbable grass, half swallowed up by it. "Why's that?"

Robin pulled his green hood further over his eyes and did the same with Will's red cloak. "Last I heard, they wanted no part of the mainland, since both Arbore and Armorica kept trying to drag them into the war. Let's not draw attention to ourselves."

Leander muttered under his breath so only I heard him. "Who's not going to stop and gawk at the traveling pack of two armed men, their monsters and pixie?"

Before, the comparisons to gnomes and pixies had warranted nothing more than a roll of my eyes. But ever since I'd found my name in that book, they had become scary possibilities.

And I might get my answer here. If the fairy denizens of Nexia didn't recognize me as one of them, then that theory could be laid to rest.

Robin took the lead with Will behind him, who was discussing with Clancy the possibility of finding his sister Marianne, along with my family. Leander seemed both fascinated and unsettled by the place, while Jessamine's wings twitched ahead of me, no doubt aching to spread and fly over the fields as she'd said she longed to.

As we entered the town, the signs of life we'd glimpsed

from the distance had disappeared. All doors were shut and the carriages were empty, left standing in the middle of the road, like the place had suddenly been abandoned.

"And *that's* not odd at all," Leander mumbled. "Fairies!"

As we walked in, we passed by a doorway of one house that resembled a wide-open mouth. Leander was closest to it, and he peeked inside. Whatever he'd seen inside made him tense up. Before I could ask, a flap of wings and a scream had me swirling around in fright.

Jessamine had shot up into the air and was flapping about in zigzags above a section of the road that had soundlessly caved in.

Stumbling away from the edge of the crater, Robin and Will stood back-to-back, dropping into fighting stances. Leander scooped me up as Clancy shouted directions for Jessamine on how and where to land. We all kept our eyes on the ground in trepidation, expecting more areas to disappear.

Instead, the ground started rising and dipping beneath us like waves, knocking us all off balance. While Leander and I hit the ground in one mass as he squeezed me closer, protecting me within his envelopment, Will and Robin rolled down apart from each other.

Jessamine swooped down to push Clancy after them. "We have to get away from here!"

"How?" I shouted, heart blocking my throat, eyes darting around the warping landscape. This place seemed bound on tossing us around.

Suddenly, in the middle of the road, vortex after another of crackling light and wind yawned wider. Some had sinister glowing eyes like those I'd seen in the Hornswoods, others had glimpses of other locations, either the rest of Nexia or places beyond it.

Portals! Like the one that had showed me Adelaide!

Before I could think of rushing towards one, to look inside, the ground bucked beneath us. It catapulted us in the air, making Leander lose his grip on me, before it ducked back, like the earth had sucked in its gut. I plummeted to the ground, flapping my arms with a startled scream. Leander caught me at the last second, and we hit the slope as he broke my fall, slid down to where the rest had landed in a heap.

"Is this some sort of trap?" Leander grunted as soon as we disentangled.

"I'd say it's a security system," Robin panted. "I've bypassed plenty, so now I know what this one is like, I can see the pattern. I can lead us through, no problem."

"Circumventing stationed guards or long-jumping a moat full of crocodiles isn't the same as whatever this is," Will snapped. "The people here want us out of their town! This *town* wants us out!"

Jessamine landed with a squeak and a stumble, slamming into Robin. "Then let's leave and find our next stop fast!"

"Follow me!" Robin slid down the slope leading away from the massive cavity.

As we followed, I searched every doorway we passed for any sign it could be our way to Faerie. I couldn't fathom what I saw inside, until my attention was snatched away as we approached a fountain that seemed to be folding itself in half, like a giant clam.

It would have snapped shut over Will's head if not for Robin. He pushed Will aside, and it slammed over his forearm instead, with a thunderclap that rumbled around us and made my joints lock up.

Robin's roar of pain melted my shock into horror. I was afraid it had cut off his arm when he pulled it from between its lips. It was there but clearly broken, and his hand was bright red and swollen as he held his limp forearm to his chest, heaving and groaning in agony.

The men rushed to his side. But when Clancy tried to examine his arm, we all fell down again as the ground rose back up like a cresting wave, this time with an inhuman chorus.

"HUMANS OUT!"

The distorted ground rolled us down the steep slope, slamming us back at the start in a pile of limbs and cries of pain, none louder than Robin's agonized shouts.

Will got up first, trying to drag Robin away. "We must fall back!"

Robin struggled. "No, we can't!"

"Yes, you can," Leander insisted. "This was a stupid idea. We know nothing of this place except from the vague and clearly inaccurate books we have. We need to regroup and investigate before taking one step further. And *you* need to go home."

"No," Robin groaned.

"Your arm's broken." Leander lifted him to his feet, setting him by Will, so he could put his good arm around his shoulders and lean against him. "Unless you can shoot arrows with your teeth, you're going home." He looked back at me, eyes feverish with anxiety. "We all are."

I stopped nodding along, all thoughts of encouraging Robin to postpone his rescue of Will's sister gone. "We can't go back! We need to try again!"

Leander's agitation rose, skin pale against his messy hair and beard. "If we do, then the inhabitants will get angrier and more brutal with us. This was just a warning."

"We were taken by surprise this time," I insisted. "But

now we know what to expect, we just need to anticipate the distortions and ride them, till we find out which portal leads into Faerie."

Leander shook his head vehemently. "We can't anticipate random changes to reality. And that's when we're only on the edge of Faerie. Things will only get stranger and more dangerous as we go on."

"Then we deal with what shows up."

He pointed at Robin, whose knees were buckling under clearly worsening pain. "I can't deal with this happening again, or worse."

I couldn't deny that this was scary. Structures that warped and tried to eat us made passing through this place again the last thing I wanted to do. But we *needed* to. We must get to the one place that could solve all our problems.

Knowing there was no use arguing with him, I sidestepped him. The ground had stabilized, and we must take advantage of that. If I ran, they'd follow, and this time we had to jump through one of the portals before the town swatted us around again or tried to devour us.

Clancy and Jessamine blocked my way until Leander came after me.

"They want all *humans* out of here," he said as he crowded me back towards the first house we'd passed. "Which means if you try to defy them, they might take out an eye this time or even snap you in half. But since it's only you three they have a problem with, they might let *us* pass."

I still shook my head. "We haven't figured it out yet, but there must be a way around this."

"There isn't."

"No! I can't leave you. I'm the one who can negotiate with

the fairy queen on your behalf. I promised to help and I will do it at any cost."

"Not at the cost of your life." He sounded adamant, yet looked more anxious by the second, as he curled one large hand around my shoulder and ran the other through my hair. "I will never let you put yourself in danger again."

Frustration burned through me, rose in my throat. "I must save you."

"You have already done more than I could have imagined, Bonnie, and I want you to not be burdened by me anymore." His turquoise eyes shone with what looked like unshed tears in a face I suddenly found so appealing, so dear. "Now I want you to go back to your father."

There were too many things I wanted to blurt out. That he wasn't a burden, that I needed to save him, that I wouldn't abandon him. I wanted to ask what he was talking about, to point out that he'd finally called me by my name, and why now.

But I only said, "What are you looking at?"

He was staring at something behind me, through the door shaped like a gaping mouth. I looked over my shoulder to see what it was, and saw a swirling portal inside.

Before I could react, Leander pressed a kiss to my forehead and pushed me into it. "Goodbye."

THERE'D BEEN nothing I could have done to fight against the pull of the portal.

I'd fallen back into the whirlpool of sound and sights, unable to even scream as I'd watched Leander shrinking into nothingness.

Emotions had rushed through me faster than I could register, fiercer than I could bear. But unlike the first time I'd gone through a portal, when I'd evidently been so overwhelmed, my mind had failed to record the experience, I'd remained aware of every second, every nerve, every flicker of sensation, in what had felt like an eternal plummet.

But even eternity ended.

My endless spiral abruptly stopped with a heart-bruising thud. Then I lay unmoving on green grass, gazing into the empty heart of the vortex that had just spat me out.

Just like in the library, the portal winked shut with a flash, and I was left staring up at the afternoon sky of an entirely different land, only two things left inside me—paralysis and disorientation.

After a minute or a day, breathing shallow and heart stumbling, I rose on shaking legs—and found myself staring down a road I knew well.

The road leading to my house.

Leander hadn't just pushed me out of Nexia, he'd sent me home to Aubenaire.

Time again warped, no longer working as I remembered. I had no idea how long I remained gaping down that road.

Eventually, the maelstrom of emotions at finding myself back here dissipated, leaving nothing but drowning sadness.

Leander had waived my promise, had disregarded my insistence that we'd find a way around the threats of Nexia. He'd cut me out of the quest, pushing me away at the first instance of danger. He'd done it to spare me.

And I hated him for it.

He'd torn us apart, unraveling our plans for heroic rescues, family reunions, and broken curses. Without giving me a choice, he'd sent me home. The place I'd always wanted to leave. Leaving me with no clue of what he'd do without me.

If merely crossing Nexia, a part of the Folkshore still, had seemed that impossible, what would await them if they reached the Summer Court? I could only hope the surreal turmoil the place had put us through, had been on my and Robin's and Will's account, that once the humans had left, Nexia would let Leander and the others move on to Faerie unharmed.

But now I was by myself, and stuck here away from him, without Dad—without Adelaide...

"Welcome back, Bonnibel."

My sluggish heart couldn't bring itself to stir as I looked up, found Miss Etheline, the owner of the Poison Apple tavern where Adelaide had worked approaching me. I couldn't even bring myself to say hello.

Her seafoam eyes regarded me with some strange expression as I trudged nearer. As if she was waiting for something, or as if she knew something I didn't. But she always seemed like she was lost in thought about things no one else knew anything about.

That absentminded lady with no discernible accent, who'd moved here a few years back, but whom everyone treated as if she'd always been there, had always inflamed my curiosity. But as Adelaide's employer, I hadn't been allowed to snoop around or ask intrusive questions while I hung around during her shifts, reading in booths, waiting for her to clock off to walk us home.

I'd always had far-fetched theories about who she was, and how she'd come to be here, all worthy of a mystery novel. Now even if she stopped me and volunteered her life story, I wouldn't care.

I had nothing left to care about.

"Are you well, Bonnibel?"

I nodded, shook my head, cringing at hearing my name, what might signify I was a changeling. I might not be, since Nexia had seemed to consider me a human to be cast out. But there was other evidence that I might be. And now I'd never know.

Now I was exiled here, in the one place I'd always wanted to leave, without everyone I loved.

"I trust this is a passing visit? You'll leave again, hmm?"

Before I could say anything to those strange assumptions, Miss Etheline gave me a faraway smile and passed me.

I turned to watch her walk away, realizing with another blow to my heart that she was suddenly the closest person I had in the world.

Memories of my father and Adelaide, then of every moment I'd spent in Leander's castle assailed me. I already missed that place, missed my meals with them—missed Leander—and it might have only been a few minutes since I...

A realization hit me, almost making me keel over.

I still had the rose with me!

Hands shaking, I opened my bag, reassuring myself the jar was still intact.

It was, but I found one petal starting to wilt. At least hours of the month we'd set for our quest had passed.

I couldn't bear the idea of more time going by with us apart. And that he didn't have the rose with him so he could keep track of it.

But since he'd sent me home with it, it seemed he no longer thought it mattered, since he had no control over how long it would take to reach the Spring Queen. And if he did, he'd either convince her to spare him, or at least his people, or he would fail.

And without me, he *would* fail.

I had to go back, be with him. And there was one place that could take me where he was going. The one place I'd always wanted to go, the edge of the human world, the nexus into Faerie. The Hornswoods.

The thought solidified into a decision in a heartbeat.

Then actually wishing I *was* a changeling, so whatever lurked in the woods would let me pass, I started walking towards them.

With every step, the story of Amadeus and Gratia came back to me, vivid with parallels. Between what Gratia had done for her husband, and what I was trying to do for Leander.

Just like Gratia had stood up to the goddess, had done all she could for Amadeus's freedom, I would do so with the Spring Queen for Leander's life. It didn't matter that he'd pushed me away to protect me. It was my life and he had no right deciding if and for whom I would risk it. From now on I was making my own decisions.

And it also didn't matter that he'd set me free of my promise to him. It was my promise and the only way I would be free of it was when I fulfilled it.

As he liked to tell me, I was discovering I *was* stubborn and single-minded. I was ready for any dangers so I could reach Faerie, reunite with Leander—and give him a piece of my mind. I would go through any tests to rescue him, and my father and best friend.

Heart thundering with an amalgam of dread and excitement, I silently made another pledge. To myself this time.

From now on, I would never again be a burden to others, a

source of worry for them. I would never stay in the shadows, safe and protected and held back from life. I would do anything to pull my weight, and do all I could for those I loved, no matter the obstacles or the cost.

I'd read enough about heroes. It was time I became one myself.

NOTE FROM THE AUTHOR

I hope you've enjoyed BEAST OF ROSEMEAD, the first installment in the *Rosemead Duology* as much as I enjoyed writing it!

Reviews and word of mouth are the life-blood of Indie Authors, so if you enjoyed the book, please help me spread the word! Even a line on Amazon, Goodreads and Bookbub would be vital to my success and to the book's sales, and would be hugely appreciated.

If you haven't yet, please read where it all began in the #1 Amazon Bestsellers, *THIEF OF CAHRAMAN and PRINCE OF CAHRAMAN and QUEEN OF CAHRAMAN*

The final and climactic part of Bonnie's story comes in *BEAUTY OF ROSEMEAD!*

Ella's story comes next in PRINCESS OF MIDNIGHT which is a STANDALONE book!

For exclusive content, news, updates and offers, please sign up to my VIP Mailing List.

I also love to hear from my readers, so please contact me at lucytempestauthor@gmail.com

Thank you for reading!
Lucy

PRONUNCIATION GUIDE

— People

Bonnibel: Bonna-bell

Etheline: Eth-ell-leen

Fairuza: Fay-roo-zah

Jessamine: Jess-ah-meen

Leander: Lee-ann-durr

Ornella: Ore-nell-ah

Ossian: Oh-sheen

Seamus: Shay-muss

— Places:

Ericura: Air-ree-cue-ruh

Almaskham: Ul-maz-kham

Arbore: Are-bore

Cahraman: Quh-rah-maahn

Campania: Kaam-pahn-yuh

Nexia: Neck-see-yah

ABOUT THE AUTHOR

With one foot in reality and the other one lodged firmly in fantasy, Lucy Tempest has been spinning tales since she learned how to speak. Now, as an author, people can experience the worlds she creates for themselves.

Lucy lives in Southern California with her family and two spoiled cats, who would make terrible familiars.

Her young adult fantasy series FAIRYTALES OF FOLKSHORE is a collection of interconnected fairytale retellings, each with a unique twist on a beloved, timeless tale.

Visit her and sign up to her VIP mailing list at https://www.lucytempest.com/newsletter

And follow her on